Heart of GOLD

JENNY BUNTING

Editing: Lopt & Cropt Editing

Cover: Kari March Designs

BOOKS BY JENNY BUNTING

Here in Lillyvale

Happiness (Caroline and Brady)

Here (Zoey and Jonathan)

Hustle (Taylor and Malcolm)

Home (Addison and Kirk)

Hubby (Makenna and Dan)

Stuck in Love

Please Be Seated (Erin and Landon)

In Case of Emergency (Cassie and Smith)

For Your Safety (Raegan and Henry)

Finch Family

Fool's Gold (Annie and Cameron)

Gold Rush (Whitney and Reid)

Golden Hour (Shiloh and Jackson)

Heart of Gold (Emily and Max)

Standalones

Safe with You (Izzie and Eugene "Thumper")

For anyone who's ever watched a door, wishing they would come back.

A NOTE FROM JENNY

Thank you so much for reading *Heart of Gold*! I hope you enjoy it.

This book contains discussions of parental abandonment, pregnancy termination, an unplanned pregnancy, depictions of gaslighting, uneven power dynamics and brief instances that could be interpreted as postpartum depression.

Additionally, while both main characters are in relationships with other people at the beginning of the novel, there is **no love triangle** and there is **zero cheating** in this book.

If you are sensitive, please take care of yourself.

PROLOGUE

EMILY

Ten Years Ago

"**Y**ou look very, very pretty," he said, tucking a strand of hair behind my ear. He was sitting next to me in this half booth, rather than in the chair facing us, lonely and vacant.

I didn't mind, though. Who knew the next time he'd be next to me.

He leaned in, sneaking a peck that turns into a torturous kiss, his fingers tracing my jaw. It didn't matter that the restaurant was full, that our food was cooling because the heat between us was unbearable. All that mattered was that his lips were on mine.

"Where did you come from?" I asked when we pulled apart, my eyes flicking from one corner of his to another.

"La Jolla, California," he joked, kissing me again. He looked down at my plate of spaghetti and back up at me. "You know what this means?"

"What?"

"We need to *Lady and the Tramp* this," he said, picking up a lone noodle to offer me one end. I laughed, and he nuzzled my neck.

"We can't be that couple," I said through wheezing giggles.

"Okay, fine." He kissed me again and pulled me in tighter.

The owner of La Scarola eyed me from the corner. He had known me my entire life—since I was a kid in pigtails to my awkward teenage years of sharp elbows and a mouth full of braces. And in that moment, he got to see me in love for the first time.

Love. Was that what this was?

I'd only known him for a week.

The owner stared us down, and Max froze. He pointed to the chair, and I nodded as he stood up and took the seat across from me. So far away.

"Tell me what your biggest dream is," he said, stabbing a piece of pasta with his fork.

I spun the spaghetti and took a bite. "You already heard it."

"Come on, Martini. I love the way you light up when you talk about it. Tell me again."

"Okay." I smoothed out my napkin on my lap. This was the fifth time I'd repeated this story, but I couldn't get enough of how Max listened to me, like he'd do whatever it takes to make it happen.

After one deep breath, I said, "I want to live in a big city. I haven't decided yet—Chicago, New York, Boston. Nothing on the west coast. I want to go somewhere new. Somewhere completely different."

Max nodded and took another bite, but those hypnotic blue eyes, icy like Antarctic waters, stayed on me. Ever since we met at the snack bar at Tin Lake, I hadn't stopped trying to swim in them.

"What else?" he asked, but he knows the rest of the fantasy.

"I will have a nice apartment overlooking the city. In the mornings, I will drink coffee and just watch the city go by on my balcony. My job will be in advertising or marketing and it will be hectic, but I will take a slow morning. Always."

"And at night?"

"At night, I will grab martinis with friends. With three olives." This was why he calls me Martini. Goosebumps crawled up my arm every time he said it.

"Because you love olives."

"I love them. So much." I patted his hand. "You've never told me what your dream is."

He shook his head. "You'll think it's weird."

I tilted my chin down and looked at him from under my lashes. "Try me."

He took a deep breath. "I want to be a dad."

I didn't expect that. My stomach churned. He looked at me with such vulnerability.

"You know my dad left, and Fred is great and all, the absolute best. Who knows where I would be without him. It's just…"

"You want to be the father you didn't have," I finished his sentence.

"Exactly." His jaw tightened and flexed. His fork dropped to his plate with a clank, and he wiped his mouth.

"Is everything okay?"

"I've never told anyone that before. This is wild, but I think I love you." He looked up, his eyes piercing me through the heart again. "Like I really love you, Em."

A big grin crossed my face. "I think I love you too."

"It's only been a week."

"I know."

"This is crazy." He reached across the table and opened

his palm. My hand met it, and he squeezed. "I had no idea this was going to happen."

"Me neither."

His smile dropped, and I could tell what he was thinking. We were going to be apart. It would be hard, but I knew we could make it through. Everything in my gut and my intuition and my heart was telling me *yes, yes, this is right*.

He grabbed my hands and rubbed my knuckles with his thumb. "I don't want to leave."

I shook my head. "This is important to you. It's two months. A drop in the bucket."

"A drop in the bucket," he repeated.

"We'll talk as much as we can. I'll give you my email," I said. "I'll have your number. I'll make sure to fill up your voicemail so when you get back…"

"I can't wait to be back here." He stood up and leaned over the table, kissing me again, the tomato sauce on both our breath. I held his cheek as his tongue breeched my lips, and we heard a grumble from the table over.

He sat down and held up a hand. "Sorry. I'm absolutely gone about this woman."

I was nineteen years old, almost twenty, not even old enough to have a drink. Still, the way Max looked at me, so hungry, his eyes telling me that he wants all of me. That he saw *me*, not just a gawky girl with frizzy, dull brown hair and freckles. It's corny, but he made me feel like a woman.

I felt grown up, sexy, sultry. It was a new feeling.

"You know, my parents are gone for the night. The lake house is empty," he said.

I covered my mouth so I don't spit out my food. We'd kissed, and his hands had traveled to places no other guy has touched, but that's it. While my friends lost their virginity left and right in high school, I always held out. "I want to be in love," I told them, and then *he* happened. I'd been waiting for him. I may have been older than all of my friends were at their first time, but Max was worth the wait.

"I'm ready," I said. He knew I was a virgin, and he'd been nothing but respectful. Before his hand palmed my breast behind my parents' house, he asked if it was okay. Now, I was ready to give all of myself to him.

His eyes twinkled with mischief as he looked up. "You are?"

I nodded once, rolling my lips together.

He took a huge bite of pasta. "Well, we better finish up, then. Plus, my meal got cold."

"Mine too."

"I can't wait."

My cheeks heated to fire. "For tonight?"

"For forever."

EMILY

NOW

Sunday

"**D**o you have your penny?" I ask my daughter as we take our first steps in the forest behind the bookstore. Her hand is in mine, but Olive is studying the ground as her sneakers hit the brush.

"Yes, Mom, I have it." She holds up her hand, the copper circle stark against her pale palm.

"Excellent."

"Mom, is thirty old?"

"No, no, it's not, honey." At least that's what I've been telling myself for months. Thirty is not old; it's just a new decade. My sister-in-law Annie has reassured me the thirties are her favorite so far, and I have to believe her or I'll hyperventilate.

"You *are* younger than the other moms."

"That is true," I say. Olive's best friend Kenzie's mother Talia is forty-two, and when we get together for play dates, she tries to relate to me, but we have nothing in common. I spent my twenties raising a child while my friends got drunk and hooked up. My first time sleeping with a guy, I got a souvenir. Talia's Europe backpacking stories used to make me sad, but I decided a long time ago to play the hand I was dealt.

Olive hops over a fallen log. "I'll make a super good wish for you. Since thirty is a special birthday. A new decade!"

Olive's birthday is not for another eight months, but it'll be a big one. Ten. We talked about decades and how it's special to enter a new one. When my daughter's not watching, I'm breathing into a metaphorical paper bag.

No matter how many people tell me thirty is not old, I feel old.

I skipped ten years of being dumb and doing dumb things. That's what your twenties are for, but I did none of it. I couldn't drink on my twenty-first birthday because I was breastfeeding. When my mom babysits, I can drink and call one of Goldheart's two Uber drivers, but it's not the same.

Still, the little girl holding my hand and a penny in the other is worth it.

We reach the wishing well. As a girl, I would visit here with my mom on our birthdays. We would lean over and talk into the depths of the well, hoping for an answer to our questions. When my daughter was old enough to know what was going on, I started this birthday tradition with her. We would make wishes for each other. Around age six, Olive became very secretive, never telling me what she wished for, and whether it came true.

The well has seen better days— bugs have left holes in the wood, which has loosened from the nails, but it brings back so many memories. Olive at four holding my hand, me pregnant with her, visiting on my due date with a quarter in my hand. I wanted to make sure my wish was heard.

I got my wish. My daughter is happy and healthy. Who

needs a dad when you have three loving uncles, adoring grandparents, and a beautiful house on acreage?

We look over into the darkness, the creaking of water echoing.

"Are you ready, Olive?" I ask.

"Yes, Mom." She closes her eyes and parts her lips, her mouth moving with the words. When she opens her eyes, she flicks the coin, and it disappears into the pitch black.

"I wished extra hard today," she says.

"For what?"

"You know I can't tell you, Mom."

"You never tell me if it comes true."

"It hasn't," she says with authority. I wrap my arm around her thin shoulders, and she leans into my side. "I make the same wish every year."

"You want me to get you a pet raccoon?"

"No, I'm over that. I've matured."

I roll my eyes. My daughter's raccoon obsession lasted for three years, just because we had a pair of friendly raccoons in our backyard we named Thelma and Louise.

After my brother's girlfriend Shiloh was attacked because Olive let another raccoon into our family business, Woody Finch Brewery, I grounded her, then desperately steered her to another obsession. Lately, it's been Pixar and *Monsters Inc.*, specifically Mike Wazowksi, the one-eyed short green monster.

Mike had made her mostly forget about raccoons, thank goodness.

"Can you give me a hint?" I ask.

"No, Mom. Even a hint is telling the secret."

"Okay." I hold out my hand, and Olive takes it. It warms my heart that Olive still wants to hold my hand, even though she comes up to my chest now. She pushes the hair from her face, and I get a flash of her father. She got my brown hair, the same freckles dusting her nose, but her flatter cheeks, thin nose and eyes came from him. His face has faded over the years, but I'm reminded every time I look at her.

"Are you going to be nice to Burke?" I ask. We reach the car and get in. Olive is quiet as she buckles herself in behind the passenger seat. She doesn't answer me.

Burke is my boyfriend.

Well, kinda.

We've been dating for two months, ever since he came into the brewery with some friends and asked me out, hands in his pockets like a shy schoolboy. Burke is nice enough. He owns his own restaurant in town, Bistro 530, and he's objectively handsome with wavy brown hair and soft brown eyes. He's been nothing but a gentleman, and I enjoy spending time with him.

Meanwhile, my nine-year-old daughter treats him like she's an overbearing father with a room full of shotguns.

"Nice? To Burke?" I ask again.

I catch her folding her arms in the rearview mirror.

"He calls me kiddo."

"I call you kiddo."

"You're my mom."

"What do you prefer him to call you?"

"Martini. Or *my name*." I was not this much of a smartass as a kid. Why does she insist on that nickname? I should've seen it coming, after I named her Olive as a little Easter egg for myself. That backfired.

"I'll tell him you prefer Olive," I say.

"Why don't you like Martini, Mom? Uncle Cam gave me that nickname."

I study her in the rearview mirror. Her arms are still folded as she watches out the window.

"Because…" I say. *Your father used to call me that.*

Thankfully, she lets it go as we make the short drive to Woody Finch Brewery for my birthday brunch.

We pull into the rear parking lot of the brewery, where my family and employees park. Cam and Annie are already here, as well as my parents. Burke's sleek BMW is parked there too.

Burke is an amazing cook, but his breakfast food is my favorite. When he asked me what I wanted for my birthday, I simply asked for eggs Benedict and his biscuits. He one-upped my request and offered to cater a birthday brunch for my entire family.

Guilt gnaws at me. It's too much to ask of him. Still, he insisted and coordinated with my brother, Cameron, and his wife, Annie. I was told only to show up.

"Please be nice to Burke," I repeat.

My daughter stares out the window, and after I park the car, I turn around.

"Olive, did you hear me?"

"Yes, I heard you." There's a hint of sass in her voice. I'm scared for the teenage years if she's like this at nine. When she looks my way, her blue eyes are arresting. "Is he going to be my dad?"

My stomach drops and my mouth goes dry. Turning around, I say, "You don't need to worry about that now."

My daughter's eyebrows scrunch together as she whispers, "He tries to act like my dad."

"I'll talk to him about that too." Olive continues her forlorn act in the backseat.

"Are you excited to see Uncle Cam?"

"Why did he have to move out?"

I sigh. A month ago, Cam and Annie moved out of the tiny house on my property to a bigger house in town. Olive had been quieter in the mornings lately without Uncle Cam there to entertain her.

"You know the baby is coming any day now."

"Yeah," she says with a sigh. It's too quiet in here. I check the rearview to make sure she didn't jump out. While I'm elated to be an aunt, finally, I'm not looking forward to how Olive will react. Cam has been the closest thing to a father to her, and sharing him with Annie has already been challenging. Add in another girl who will inevitably take priority, and it's going to be rough for Olive.

You can handle this. You are strong and capable, I tell myself.

The day promises heat with a touch of humidity, and sweat already collects at my hairline. After locking the car, I walk with Olive to the rear entrance. From the taproom, I hear commotion, mostly clinking and talking. I plaster a smile on my face as we walk down the hallway.

"There's the birthday girl!" Burke yells when he sees me. He's wearing his chef's whites and a mega-watt smile. I smile too as he approaches me and kisses my cheek. He ruffles Olive's hair and the scowl on her face says it all.

"Hey, kiddo, how are you?" he asks.

"I'm good."

"Hey, Burke," I say as my daughter drifts towards my mom. She immediately pulls Olive in and smothers her with kisses.

Burke gestures to the extravagant spread and sets his hands on his hips. "How does it look?" There's serving trays with hints of steam, piles of croissants and biscuits, coffee carry-outs from Gold Roast, and carafes of orange juice and champagne sitting at the end of the table. It's all wonderful and so thoughtful.

I'm not sure why I feel a heavy pit in my stomach.

Burke can't get away from the restaurant tonight, so we decided brunch would be the next best thing.

I rest my forearms on his shoulders as he holds my waist.

"It looks wonderful. But I have something to talk to you about."

"Okay." Whenever I say something like this, Burke always looks like I'm about to break up with him.

"Olive doesn't like it when you call her kiddo."

Burke's expression collapses into concern. "I'm sorry, I…"

"It's fine." I kiss him quickly to end the conversation. Pulling away, I feel his hands stay on my waist until I'm out of reach.

"Happy Birthday Emily!" I hear from the hallway, and it's my brother's girlfriend, Shiloh. She's wearing a cute striped dress, and her blonde curls are down, not in her usual braids. Shiloh is shorter than me by a few inches so she has to jump to wrap her arms around my neck.

"So, your boyfriend is here," Jackson says, pulling me into a hug. When Jackson, the oldest in our family, first came home to Goldheart, he didn't socialize much. Thank God for Shiloh. She brought him out of his shell, and he's the Jackson he was when we were kids.

Shiloh looks behind me to the spread. "Wow, Burke did all of this?"

I shrug. "He wanted to, I guess."

"That's so nice! He's a keeper!"

"I think so," I say, injecting fake cheer into my voice. Burke is everything a girl could want and one of the few eligible bachelors in our small town of Goldheart. He cooks, *and* his apartment is immaculate.

When he kisses me, he acts like I'm a gourmet meal to devour. He leaves the toilet seat down and calls his mother every Sunday. On paper, he's perfect.

Still, there's something missing I can't put my finger on.

My experience in dating includes a fever dream from ten years ago, so I assume the missing piece will slide into place eventually. Burke is perfect.

There's a knock at the brewery's front door and we all look.

"Don't they see the sign on the door?" I ask, shrugging one shoulder. Jackson kisses Shiloh on the head and walks to answer it.

Shiloh beelines for my mother and daughter. As a group, they walk to the bathroom. I bet Olive wants company. Or an escort.

"What's going on?" I call to Jackson.

As I get closer to the door and my brother, my throat tightens. In the entrance stands a man, blond, broad shoulders, wearing a crisp gingham shirt and pants. The way he holds his hands in front is familiar, and my eyelashes flutter.

Olive's cheeks. Her mannerisms. All on this man I haven't seen in ten years.

He notices me, and our eyes lock. I feel woozy.

He breaks into a huge grin. "Hey Martini. It's been a long time."

2

MAX

"How was the party?" my mom asks over my car's speaker as I drive.

"It was great. A truly wonderful send-off."

"Moving to Paris. Wow. That's so great."

"Yeah, no time like the present. They want to do it before they have kids."

"I'm so glad you stayed friends with Henry. He's been such a good friend to you."

"It was a really nice visit," I say, feeling the most relaxed I've felt in a long time.

Henry and I visited our favorite haunts with his wife, Raegan—we got cheap burritos in Mission and walked around the city, talking about old times. They both love San Francisco, but Raegan always wanted to live in Paris; she is fluent in French and had studied abroad there.

Never did I think Henry would move across the world, but Raegan talked him into it.

After the party, Raegan went to bed, and Henry and I walked to the bar in his neighborhood.

"We might eventually settle down where Raegan's from, Goldheart," he mentioned casually.

"Goldheart?" I asked. That's a town I've tried not to think about for years.

"You know it? Have you been there?" Henry asked.

"Once."

"Her sister is pregnant. Married into a well-known family there. They'll keep me flush in beer." He holds up his pint glass, frosty with condensation. I must've looked confused, because he said, "They own a brewery. Woody Finch. Really good beer."

I freeze and choke on my sip. "Finch?"

"Yeah, that's the family's name. Finch."

All the moisture evaporates from my mouth. "Is there an Emily in that family, by chance?"

"Yes, do you know her?"

"Kind of," I said. I changed the subject to anything else, but that night, I couldn't sleep. Emily. Goldheart. Two things I've tried to forget, but have always failed at. After breakfast, I climbed in my car, frozen in my seat.

"Are you driving home right now?" my mother asks.

"No, I'm a... Henry asked me to stay a little longer. Who knows when I'll see him again."

The lie coats my mouth.

"Sounds like you won't make it for dinner. Rats. I'll be stuck with your father."

I wince at the dig. "You probably will."

"Oh well. We were going to suggest going out anyway." She changes the subject. "Is it over yet? This nonsense with Noelle?"

"Not yet." My jaw grinds at the mention of Noelle.

"You're being ridiculous, Maxwell. That girl is perfect for you."

I cough into my hand, braking for traffic. "It was her idea, Mom."

"That girl *had* to give you an ultimatum. You're thirty-five. You've dated her for three years. It's time, honey."

"Mom," I say sternly, coming to a complete stop. My temples pulse with this conversation.

"That girl wants to be your wife."

But do *I* want that? I keep that thought to myself.

This break started thirty days ago, when Noelle mentioned her recently engaged friend, Kira. Noelle described Kira's engagement ring at length, including the carat, cut, and the other C's, while I stayed silent.

"You're not listening," she claimed.

"I am," I said with an involuntary eye roll, and then Noelle exploded.

"Why won't you marry me?" came out during tears, and I didn't have a good answer for her. It led to an explosive fight, and through tears, she said, "I'm going to give you thirty days to figure out if I'm the one. No talking, *no sex*. If you don't propose by the end of thirty days, I'm gone."

I tried to talk her out of it, but she stood firm. "You can't see me. You can't text me. You can't call me. I want you to be sure of your decision. That I'm the one."

The last thirty days has been lonely, but I'm just as confused as I was a month ago.

The last time I wasn't confused about someone, I turned out to be completely wrong.

It was a week. One week. Nothing in comparison to the three years I've been with Noelle, the experiences we've had, the ways we've grown as a couple. I love Noelle.

Still, a girl named Emily still haunts me, even ten years later.

"You know," my mother says, "my friend Rita just had the most delicious grandbaby."

"Are you going to eat it?"

Mom chuckles. "No, silly. I'm just saying. All my friends are becoming grandparents. I'm getting old, Maxwell."

I roll my eyes. She sounds like Noelle. Sometimes I catch Noelle and Mom conspiring, studying me like a sperm donor in a book. Noelle would make a wonderful mother, and my children would be so lucky.

Still, I hesitate.

"Are you going to call Noelle?" my mother asks, shaking me from my thoughts.

"She's my next call." We discussed over text that I would call her today to discuss meeting for dinner to give her my answer. I still don't know what I'm going to do.

"I'll be anxious to hear what happens. Do something romantic for her. She loves that." I roll my eyes. My mom would love a daughter-in-law. "Remember, your father is retiring this week. His party is Saturday."

"I know," I say. My mother has given me a week-by-week countdown for months. It's finally happening. Fred Sawyer is hanging up his fluoride. The longer he delayed it, the more relieved I felt. Meanwhile, he came close to being the subject of his own *Dateline* murder special because he works so much and my mother is fed up, to say the least.

"I love you, Mom."

"I love you too, Button."

We hang up, and my thoughts drift as I sit in stop-and-go traffic.

I have the specs for Noelle's dream ring in my phone. Halfway through our break, I made an appointment with a jeweler, but something came up at work. For the first year and a half, our relationship was so fun, and I fell in love with her without trying. Then, the wedding bug hit her, and it was all about getting engaged, buying a house, babies. I was in trouble whenever another man dropped to one knee for his woman. We didn't go to Henry's wedding because Henry and

Raegan got engaged after six weeks and Noelle thought it would be too triggering for her.

"I don't get why they got engaged so fast. It doesn't make sense," she said, staring off into a corner like someone died.

I shrugged it off at the time, neither agreeing or disagreeing. Noelle didn't know that I understood it, a little too much.

I should marry her. Noelle is perfect.

I dial Noelle. She picks up after one ring.

"Hey, baby!" she says through the dashboard. "I missed you!"

"Hey, baby. I missed you too," I parrot. It's silent between us. I'm not sure what she's been doing, but I have no more clarity since our fight twenty-nine days ago.

"So..."

We had no plans, but I blurt out, "I won't be able to see you tonight. I'll be home late. Henry and Raegan had a going-away party in San Francisco, and I stayed a little longer than I planned."

"Oh, how are they?" Noelle's cheer sounds fake.

"Great. I'm sorry I stayed longer."

"No problem. I'll miss you." She's quiet for a second, so I glance at the connection. Traffic is picking up, moving at a good pace, but I keep my eyes on the road. She finally says, "I've thought long and hard about it, and you can move in. I can be patient a little longer."

My throat constricts. "I thought you wanted to be engaged first."

"I do," she says. Noelle had lived with a boyfriend for five years who never pulled the trigger. When we started dating, she made that rule. "Our time apart was really eye-opening. I love you, and I can compromise. I would be happy living together for now. It'll give you time to plan the perfect proposal. I'm sure the ring I want will take time, and I want you to have it when you propose."

Scratchiness creeps into my throat. "We can talk about it tomorrow. Let's go to that Japanese place you like so much."

I've never been a fan of that place, but Noelle asks constantly if we can go.

"Really?" she asks, brightness in her voice. "I'll see if there's any reservations."

"We can always sit at the bar, if not."

"Great," she says. "I'll see you tomorrow. I love you."

"See you tomorrow," I say, and the guilt hits me in the gut. I should tell her what I'm doing, but it'll create a Chernobyl-sized explosion. Going to the town where the girl I dated for a week lives is beyond insanity, but I need to know. For me, for my relationship with Noelle. All I need to do is see her in a relationship, with a kid or two, and I can move on. Noelle wouldn't understand if I told her now, but if it gets a two-carat cushion-cut diamond with a halo on her finger later, she'd be fine.

At least, I hope so.

When I pull into Goldheart, I'm overwhelmed by memories. I notice some changes to the facades of the main street businesses, updates to signs and fresh coats of paint, but it still holds the charm I remember. The gazebo in the middle of town gleams white, and residents and tourists are already out and about, holding coffee or shopping bags full of souvenirs or treats.

A sign tells me, *Woody Finch Brewery, up ahead.*

Just like Henry said.

I remember conversations with Emily, in the afternoon sun, watching Tin Lake, swapping stories about our families. She mentioned her dad's hobby of microbrewing, and we even tasted some even though Emily was under twenty-one.

A coffee shop appears, and angels sing. My eyelids feel

heavy from the alcohol last night and the lack of sleep at the hotel. If I remember correctly, this town was settled because of the gold rush, so this looks like a building left over from that time, refurbished for modern businesses. I open an outside door to a hallway, and then open the door to Gold Roast.

A pretty woman around my age stands behind the cash register with a welcoming smile.

"Welcome to Gold Roast. What can I get you?"

"Coffee, black." I pull out my wallet from my back pocket.

"Two-fifty." I pull out a five and hand it to her. Once she places the change in my hand, I stick a dollar in the tip jar.

"Can I ask you a question?" I ask.

"Sure," she says. Her name tag says *Tara.*

"When does Woody Finch Brewery open, do you know?"

This is easily Googleable, but I just need to say it out loud, to make it real.

She looks at me like I'm dense. "I think it's closed for an event today. It's Emily's birthday."

Her name hits me straight in the heart.

"Emily's birthday?" Should I show up? Is that weird?

Tara cocks her head to the side, like she's studying me. "Do you know Emily?"

I pull out another bill and stick it in the tip jar. "Kind of. Thank you for the information."

Tara's eyebrows knit together as she turns to pull my coffee. When she turns back, she sets the cup on the counter.

"Thanks."

"You're welcome." Her look is curious. I don't immediately recall her from ten years ago, but my memory can be bad. The coffee hits my throat, dark and rich, and when I turn back, she stares at me.

I hold up my hand in a farewell.

When I get back into my car, I pull out of a parking space

and go in the direction of the sign. At the end of Main Street, there's a large field and a red barn with white trim in the distance. A paved road winds through the grass and I'm at the entrance.

Woody Finch Brewery, where dogs and their humans are welcome is scrawled across the sign directly in front of the bar. Picnic tables litter the front, and the front parking lot is empty. A few cars are parked at the rear.

I wonder if one of them is Emily's.

I sit for a few minutes. What should I say if I see her? Will it be weird? Are they even open?

She probably doesn't remember me. After I left for Costa Rica, I never heard from her, and my emails went unanswered.

I tried to find her once in Goldheart. It didn't go so well.

I bet she's married now with a couple kids and is happy.

"What are you doing?" I ask out loud. Turning off the engine, I sit, staring at the red siding. Is this a good idea? She might not remember me or want to see me. It's her birthday, for Christ's sake.

I stick my key back into the ignition.

"This is insane." My car roars back to life, but my hands stay planted on the steering wheel. They don't move; they don't shift my car to reverse.

No, I came all this way. I need to know she's okay. If I see her happily married, I will take it as my sign to commit to Noelle. A woman who has been more than patient with me.

"Let's do this," I tell myself as I switch off the engine again and open the car door. I adjust my pants and check my shirt. Shaking out my hands, I walk to the entrance.

I'm not proud, but I try to look in. The door is dark, and I can't see much.

Before I lose my nerve, I knock. If no one answers, I might take that as a sign as well.

There's noise inside as a man walks to the entrance. He's a couple inches taller than I am, and he's imposing, all shoulders and brawn. I work out, but I've always been on the leaner side.

"Can I help you?" he asks. "We're closed for a private event."

He looks like Emily in male form. I smile, to mask the anxiety coursing through my entire body. "Hi. You're one of the brothers, right?"

He studies me. "Yeah, but we're closed…"

"Is Emily here?"

"Yes, but…"

"I was wondering if I could see her," I ask. "Just for a second."

"What's going on…" I hear from the voice that's haunted me for ten years. She steps to the side and the wind is knocked out of me.

She looks exactly the same. The wild brown hair I remember that I ran my fingers through. Her full pink lips I couldn't leave alone for a week straight. Her cheeks are rosier, but I can still see the sprinkle of freckles across her nose. Her body is softer than I remember, but she's wearing a sundress, with strings tied at her shoulders. I don't know what to say. How to act.

All I do is raise a hand and finally say, "Hey Martini. It's been a long time."

3

EMILY

I must be dreaming. There's no way Max is standing in front of me, at my family's brewery, on my birthday. This can't be happening. Just when I gave up any fantasy of him popping up in town, he shows up.

And he looks like *that*.

He's well-dressed like he always was, in khakis and a tucked-in, button-up shirt. His jaw is clean-shaven, his blond hair perfectly styled. When we dated, I joked he was my Ken doll, always perfect. The past ten years had been kind to him. His boyish good looks have morphed into a man's, distinguished and poised. He fills out his shirt now, with broader shoulders, tapering to a slim waist. His eyes crinkle at the sides as he smiles.

I've seen him naked is the first thought I've had. The second thought I had is *Holy shit, I don't want Olive seeing him. Not yet.*

"Hi, um, can you excuse me for a moment?" I ask, holding up a finger.

"Emily, who is this?" Jackson asks. My eyes widen, and my brother's mouth drops in realization and he nods. "Say no more. I'll watch him." Jackson jerks his head to a table. "We're going to sit over here."

"Why? I…"

Jackson's voice grows sterner as he clamps his hand on Max's shoulder. "We're sitting over here."

I mouth *thank you* before I run off to smuggle my daughter out of here like a rescue mission for a hostage victim.

My mother and daughter are walking down the hall back towards the taproom, laughing like two ladies out for a shopping date and a light salad lunch. Shiloh is several steps behind.

"Mom, Olive, come here. Shiloh too."

"What's going on?" My mom's face tells me Mom has gone to the worst-case scenario in her thoughts. Fires. Gunmen. Clowns.

"I need you to go into the office," I say. The nearest office is Jackson's, and it's locked. I rattle the door handle several times, like jiggling it will open it.

"I have a key," Shiloh says, wedging herself next to me to put the key into the lock from her keyring.

"Thank you," I breathe out. I'm not sure if I should cry or scream. Maybe both.

I honestly didn't ever come up with a game plan if he ever showed up. As the years passed, I grew less and less hopeful, sure I would never see him again. Olive would never meet him. It was easier than being disappointed.

Then, he shows up today, of all days, and I need my daughter out of here as quickly as possible.

I kneel in front of Olive. "Honey, we need to go home."

"What about the party?" she asks, her blue eyes widen and glazed. Tears are coming.

"Honey, just trust me." Olive's chin quivers, and her bottom lip juts out.

"But why, Mom?"

"Emily, what is going on?" Mom asks. Both her and Shiloh look at me with concern.

"Mom, he's here," I whisper.

"Who?" Her face suddenly morphs into one of understanding and shock. "Olive, listen to your mother."

"But I want biscuits. It's the only thing Burke does right…"

"I'll bring you some, honey, I promise."

"You stay here. I'll take her home," my mom offers.

"What's going on?" Shiloh asks, her smile so innocent. My daughter is distraught, staring into the corner, so I point to Olive's head.

Her dad, I mouth.

"Oh," Shiloh says. Shiloh knows enough about Max so she kneels down in front of my daughter. "How about we have a special day, just the two of us? I'll take you for some ice cream, and then we can take Bubba for a walk." Bubba is her pit bull rescue, and my daughter talks about him incessantly after she sees him. Olive is also obsessed with Shiloh, and a day just the two of them trumps any family gathering.

Olive looks up. "Really?"

"Sure," Shiloh says, standing up, placing her hand on Olive's back. I could cry at Shiloh's quick thinking and kindness. She reaches over Olive's head and takes me in a hug. "Keep me posted, but we'll do lots of fun things."

"Okay," I say.

I hand her my keys since Olive's booster is in there, and Shiloh places her hand on my cheek so tenderly, I hold back tears. "You got this."

I nod against her hand, and Shiloh takes it away, offering it to my daughter. Olive slips her hand into Shiloh's without hesitation. "Come on, Miss Olive. We're going to have a fun adventure day! It'll be better than this old party."

When they leave, I collapse in half with a long exhale and lean over, bracing my hands on my thighs. The tightness in my chest spreads to my throat, and I can't breathe. My mom's hand on my back does nothing to reassure me.

"Honey, just breathe. It'll all be okay."

"Why now?" I gasp for air. "Why did he have to show up today?"

"Did he know it was your birthday?"

"No. I don't think so." I stand up and stick my hands on my hips, wheezing. "Do you think he's still out there?"

"Probably. He came all this way."

"Mom, I don't want to deal with it. Can you tell him to go away?"

"No, Emily Jean. You're dealing with this." Mom steps in front of me and rests her arm around my shoulders. I want to unleash the biggest sob. She pats my shoulder like I'm being ridiculous. I don't think I am. A guy I slept with ten years ago is back, and a child he didn't want is actually walking and talking and about to be so hopped up on sugar that she won't go to bed tonight because the angel my brother chose bought me some time.

"Come on. You need to face him," Mom says as she ushers me to the door. I brace my hands on the door frame so I don't have to leave. Mom tries to yank me, but I've dug my heels in.

"Mom, I don't know what to say to him."

"Tell him you'll meet him for dinner," Mom says. "That way you can enjoy the party."

"Enjoy the party. You want me... to enjoy the party. With *him*?"

"Hell no, we're not inviting him to stay. Absolutely not. You will go out there and tell him that you will see him tonight. You will enjoy the gorgeous meal your *boyfriend* prepared for you, and then you will go to dinner with him tonight to figure out what he wants. I will babysit and put Olive to bed after God knows what Shiloh will feed her."

"Mom, I don't want to do this."

She takes my face in her hands so I can focus on her. "You have to do this. For Olive. You need to see what he wants."

My chin quivers. My mom's the only person who knows the full story, outside of my good friend Caroline, who was my best friend when I got pregnant.

"You will be fine."

My mom's hand on my cheek tips me over the edge, and I let out a sob, my face contorting into an ugly cry. Emotion I've repressed into my bones billows out like steam from a sewer crate.

Without saying anything, she envelops me in a hug and pats down my hair.

"He didn't want us," I say between sobs against my mother's chest. "He didn't want me. I thought he did, and I was wrong."

"Shh," my mom soothes as we stand there, in Jackson's office. She holds me until my sobs quiet and then pulls away.

"I know you did not expect this today," my mom says. "You don't know what his motives are. Maybe he had a change of heart."

"I can't think like that, I…." I unleash another sob.

"Emily Jean Finch." Mom pushes me away, but still holds my arms. "You need to face this. I'll be there with you. I promise."

She's right. I nod, and my mom cages me with one arm around my shoulders and her other hand holding my arm, shepherding me out in the taproom. Max is still there, sitting at the decorated table. Jackson is acting like an air marshal with a criminal, waiting for landing. Burke stands over the food, inspecting it, but he gives an unsure smile when he sees me.

When Max notices me, he shoots up, walking toward me.

God, he's handsome. It's unfair he's still as good-looking as I remember.

Maybe more.

I summon the demeanor I've had for the past ten years. Strong, capable, unfazed. Even though I cried in my mother's arms literally forty-five seconds ago, I walk away from my mom's clutch and approach Max.

This is a business transaction. Don't look at the chiseled jawline.

"Let's talk outside." I point to the door. Jackson takes a step to follow, but I hold up a hand. "I promise, I'll be fine."

You don't have to talk about specifics. Just ask him to meet you for dinner to discuss, and then you can pretend like this didn't happen for four hours. You can do this. One step in front of another.

The heat in the air is oppressive when we walk outside, but I still cross my arms so tightly around myself, I might bruise.

"If I would've known it was your birthday, I would've gotten you a gift." He chuckles nervously.

All I can do is look at his shoes. His lovely, well-made cognac shoes.

"Listen, Max, this is a family thing, so ..."

"I just want to talk." He holds his hands out like he comes in peace. "It doesn't have to be now. We can meet..."

My gaze drifts from his shoes to the gravel. "Sure."

"How about that Italian place we went to on my last night? Is it still open?" he asks. There's cheer in his voice, but I don't look up to see if there's a smile attached. Heat simmers low in my belly. How I tried to remember his voice for years, and now it's here, huskier and deeper, still strumming something inside of me.

"Sure," I say. *Keep your eyes down. Don't look.*

"Do you want me to pick you—"

"No!" I shout. I look up for a quick second, and that's a mistake. His eyes are arresting and so much like Olive's I have to look away. I can't blurt out my secret right now. I will do it in a classy way. A dignified way, after two to three cocktails.

"I'll meet you there. Six o'clock. La Scarola. It's on Rosella Drive. In Auburn," I say.

"Perfect. I can find it then. Can I get your number?" he asks.

"Sure," I say. Of course he wouldn't have my number, still. Even then, I changed it a long time ago, right after the *incident*.

Taking Max's phone, I notice the lock screen of a photo of him with a blond woman, smiling, both holding glasses of wine.

Swallowing, I hand it back to him. "I need your passcode."

"Oh, sorry." He types it in, and the screen is now filled with apps.

He has a girlfriend. Or a wife. I glance at his left hand, trying to be as casual as possible, but there's no wedding band. Maybe he's the kind of guy who doesn't wear one or loses it. Why is he here if he has her?

I type my full name into his contacts and enter my number. Max takes his phone back and types something in. My phone in my purse vibrates, and my eyes close.

"I just texted you," he says, shaking his phone at me. "Did you get it?"

"I think I got it."

"Can you check?" He smiles, and my knees go weak.

I pull out my phone. *Hi* from a 619 area code.

"Got it."

"Great," he says. His smile is unfair. Completely unfair. I'm not sure how I'll survive a dinner with him, after I tell him everything, knowing he has a hot girlfriend who he decided to stay with. He may even have a child or two. He sure had strong sperm.

Thinking about Olive potentially having a sibling makes me woozy. Baby steps. First step: Get through party. Second step: Freak out in private. Third step: Prepare every possible scenario for dinner tonight. Maybe prepare a flow chart.

Max's smile spreads to a grin, and I lock my knees so I don't fall. He's still so handsome. No wonder my daughter is so good-looking.

"I'll see you tonight at six o'clock at La Scarola on Rosella Drive in Auburn," he says. He shoves his hands in his pockets and hesitates. Does he want to hug me? Why is he here? What does he want to say?

The moment fades away as he walks away toward what I assume is his car. It's a gray sedan, modest, unlike Burke's car.

He stops, turns around, and I brace for whatever he has to say.

"It's really good to see you. To know you're real. That I didn't imagine it."

My mouth flops open as he nods with a closed mouth smile and walks away. My hands shake against my legs. As he pulls away, gravel sputters from his tires, and I let out a sigh so loud it startles me. Ripping open my purse's zipper, I pull out my phone.

I tap to open my contacts and find the Bs. I haven't talked to her in a few months, since she recently had a baby and I know how discombobulating that can be. Still, she needs to know. She was there.

It rings three times, and I think it's going to voicemail. Instead, she answers, and I gulp air because I've been holding my breath.

"Emily, hey, what's going on?" Caroline asks. "It's been ages!"

I take a deep breath. "Caroline, he's back."

The line goes dead like she hung up on me. Then, I hear an "Oh *shit*."

4

EMILY

TEN YEARS AGO

"You can do this," Caroline said.

I cradled my phone in my left hand and a positive pregnant test in my right. I found out I was pregnant two days, three hours, and fifty-three minutes ago. My finger hovered over the number in my phone, and I let out a huff of air.

This was a nightmare. The first time I ever had sex, and I got a plus sign. Just my fucking luck.

I had just turned twenty, still home from school for the summer. My roommate at USC, Caroline, was up for the day from her parents' house in Lillyvale, a town about an hour from us. At lunch, I told her I didn't feel good, and we did menstrual math together. She knew about losing my virginity to Max, and she had joked, "What if you're pregnant?"

"That's not even funny, Caroline. We had sex once."

Caroline's chin lowered, and she gave me an all-knowing look through her eyelashes. I threw my hands up. "Okay, more than once. However, condom, every time."

"One didn't slip?"

As I took a bite of salad, I remembered an "Oh shit" from Max the first time. At the time I didn't think anything of it.

"The condom just slipped, no big deal," he said as he readjusted it. Then, he sunk into me again, and all the worries flew out of my head.

"Let's get a test. Just for fun," she suggested.

"What a waste of ten dollars," I said.

It wasn't fun as we watched a distinct, opaque pink line join the line already there.

"I was *joking*," she said, looking up at me with wide eyes and parted lips.

I burst into tears, and Caroline held me. "It'll all be okay. He said he loves you, right?"

"Yeah," I said through sobs.

"It'll be fine. Everything will be okay," Caroline said, handing me my phone, perched on the bathroom counter. "Be brave."

When Max left me for his dental mission in Costa Rica, he promised he would email me, since he had no idea what the service would be like in the mountains. It had been six weeks since he left, and I assumed he was getting settled.

We always figured I would get his email once he sent me one, and I really wished I had gotten his email at the same time as he got mine.

His phone number was all I had.

I take a deep breath and shake my head. "You know, I should wait until he gets home, because he told me the service is terrible in Costa Rica..."

"You're stalling."

"Well...I'm just not trying to get my hopes up because I haven't gotten an email and we might get voicemail..."

"Emily, you're my dearest friend, but if you don't stop talking and call him, I will murder you."

"Okay, fine."

My thumb shook as I scrolled to the Ss, to *Sawyer, Max*, a

small heart after his name. I pressed on it and held it to my ear. An automated message startled me.

This person is unavailable right now. Please try again later.

Pulling the phone away from my ear, I dialed again, just to be greeted with the same message.

"Told you. His phone isn't taking messages." I couldn't think. Looking up at Caroline, her shocked expression alarms me.

"Did he block me?" I asked.

"No, no, no," Caroline said. "There has to be an explanation."

She grabbed the phone from me and tried again, just to receive the same message. Her face grows long.

"What?" I asked.

"You remember Brett from that party last year? He blocked me, and I got that very message."

"No," I responded, but the inkling invaded my mind. What if he blocked me? What if I'm being ghosted right now?

"Oh my God." I covered my face because the tears were inevitable.

"Don't cry. There's other ways to get ahold of him."

"How?" I squeaked out between sobs. "This is hopeless."

"That is quitter talk," Caroline said. We sat in silence for minutes, in my childhood bedroom, as we thought. My gaze drifted to the pregnancy test, sitting on my stack of summer reading.

Caroline snapped her fingers. "I got it. I know how we can get ahold of him."

5

MAX

Well, that was interesting.

After I walked back to my car from the brewery, I shake out my hands and try to wrap my brain around what just happened.

I saw her. As expected, she looked stunning and just as beautiful as I remember her. Maybe even more.

Her hair was slightly longer and wavy, falling like scrunched silk on her creamy shoulders. The eyes were what I remembered the most. The color of jade, staring into mine when we saw each other for the first time ten years ago. Sundresses have always been my weakness, and the one she was wearing hugged her figure—her small breasts, her hips. I had to tell myself to look from the neck up. The whole situation was unfair, and a laugh in my face.

What I feared would happen happened. When I saw her, it was like no time had passed. I was twenty-five again, rattled by a girl who took over my world with a Diet Coke and a smile.

I agreed to dinner, considerably later in the day, and now I need to figure out how to get back to San Diego in time for my eight a.m. patients tomorrow, folks who had appointments for weeks. I work as a partner at my dad's dental practice, with the intention of taking it over when Dad retires later this week.

My dad always instilled in me that our patients come first, above all else. If we have personal appointments, we do it outside of practice hours. I've taken exactly one vacation since I started at the practice eight years ago, besides my annual dental missions to Costa Rica. I went on my first one the year I met Emily, after my first year of dental school.

My dad allows it because it looks good for the business to take a break from our well-off clients once in a while. I do it because it's the only time I truly love being a dentist. Helping people gives me so much joy.

Sawyers do not get distracted. My mother works at the office as a receptionist, so the Sawyer Dental Practice is a family affair. She never books serious procedures, like root canals or veneers, on Monday. So at least there's that.

Guilt roars through me as I look up maps and timeframes of how fast I can get from rural Northern California to San Diego after our dinner. It will be ten hours, at least, of driving, mostly through the night. For all my mom knows, I'm on my way back now, probably north of L.A. Not in this tiny town we went to once for the rare vacation my mom practically threatened divorce over.

Time moves slowly as I wait. I try to nap in my car since I'll have a long drive ahead of me. Every time I close my eyes, I see her, terrified at my presence. Pulling me aside to ask me to go to dinner. Why was she so scared to see me? We did make all our promises to each other, and then she never responded to my emails and changed her phone number. There's hope, though—she wants to have dinner with me, and on her birthday no less. Maybe this has been eating at her like it's been eating me.

Dinner is a big deal. If I were nothing to her, she would've told me to go away. She wouldn't be meeting me.

Five o'clock rolls around, and I drive to Auburn, pulling into the parking lot of the restaurant. It's nondescript from the outside, but inside holds some of the best Italian food I've ever tasted. I arrive twenty-five minutes early, my body twitching from anticipation and the long drive I have back to San Diego.

It will be worth it, though. This dinner will answer questions I've had for a long time.

I plan to leave for home with zero questions. Clarity. The ability to go back to my life and close this chapter forever.

After this, I can commit to Noelle, and I can finally stop thinking about Emily Finch.

Two minutes before six, a dark SUV pulls in and parks next to me. When I turn my head, Emily turns hers at the same time. Her face is long and terrified. I hope she's not scared of me.

I wave, and she waves back tentatively. Maybe it's just nerves.

I exit my car first. Emily stays in hers, her hands glued to the steering wheel.

I stand at my trunk with one hand in my pocket, waiting for her to come out as well. She doesn't.

After I walk to her window, she's staring out her windshield. There's nothing to look at, just cars and a lone potted tree. I knock at her window.

Her door finally opens, and she steps down, her knee buckling under her. I reach for her, but she holds up her hands.

"Are you okay?"

"I'm great. Dandy. Never been better." Emily's whole throat moves with a swallow.

"Are you sure this is okay? It's your birthday, after all. I got you something."

I pull out a can of Diet Coke with a bow on it. The gas station attendant I bought it from looked at me like I was nuts.

Emily's whole face melts at my gesture. I wonder if she thinks about how we met as much as I do. "Thank you," she says. She drops it in her large purse, hitting something inside with a thunk.

"Are you sure this is okay? Did you have other plans?"

"There's no one I would rather spend it with than you," she says. I squint at her, but brush it off. For some reason, she's on edge and I don't know why. She points to La Scarola. "Besides, this is my favorite restaurant."

I look up at it. It always looked like nothing from the outside. "I'm excited. I remember this place being excellent."

"Oh, it still is!" Her voice hit a high note and cracks.

"Are you okay?"

"Yup, why wouldn't I be?" She laughs, but it's a machine gun of awkward chuckles.

"Okay," I say. She's acting so strangely. "Are you sure?"

"Perfect. Never been better." She lets out an exhale, hitting a low note as she leads the way to the restaurant.

She talks to the hostess, who leads us to a small table. The table we sat at on my last night in town is next to us. I remember how I wanted that night to never end. Instead of sitting next to her on the half booth like our last night, I take the outside chair.

"I never thought I'd be back here. It looks exactly the same."

Emily opens the menu like she's never been there before. "That's part of its charm."

"It's been a long time," I say, holding my menu, looking at her.

"It sure has."

"Hi, Emily," the server says. She turns to me and points back to her. "New man?"

"Well—"

The server nods once and pulls out a pad of paper. "What can I get you to drink?"

"Coffee. Black," I order.

"Double gin and tonic."

"Oh, it's one of *those* nights," the server says with a chuckle as she walks away. Emily's chest is bright red. She's changed out of the sundress to a tank top and shorts, and I tried not to look, but the red is spreading down her neck and arms.

"Emily, you're bright red."

Her eyebrows lower as she extracts a black rectangle from her purse and flips it open. It must be a mirror.

"Oh my God," she says once she takes a look at herself. Then, she drops her elbow to the table with a thud to drop her head into it, a loud clank of the centerpiece and the silverware vibrating through the restaurant. She lifts her arm to hold her elbow. "Ow."

"Let me look at it. I am a doctor."

"You're a dentist," she points out. "Right? That still happened?"

"Yes," I say. "I've been practicing for eight years now."

"Did they teach you about elbows in dental school?"

"I learned elbows on the streets," I joke. She giggles, and it breaks the tension. She flicks her hands out.

"It's fine. Never better. I need alcohol, like right now." Her eyes scan every direction but at me, and I fail to catch her gaze. Her hands tuck under her thighs. Is she being followed? Did she have to go into witness protection right after we spent time together? Is her name actually Emily Finch?

"I don't want anything," I promise. "Just all these years, I was curious. About you."

"Oh, okay." More sarcasm. Holding in everything I want to ask, I fold my arms in front of me. We can ease into the tough stuff later.

She fidgets, and I can't focus.

The server returns with Emily's drink and my coffee, steaming billowing from a white ceramic mug. Emily throws the black, tiny straw over her shoulder and takes a glug from the side, draining half of it. She winces as she slams the drink back down.

"I have something to tell you," Emily finally says.

She rests her laced fingers on the table. She stares at the centerpiece as I lean down too.

"You're making me nervous."

She lets a long guffaw. "Just wait. Just you wait."

After letting out a laugh reserved for deranged serial killers, Emily takes another huge swallow of her drink. Only a thin layer of liquid rests amongst chunky ice cubes.

"You're drinking that really, *really* fast. Whatever you have to tell me can't be that bad."

"Oh, it is."

She tucks her hair behind her ears, ears I always thought were adorable since they flare out slightly. God, she's pretty. She closes her eyes and breathes in and out like she's in a yoga class.

"So," she says, her eyes opening but staring at the ceiling. "Remember, when we…you know…did it."

"Yeah." My cheeks grow hot, and my cock swells against my zipper. Over the years, I've played that night over and over again. It was awkward and weird and…perfect.

"Remember when you weren't sure what happened to the condom but told me not to worry about it?"

"Yes…" Oh my God.

"Well, surprise," she says, her eyes flashing open to look

6

MAX

I am numb. My mouth opens but no sound comes out.

I had the baby.

After all those years of wondering why she never reached out, it's because she had a baby and didn't tell me.

I look up, my mouth agape. "Is she mine?"

Emily nods, her hair escaping and falling into her face.

Staring at the tablecloth, I feel my limbs buzz. My breath is irregular as the room grows warm. I pull at my collar since my throat constricts.

"I bet you didn't expect that," Emily says with an audible sigh as she picks her glass up again, the ice hitting her teeth.

Fuck no, I wasn't expect that. Driving home tonight is not happening. I need to stay, I need to understand how the fuck I have a nine-year-old child I didn't know about.

She told me she was a virgin when we slept together, and I believed her. Even if I saw her with a guy several months later, she wouldn't lie about this.

The server walks to our table. "Are you ready to order?"

"One more, please." Emily holds up her tumbler.

"Do you have bourbon?" I ask.

The server, a woman in her fifties, stares at me. "Of course. What kind?"

Shaking my head, I close my eyes. My brain needs to work, words need to form. "The strongest kind. One ice cube. Fill 'er up."

"Are you ordering food as well, or just drinks tonight?"

"I don't know what I need," I say.

"We will. Just give us a moment," Emily says, another high-pitched laugh accompanying it.

My mind clears, and consciousness leaves my body. Time has stopped.

I missed nine years. Her birth. Her learning to walk. Her saying "Dada" for the first time and meaning me.

My worst nightmare has come true. I abandoned a child without my knowledge.

My shock morphs into white-hot heat. Pressure boils in my temples; my fingers quiver. How dare she keep this from me. She knew how to get ahold of me. I sent her an email every day I was in Costa Rica. She had a million opportunities to tell me. To find me. To give me a chance.

She didn't.

Our daughter suffered.

My daughter.

I can't look at Emily. All I can do is stare at this fake flower centerpiece. What do I say that is measured, that is appropriate for the news I just received? I want to lash out. Show my rage. However, I'm not that guy. Suffering in silence is my go-to.

So, silence it is.

We are still sitting in a staring contest when the server swings back around with Emily's second drink and my bourbon.

"Soooo," Emily says, letting the O drag out.

"Give me a moment." I take a gulp, the liquid searing the

back of my throat. My trip home be damned. All my patients tomorrow need to be rescheduled. I need to stay to figure out how the fuck this happened.

I look up to really study this woman. A woman I thought I knew. We spent hours getting to know each other that week, but I guess that's not enough time. Inside her was a person who decided one day she was done with me.

My gaze flicks to her and she smiles to break the tension but it's palpable, like a rubber band pulled too tight. This will snap.

"Why didn't you tell me?" I run my hand down my face.

She shrugs one shoulder. "At the end of the day, I couldn't do it."

I stare at her. "Couldn't do what?"

"Get rid of it. Of her." She folds her hands and looks down.

"I didn't expect you to." I shake my head and take another swig of bourbon. It made my mouth twitch as it hit the back of my throat. "It's your body. I wouldn't have a say if you did."

"Really?" she asks. Her eyelids shrink her eyes to slivers as she peers at me.

"Yeah," I say. "What's she like?"

Emily shakes her head, and her eyelashes flutter. "She's perfect. Completely healthy. Happy."

My throat constricts and I cough, emotion tugging the back of my eyes. I could fall apart, right here. Instead, I center myself. Displays of strong emotions are never an efficient way of getting things done.

"Where is she right now?" I ask.

"She's with her grandmother. My mom."

I start laughing, uncontrollably, manic tears leaving the corners of my eyes. Taking the cloth napkin, I dab my cheeks, but the tears still stream down as my laughter fills the restaurant. Other patrons turn their heads to look.

"What's so funny?" Emily's face mirrors my own mixture of confusion and rage.

"My mother asked me this morning when I would make her a grandmother. She manifested it," I choke out between the giggles. Taking a deep breath, I calm down and take another sip. The bourbon churns in my stomach, ripping up the lining, making me hollow. I haven't really eaten anything today, but I doubt I could stomach anything right now.

Everything about this situation feels like a punch to the gut.

"Are you married?" Emily asks.

"I have a girlfriend."

Emily's face falls. "Okay."

"You?"

"I have a boyfriend," she whispers. "Burke."

The gnaw in my stomach morphs to nausea. I take another sip. "When can I meet her? Olive?"

"Are you staying in town?" Emily asks.

"Now I am." My tone is harsh, but I don't care.

"Okay. Let's plan for tomorrow. You can come to the brewery."

I clench my jaw and knock my fist on the table. "Are you going to tell her? We're going to tell her? That I'm her father?"

Emily's face crumples as she traces an invisible circle with her fingernail on the tablecloth. We both stare at the same spot on the table. "You can meet her, but we can't tell her. Not yet, anyway."

I cough against my fist and grab my phone. "Excuse me. I have to make some calls and rearrange some appointments for tomorrow."

"Okay. I'll be here. Drinking."

Standing up with force, the chair tilts violently from my body. My hands shake as I unlock my phone, scrolling for my mother's number. My thumb hovers over her contact.

Focus on the call. Focus on the step immediately in front of me.

My mother can't know right now. I need time to process this. To figure out what the fuck I'm going to do. My parents will try to fix this, and this is something I need to fix, without their input.

The phone rings three times before my mom answers. "Hi, Button. What's going on? Are you on your way home?"

"No," I say. "Something came up."

"Oh? What happened? Are you okay?"

"I'm fine, Mom. Listen, I can't tell you what it is, but I can't come home just yet. Can you arrange my patients for tomorrow? Apologize for me?"

"Honey, you're scaring me."

"Don't be scared. I just need some time. Dad's retiring this week, and I want to be refreshed..." The lie tumbles out, cool and believable. I hate lying to my mother, but I need space without her or Fred breathing down my neck. Because he's retiring, it's a light week with no involved procedures. He looks for any excuse to work so he won't mind.

Fred Sawyer, the man I call my father and took my last name from, stepped up when I was two. He's the man who inserted himself into my mom's and my life without an agenda. He loved us. He's handing over his life's work to me next week when I take over his dental practice.

He gave us everything.

Still, every family has its problems. Mine values work over everything else. Even happiness.

"Say no more. You haven't taken a vacation in how long? How about I move all of your patients for this week? It won't be too hard. Noelle and you can get away. I'm sure he would love a chance to see everyone one last time. Then he'll be all mine, and he doesn't have work as an excuse anymore."

"Are you sure Dad'll be okay with that?" I ask. I can't remember the last time Fred or Mom said it was okay to rest. When Noelle and I planned a Hawaii trip last year, my stepdad complained for four months straight, saying he hadn't taken a vacation in thirty years.

My mom rolled her eyes whenever he got on his high horse, because all she wanted was to travel. She was the one who encouraged my dental missions to Costa Rica and convinced Dad it was a good look for our practice.

"I'm getting nice in my old age," she says. "Go somewhere. Reconnect with Noelle. Just be home by Saturday for Fred's party."

"Will do." Another lie. Instead of reconnecting with Noelle, I'm taking this week to reconnect with the mother of my child.

My mother promises to apologize to my patients and let Dad know. Slipping my phone back into my pocket, I hover near the entrance.

I told her, "You know my dad left and Fred is great and all, the absolute best. Who knows where I would be without him. It's just…"

"You want to be the father you didn't have," she finished my sentence.

"Exactly," I said, looking into her eyes.

Emily *knew* this about me and she kept our child a secret, and I became what I hated.

I became an absentee father.

The woman I fell in love with betrayed me.

Maybe I never knew her at all.

Even though I have the best stepdad a guy could ask for, I never forgot the man I'm one-half of disappearing, not caring if I was dead or alive. My mother loved him with her whole soul, and sometimes she looks off into space, and I wonder if she's thinking of him.

There's a reason I don't crack myself open. This hurts even more than keeping myself shut.

When I walk back inside, Emily looks up as I walk to her. I pull out the chair and sit down, placing the napkin across my lap.

"I'll be staying in town for a little bit. So we have time."

"Great. That's wonderful." Emily hesitates. "Do you have a place to stay tonight?"

"No. What kind of accommodations are around here?" Logistics is a safe topic. It will keep me from getting emotional.

Emily contemplates for a moment. "If you want, I have a tiny house on my property. My brother used to live there, but he recently moved out with his wife. It's summer, so it might be tough to find a place to stay in town."

I don't question it. If I'm on her property, she can't run away again. "That would be great."

"Great." She raises the glass again to drain it and then drops it to the table. "I'm not very hungry."

"Me either," I say although my stomach feels like it will turn inside out. I grabbed a breakfast burrito this morning, but after the excitement of seeing Emily and now the shock, I can't fathom eating anything right now.

"My daughter will be there, but I'd prefer you don't meet her until tomorrow. I want to set it up so it's not an ambush."

"I understand." I lean back into the chair, staring at my drink. I look at her, and I can't read her expression. Is she excited? Is she mad she couldn't keep this secret forever?

Her cheeks are flushed, her eyes glassy. She smiles, but her lips drop to a downturn.

"Better late than never, right?"

"Right," I say, my lips tight from this conversation. I crumple the napkin from my lap and throw it on my empty plate. "I'm done."

"Are you mad?" she asks.

"I'll get over it."

"That's fair," she says. "We should sleep on it."

That pulls me back. Noelle hates fighting so we've stayed up until the wee hours of the night, hashing and rehashing disagreements until my will bends because I'm just over discussing it. Emily recognizes anger and lets it exist. Although I'm furious for what she did, at least she gives me space to feel it.

"Okay," I say, my blood pressure already lowering. I pay our bill, and we walk out, several feet from one another. She gives me the address, and I walk to my car after a nod. No touch, no goodbye. When I reach my car, I turn back and she's still standing outside her driver's door, arms folded, with eyebrows knitted together. She looks confused, maybe hurt.

A small part of me wants to go back, but I start my car and drive off.

7

EMILY

I spread peanut butter on a Ritz cracker and make a sandwich with another. A tear hits the treat as I bite into it. I must look pathetic, drinking a lukewarm can of Diet Coke with a bow on it and eating crackers for dinner. My tears started when I hit the threshold of my house and haven't stopped as I polish off a full sleeve with gobs of peanut butter.

Some birthday dinner.

This birthday has sucked ass. I didn't think my twenty-first birthday could be topped, but no. This is hands-down the worst birthday I've ever had.

When I close my eyes, I see Max's shock. The utter disbelief on his face when I told him about Olive burns my brain. He shut down to a deadly silence and fury brewed in his gaze. I thought for a moment he would stand up and leave once I told him I couldn't get an abortion, and our honest mistake is now a human. When he left to make some phone calls, I knew there was a chance he might never come back.

But he did, and now he's in the tiny house. On my property. Absolutely furious with me. He still wants to meet her, even though I was certain he wanted nothing to do with her or me. I'm not sure why he's here. Why he's back, after all this time. Thinking about asking him, getting an answer, incapacitates me with a fear so strong, I want to flee.

But I can't because he's right *there*.

This is so fucked up.

I push the curtains away, the lights glowing against the deepening dusk. My mother is on the way here with Olive, and I'm halfway through my emergency bottle of cheap wine from the Goldheart Neighborhood Market.

Car tires roll over gravel outside, and then I hear two voices—my mother's and my daughter's. I take another deep drink as the door flies open. My daughter bounces in, blissfully unaware, while my mother is cautious, like I'm a black bear out for blood.

"Hi, Mom," Olive says, wrapping her arms around my shoulders. I kiss the side of her head as she squirms. She looks at me, and at least this set of blue eyes isn't mad at me. "Did you have a good birthday?"

"It was a birthday," I say. My mother and I catch glances, and I smile with a closed mouth. Mom takes a seat, and I pour her a glass because I should slow down.

"Olive, can you take a seat, please?" I ask.

"Why?"

"Please sit down."

Olive sighs audibly and sits down, pushing her hair out of her face. I take a sip of wine.

"We have a friend staying with us at the tiny house."

My mother points in the direction and mouths *He's here?*

I nod. Mom takes a sip of wine as her eyes bug before I turn back to Olive.

"His name is Max, and he's a very nice man. He wants to meet you tomorrow. Is that okay?"

"Sure," Olive says. "Do you have a new boyfriend?"

"No," I say with a laugh. "He's just a friend. An old

friend. From a long time ago."

"Okay, weird." Olive stands up with a head shake and walks to the exit of the kitchen. "Can I watch my iPad?"

"Sure, go ahead."

"Yes, I didn't think that would work!" She pumps her fists and runs into the living room.

I slump into my chair and pop the last cracker sandwich in my mouth.

"What a way to enter your thirties," my mom says, holding up her glass so we can cheers. "How was dinner?"

"Awful," I say. "I cleaned out a full sleeve of Ritz crackers."

"You didn't eat at the restaurant?"

I shake my head. "He didn't either. I had to sit in my car for thirty minutes so I was sober enough to drive, though."

"Now, that man is out there. Yards from his daughter."

"Yep. Hence this." I hold up my glass.

"I don't blame you." She takes a sip. "Do we know if he's, you know, dangerous?"

"Max is fine. I wouldn't be surprised if he's supine with shock for the whole night. Or anger."

"He was mad?"

"Yeah, it was weird. I can't think about it for too long, though."

"If anyone has a right to be mad, it's you." Mom pushes up her sleeves and stands up, readjusting her shirt over her hips. "Maybe I should go talk to him."

"No," I yell, grabbing my mother's forearm. "Let him be."

"I can call one of the boys to stay with you. Or I can."

The door rattles with a knock. My mom gives me a look of terror.

"It's fine. It's probably Caroline."

Mom stands and pushes the curtains aside covertly. She opens the door to my long-time friend, Caroline Brady.

"Caroline, it is so nice to see you," Mom says, taking her in a hug. Caroline has a small duffel bag in one hand and a bag from the grocery store in another. "You didn't need to come all the way out here. Where's the baby?"

"With his father. Brady can handle him."

Caroline had a baby eight months ago, and we haven't seen each other since after her wedding. My family was invited but was unable to go. I heard there was a fight that was pretty epic.

Caroline's strawberry-blond hair is tied at the base of her head, and she's wearing comfy athleisure, a shirt off the shoulder with a bra peeping through, and tight black leggings. I should change, but I have no energy whatsoever.

"We made a pact," Caroline says. "Hence, why I brought two more bottles of wine."

I sigh. "You're an angel."

"Pact?" Mom's eyes shot to me.

"When it looked like Max wasn't going to be in Olive's life, Caroline promised she would come immediately if he showed up again," I say.

"Also, happy birthday!" Caroline shouts. She dips her hands into the brown grocery bag and extracts a cake, decorated with white and gold frosting. "Read the top."

I hover over it. "'Thirty, flirty, and dealing with a baby daddy.' Cute."

"I thought so. It kinda rhymes," Caroline says, walking to my cabinets, opening and closing them. "Where are your plates?"

"I'm not hungry," I say.

"I can just put this in the fridge," Caroline says, opening the fridge door.

"Caroline, are you worried about the man being in the tiny house?"

Caroline spins, her hair spraying out with the velocity.

"He's here? On your property? Do you want the raccoons to get him?"

"No, no. I knew the Goldheart Inn would be full. It makes sense."

Caroline touches my arm. "Em, I know you slept with this man, but are you sure he's not a homicidal maniac?"

"Thank you," Mom says, slicing her hand through the air.

"He's fine. Don't worry. I have a sturdy baseball bat and golf clubs."

"Our only hope is the raccoons," Mom mutters under her breath. "Are you sure you don't want me to stay?"

Caroline pats Mom's shoulder. "I'm staying the night, Kit. I told Brady I'm getting drunk after I sobbed for thirty minutes against my baby's head. I need this."

"We'll be fine," I say. "I promise."

My mother hesitates before she slides her purse onto her shoulder.

"I don't want to tell her right away he's her dad. So, please don't say anything."

"I promise I won't." My mom looks at me with a senti-mental gaze and walks over to kiss my head. I hope my smile signals she shouldn't worry about me, but I know she still will. I didn't understand it until I had my own kid. When my brothers have kids, they'll get it too.

"I'll tell him three tomorrow," I say.

"Okay, I hope you girls have fun. Triple-check the doors. And put a chair under the doorknob."

"Got it, Mom." I stand up to hug her, and she sighs against my shoulder.

After saying goodbye to Olive, my mom finally leaves. Caroline and I rush to the window with our wine glasses.

"Do you think she's going to knock at his door?" Caroline asks.

"I have no idea," I say. We watch my mom get into her car

and drive away, the headlights disappearing into the trees.

"Whew." I take another sip of wine.

"I can't believe he's back," Caroline says. "What's he like?"

"Exactly the same. But different." I plop down in my dining room chair again, holding the stem of my glass. "How is he even better-looking than I remember? His eyes crinkle at the sides now, and his eyes are so *blue*. I forgot how powerful those were."

"Still has all his hair?"

"Yep," I say, nodding. "All of it. Not a whisper of thinning. No receding hairline either."

"Damn. Brady would be jealous," she says. She tucks her foot under her butt.

"He has the prettiest girlfriend. Like, what the hell?" I ask, spreading my arms.

"Ooh, Mom's cussing," I hear from the other room over a Pixar movie.

"How do you know what she looks like?" Caroline asks.

"It was the lock screen on his phone."

"I wonder why he's here?"

"Right?" I take another glass of wine, sloshing some burgundy onto my shirt. "Fudge."

"How was it? When you told him?"

I pause before answering Max's fury unnerved me. The anger I saw was quiet, measured.

"It was awful," I say. "He was shocked, to say the least. He asked me why I didn't tell him."

Caroline leans back and taps her fingernails onto the table. "Does his stepdad know he's here?"

"I don't know. We didn't get that far." I stare at my table, the knots in the wood. "This was not what I expected when I got up this morning."

"Does Burke know?"

"About Max? In very broad strokes. Thankfully, I pushed Max out of the brewery before there was any serious questions. Burke didn't ask or anything, and my family wouldn't have clued him in."

"I'm glad we stayed friends, because your life is so fun to watch."

"Shut up," I say with a groan. "This whole situation is utterly ridiculous."

"You're telling me." Caroline looks around the kitchen. "I trust you, Em, when you say he isn't dangerous, but let's wedge some chairs under the doorknobs, just in case."

"I am nowhere near ready for sleep. Let's booby-trap this whole house, like Kevin in *Home Alone*."

"Let's do it." Caroline's smile fades as she stares at the same spot on my table. "How are you? Really? How do you feel?"

A tear leaks from my eye, and I swipe it away. "I finally felt like I stopped hoping he would change his mind. About us." My voice lowers to a whisper. "Olive deserves to meet him. It's just... It's a lot."

Caroline says nothing as she takes me in her arms.

My phone buzzes on the table. I turn it over and my heart clenches.

Max: I want to bring Olive a present tomorrow. What does she like?

I show Caroline the text message.

"This is going to be rough," Caroline says, sitting back. "I don't envy you."

"I don't envy me either." I type something quickly and tell him to meet us at the brewery tomorrow afternoon at three. Going to sleep tonight will be impossible.

"I brought an expensive bottle of wine," Caroline says, pulling it out of her duffel.

"We're going to need it."

8

MAX

I've paced the length of this tiny house at least a hundred times. The structure moves with my steps as I walk back and forth. Knowing my daughter is yards from me is excruciating, even worse than knowing Emily is in there too.

When I woke up this morning and impulsively thought to visit Goldheart, I could've never anticipated all of this.

I'm a father, and I didn't know it. I missed the opportunity to see Emily grow with our child. I missed ultrasound appointments and hearing the baby's heartbeat. I missed her birth. I missed everything. Most of my friends back home have kids already, but their kids are younger, not nine-year-olds. I have no idea what nine-year-olds like or what they're into.

Every time I pass my phone, I pause. It feels wrong to miss nine years and not arrive with a peace offering, although she won't know who I really am at first.

I want to make a good impression. I want her to like me.

I pick up my phone and shoot a text about bringing a present. My hands itch to push the white curtains with tiny daisies away from the window to look at the main house, wondering where Olive is. There's lights on in the kitchen and one light on the second story. She could be in either. I saw a car arrive and then leave just after another car arrived. It was too dark to see who it was, but it looked like a woman leaving and coming.

Her text answering my present question comes back.

Emily: She loves raccoons, and she's been into Mike from *Monsters Inc.* She likes books too.

A smile crosses my lips. I loved to read as a child. I'm glad my daughter got that from me, although she didn't know it.

Emily: Come to Woody Finch at three tomorrow. You can meet her then.

I type back a thumbs-up emoji and grimace. An emoji is too impersonal for what is going on. How could I send her yellow cartoon icon for what just happened between us? How Big Life Moment it was.

My phone lights up, but it's not Emily. I hate myself for feeling a twinge of disappointment.

"Hi, Noelle," I answer.

"Max, are you driving home?"

"No." I hesitate, and I can imagine Noelle wringing her hands on the other side.

"Your mom called me and said they're giving you a week off."

"They are." I pause and brace.

"I can get some time off, and we can go somewhere," she suggests. "Tahoe? I could even meet you in San Francisco, and we can get a fancy hotel room."

"No," I say. "I have something I need to take care of."

She pauses. I can feel the fury pulsing through the phone. "What do you have to take care of?"

I can't tell her, although I want to. However, the last thing I need are other voices chiming in, telling me what to do, when I should figure it out on my own. It's for the best no one knows yet. I stay quiet.

"Where are you at least, so I can know? You're not in trouble, are you?"

"No, no, no, nothing like that. I promise I'm safe, and you have nothing to worry about. I'm in a town outside of Sacramento called Goldheart." I've never mentioned Goldheart to Noelle, so she doesn't know the significance of it or what this town holds for me. Noelle will lose her shit if she knows I had a kid I didn't know about.

"I've never heard of it." She lets out an audible, exasperated exhale.

"Let me take care of this, and I'll be home soon."

Another whoosh of breath over the phone. "I guess that reservation I have for tomorrow is no good now."

"Ask one of your friends. Have a girls' night."

"Girls' night. Okay." When we first started dating, she mentioned a few friends. Now I'm not sure if Noelle has any friends left. If I let her, Noelle would spend every free moment I had together. At first it was cute. Now it's stifling.

"Do you know when you'll be home?" she asks again.

"I don't know," I say, checking the main house again. The second car is still parked by her back door. I wonder if that person is staying the night. I wonder if it's her boyfriend.

"I'll be home for my dad's retirement party on Saturday. You'll still be my date, right?"

"Of course," Noelle says. "Come home soon. We've already been apart thirty days, and I miss you."

"I miss you too," I say, meaning it, but the words are marbles in my mouth. We say goodbye, and I put down my phone.

I'll tell her soon. Tomorrow. That piece of news might make my decision for me. I don't think Noelle ever envisioned being a stepmom.

Pulling out my phone again, I start my search for a present to make my daughter like me. As I scroll through my options and mark stores I can go to tomorrow near here to kill time, my eyes drift to the window again.

No matter how frustrated I am with Emily, there's still this pull to her I was afraid of. The nagging in my gut was correct.

She's still beautiful, even more so now. It's still her energy I'm drawn to. Although she deliberately did parenthood without me, I know she gave our daughter an extraordinary life. I may not have been there for the first nine years, but I'm not going anywhere now.

Emily has to know that. There's no way she's getting rid of me this time.

No matter how much she didn't care about me back then, and told me she did.

EMILY

Monday

When I arrive at Bistro 530, Burke's still busy, moving from one dish to another, focused on his work. The dining room is full of guests, even at two-thirty. I saw the Bad Biddies Club, a group of older women in town who love to gossip, so I shielded my face. I don't want any of them noticing me, especially their fearless leader, that evil bitch, Miriam Oliver. That woman has it out for me, and she can sniff out my drama like a bloodhound with a steak.

Caroline offered to stick around, but I hugged her and thanked her for the birthday visit.

"You call me if you need anything," she said into my hair. "Absolutely anything."

Burke doesn't have a jealous bone in his body, but it's best he hears things from me. He keeps his phone off during restaurant hours, so I find myself in his kitchen often, resting my hip against a trash can.

"What is it, baby? I'm kinda busy here." He sprinkles a finishing basil on top of a pasta dish.

"So, Olive's father showed up at my birthday."

His hand freezes mid-air, and his head swivels to mine with big eyes. He straightens to a military stance. "So that's who that guy was. I thought he was long gone."

"Me too," I say. "I went to dinner with him last night. To tell him. It wasn't anything."

"Okay," Burke says, his voice unsure.

"They're meeting today. Three o'clock."

"Should I be there too?"

"No, I don't think so. I thought you should know. I didn't want you to hear about it from anyone else." I take a deep inhale before I say, "Also, he's staying at the tiny house."

"How long?"

"I have no idea."

"Is he safe?" Burke asks, looking at his plates instead of me. He puts them both on the shelf and wipes his hands on his apron.

"Of course he is."

"Well, the way you talk about him, it seems like you barely knew him."

"We spent a lot of time together that week." Burke knows the Cliff Notes, not the memories that came flooding back when Max reappeared. The hours we talked, how we couldn't shut up around each other, the soul-bearing. I had never seen that anger from him, though, so maybe Burke was right. I didn't know him at all.

"Be safe," Burke says. He holds a skillet to sauté garlic. "Let me know how it goes."

"I'll leave you to it." I land a kiss on Burke's cheek, touching his forearm before I turn to walk away. The butterflies are absent, but I guess that is just nerves.

"I want to meet him," Burke says. "Shake his hand and look him in the eye."

"Okay. That can be arranged."

Burke's staring at the stainless steel of his counter before he looks to me. His jaw tenses, and he sets his hands on his waist. "Good luck."

"Thanks."

He nods, but uncertainty creeps onto his face.

Another reason Burke is perfect. He didn't question me going to dinner with another man, or that he's staying on my property. Burke lets me be me.

Still, I don't tell him how I tossed and turned all night. How I got up at two a.m. and checked the tiny house from my window, seeing the lights on. How my stomach won't stop grinding and tightness in my chest won't go away.

Twenty minutes to go.

"Mom, stop it," Olive says as I smooth down her ponytail for the umpteenth time. Her tone is so grown-up, my heart falls in my chest. Nine years have flown by, and I'm seeing the teenage years coming faster than I want.

"He's late," Cameron says, pacing with his arms folded.

"It's fine, Cam. It's three minutes."

"Still. No one is late for my girls."

I touch my brother's forearm. "He's probably nervous."

"Oh, he better be." Cam slams his fist into his hand. I chuckle under my breath. Cam was always a lover and not a fighter, so it's funny to see him so protective over us.

"Thanks for being here."

"Of course," he says with a terse nod. Cam asked if he wanted me there, and I said yes. In a way, Cameron has been the father Olive didn't have growing up, so it made sense to me.

My hands shake as I crack my knuckles, a bad habit left over from my teenage years.

"What did you tell her?" Cam whispers.

"He's just a friend. We're meeting a friend."

"She's going to think you're a hoe." I snicker behind my hand. Thank God for my brother. For a second, I forgot I wanted to throw up.

"Why are we meeting him again?" Olive looks up at me.

"He's...important," I say.

"Is he related to us?" Coughing against my hand, I lie and shake my head.

"This is just weird," Olive says, pressing her hands into the table.

The door to the brewery opens, and in strides Max, looking handsome and well put together. He's wearing a suit jacket over dark-wash jeans and polished leather shoes, holding a neon-green item and a single sunflower in his other hand. He looks around, and when he sees us, sees Olive, his face melts.

Don't cry. Keep it together, I tell myself.

I imagined this moment so many times over the years, and while I didn't expect it to look like this, it's perfect. I'm still in my body. I'm still present. This is a Big Life Moment, but it feels normal and natural, like it was meant to happen.

"Hi," I say as I walk to him and take him in a half hug. He's warm and his hand is strong against my back. I try not to register how strong his back feels or how he smells like woody citrus. Being this close to him brings back a lot of old, confusing memories.

When I pull away, his cheek touches mine and my stomach flops.

"Hi," he whispers. He stares at Olive, who's deep in a conversation with Cam, and his bottom lip drops.

"She's shy sometimes with new people, just to prepare you. I told her you're an old friend," I whisper.

We walk closer to the table where my family sits, and

Olive looks up at me when I'm directly across from her. "Olive, this is my friend, Max. Max, this is my daughter, Olive."

"Pleasure to meet you." He shifts the flower to the same hand as the neon-green stuffed animal so he can hold out his right hand. Olive studies his outstretched hand and finally takes it, slipping her small hand into his.

I might end up in the hospital today because I can't take this.

Keep it together. Take down the emotion by a notch.

"I brought you something," Max says, taking the stuffed animal from under his arm. "I heard you like this one."

"I do," she whispers, taking it in her hands. I've said no so many times to a stuffed Mike Wazowski, so I'm glad her father gets the honors. When I look at my brother, Cam is studying me and puts his hand on my shoulder. He knows I'm barely holding it together. *Don't cry.*

Max also hands her the flower. "Every lady deserves flowers."

"Thank you," she says, taking the flower down and resting it on the table carefully. She holds the stuffed animal by its thin arms. She makes the stuffed animal dance by pulling at its arms each which way. When she looks up at him, my heart expands.

"So," I say, pointing to the seat across from Olive at the table. "Please have a seat."

He walks sheepishly toward the other side, and Cam follows him.

"Hi, good to see you," Max says, shaking Cam's hand. They met once briefly, by accident and now Cam grumbles as he takes a seat like Max was his high school bully.

Max folds his hands on the table. "So, Olive, I want to know all about you."

Olive's face scrunches in confusion and looks up at me.

She moves closer to me as I put my arm around her. Her eyes look everywhere but at Max.

"Tell Max what grade you're in."

"Third." Her voice is barely audible.

"Who's your teacher?"

"Ms. Lyle."

"You like her, don't you?" I ask. Usually my daughter will do a full monologue about Ms. Lyle and how pretty she is and her massive Maine Coon cat, Katniss. Instead, my daughter nods once.

I swore I would never force my child to interact with adults unless she wanted to. I want to break all those promises. This going well is so important to me.

"I heard you like raccoons, and that there's a pair called Thelma and Louise," Max says. He also texted me and asked if there were any conversation starters, so I mentioned the raccoon duo I don't see much of anymore.

If this doesn't get my daughter talking, I don't know what will.

She sits up straighter, no longer pressed to me. She folds her hands in front of her, mirroring Max's posture. In that moment, they're carbon copies of one another, and there's no denying he is her father.

"This is creepy," Cam says under his breath, watching this unfold.

"Yes. Thelma and Louise are my best friends. Have you seen the film, Max?"

Have you seen the film, Max? Cam and I look at each other. You think you know a kid, and then she outs you as a bad mother.

"I don't think I have."

"It's great. You should really see it," Olive says. Max purses his lips, his look saying, *You let our daughter watch that movie?*

I shield my eyes. I always justified it by that if showing my child *Thelma and Louise* at a young age was the worst thing I do as a parent, I'm not all that bad. It's part of her Women Empowerment education. I *do* cover her eyes during the parking lot scene, but I let her watch the Brad Pitt love scene. She'll have sex one day, so I didn't see the harm. She didn't want to watch it anyway.

"Ew, his butt," she said, covering her own eyes.

"Isn't that...violent?" Max asks.

"It's a classic is what it is," Cam butts in, looking for any reason to fight. I touch Cam's forearm.

"I guess I'll have to see it," Max says.

"Mom has a copy." Olive looks up at me. "Don't watch it with her, though. She knows it word for word and then says it under her breath. It's soooo annoying."

I blush as Max's gaze fixes on my face. He doesn't break eye contact as he says, "I'll keep that in mind."

"So, back to the raccoons." Olive places both palms on the table, like she's offering a business proposal. "They helped out Uncle Cam."

"Oh?" Max asks, looking to Cam.

"Martini, please don't tell that story," Cam says, his forehead in his hands.

"Martini?" Max asks with a wide look, the blood draining from my face.

"Yeah, that's what my family calls me. Except Mom. She doesn't like it."

"I started it." Cam points to his chest with pride.

I cover my face. I told Max my dream of being a fancy lady, drinking martinis after a busy day in a big city, and he started calling me that on our second-to-last day together. The nickname "Martini" stuck for Olive, and it's haunted me since Cam started calling her that when she was three.

"Mom, you're like bright red."

"I know, sweetie," I say, smiling, but inside I want to die. "You know I don't like it."

"I like it." Max catches my gaze from across the table, and he holds it, his lips pressed together. I wonder if he's thinking of him muttering "Martini" into my ear when he was inside of me, when, unbeknownst to us, we were creating our daughter.

"Thank you," Cam says, smacking Max on the arm. "It's a great nickname."

"Can I call you Martini?" Max asks Olive, but his gaze stays on me. I can't handle this. His stare always makes me dissolve into a puddle. He can't be thinking about the sex. The awkward, condom-slipping sex that created a human being. I look away first, and my brother catches our look, his eyebrow flicked.

Olive shrugs a single shoulder. "Sure. Even though you're not family. Mom, I'm not being rude, I'm just asking. Why am I meeting you, Max?"

Cam cocks his eyebrow higher. I grit my teeth at my brother while Max smirks, but I see the discomfort in his hunched shoulders.

"Your mother and I are old friends, and we're catching up. She's told me so much about you that I wanted to meet you."

"It's because you're fabulous, Martini," Cam adds, layering over this deflection like it's buttercream frosting.

"Yes," she says, flipping her hair. My cheeks bloom with embarrassment. I have raised a confident but vain child.

"I would love to hear this raccoon story," Max says. The way these men swerve Olive away from her razor-sharp instincts make my heart glow.

"Uncle Cam, can I tell the story?"

"Fine," Cam says, covering his face.

"So, Uncle Cam used to live at the tiny house."

"The one I'm staying at?" Max asks.

"He's staying at the tiny house?" Cam mutters to me with clenched teeth. I wave it off.

"Yes. Why are you staying there, anyway?" Olive asks.

"The hotel in town is full, sweetie. He's a friend and wanted to visit," I say, pulling her to me. She wiggles out of my grasp. Cam stares at me, because we both know Olive is really close to firing questions at Max. Being suspicious of adults is part of her precociousness.

"Okay," Olive says. "So, Aunt Annie was over, and Annie's former lover and Cam's former lover…"

Add another tally mark to the Worst Mother column. Olive might as well be smoking a cigarette and have a tattoo with the rate I'm going.

"Hold on. Where did you hear that word?" I ask.

"Aunt Whitney."

"I'm going to have a talk with Aunt Whitney." I knew Whitney, my brother Reid's fiancée, was giving Olive starter romance novels, but I don't want my daughter throwing around the term "lover" all casually, especially to her father.

"Mom, it's fine," Olive continues, placing her hand on the table. All the initial shyness is gone. Now she's showboating. This is what happens when you're the only grandchild for nine years.

"So, they came over. They had a bullhorn. Then, Thelma and Louise came and scared them off. They didn't take the bullhorn, though."

"It's my most prized possession," Cam says.

"Wow," Max says.

"We're not going to talk about Darryl."

I hear snickering and look across the table at my brother, who is delighting in this meeting and the weird turn it's taken. He doesn't know that I'm worried Max will file custody papers immediately because I've been corrupting our daughter and I didn't confirm her existence with him.

However, Max takes Olive's bait. "Who's Darryl?"

"I don't know if I should tell you."

"Tell Max, honey." If she's telling raccoons stories, she's not grilling Max like she's a detective on *Law and Order*.

"Darryl got Aunt Shiloh."

I add, "Olive let raccoons into the brewery a couple times. We don't do that anymore, right, Olive?"

"Yes. Shiloh told me not to tell you that she's paying me in Skittles for every ten days I don't let a raccoon in."

I knew Shiloh would do something like this. I love her, but she has to stop giving my child sugar. My child is stone-cold sugar sober today, and she's already like *this*.

"How did Darryl get Aunt Shiloh?" Max asks as I mouth "No" to him.

"I thought it was Lena, another raccoon. She's a mom. But it was actually that sneaky Darryl. Darryl scratched Aunt Shiloh, and she needed the rabies vaccine. Uncle Jackson took her, and that's how they became lovers. They call that trope friends-to-lovers, right, Mom?"

"Yes." Covering my eyes, I make a mental note to talk to Whitney about discussing romance tropes. I can't handle imagining my older brother having sex, and now thanks to her, I am and it's so gross.

I feel eyes on me, and I look up to Max's raised eyebrow, his face red from holding back laughter. Mine is red from mortification. *It's okay, she's wonderful*, I think Max mouths to me, and my whole face relaxes. There's a shine to his eyes, and I wonder if it's emotion or the harsh lights.

He turns back to Olive. "This family really loves raccoons."

"Just me," Olive says, raising her hand.

"Should I have gotten you something with raccoons?" Max asks.

"No, I love Mike." She sits the stuffed animal, facing her,

the single eye staring her down. How my daughter can go from saying "lover" casually to playing with a stuffed animal makes my head spin.

"Well, I would love to meet them sometime."

"The raccoons?" Cam asks, his voice raising an octave. "No, you don't."

"You don't meet them. They meet you," Olive says.

Max covers his mouth with his hand and leans back. My heart melts a little bit. I hope he overlooks I showed an R-rated movie to a child and let her read romance novels so she can use the word "lover" with the right context.

We lock eyes, and he smiles as Olive yammers on, finally telling him about her conversation with Ms. Lyle about her cat scaring a Chihuahua named Zack Morris. The corner of his lips turn up as he listens. The way the light hits his eyes, I see the shine again. He smiles and the water pools in the corners of his eyes.

The way he's watching her, I can't help but entertain the thought that my pregnancy wasn't the end of the world for him. Maybe he wanted to be here.

Still, I smile. I watch. Even if he never wanted us, in this moment, I pretend like he did.

10

MAX

Olive is everything I could've hoped for.

She's smart, funny, and outgoing. Just like her mom.

The "lover" comment had me rolling on the inside. Watching how animated she is about raccoons was something I didn't know I needed. When I imagine the kind of kid I have, I couldn't have dreamt up a better one than Olive.

She's beautiful too. Looks like Emily, but I can see myself in her cheeks. She got the shape of my eyebrows and my ears. Her eye color matches mine, and my chest swells with pride that I helped create her, even if I haven't been around for nine years. I should've been. If I knew, I would've been.

Did Emily tell her family about the nickname? Something tells me she didn't. The way her cheeks flushed, I wonder if she was thinking about the last time I called her that. It was her first time, and I whispered it in her ear as I slowly thrust in and out of her.

The time we made our daughter.

My phone buzzes in my pocket, and I ignore it. Once the vibrations stop, it starts again. We all stand, and Olive takes steps to walk away, without saying anything to me.

Baby steps.

"Manners?" Emily asks.

"It was nice to meet you, Max." Olive waves without looking at me, distracted by her uncle.

"It was nice to meet you, Olive." My throat closes on that one, and I need to cough. Calling her Martini feels icky. Although I have permission, Emily will always be Martini to me.

"It was nice meeting you," Emily's very tall brother Cameron says as he stands up. "I need to get back to work. Max, how long are you planning to stay?"

"I have nothing going on this week," I say. "I have plans on Saturday, though."

"Don't fuck this up, Max," Cameron whispers in my ear as he slaps me on the back so hard, I lurch forward.

Emily and Olive whisper to each other and then turn toward me. "We want to ask you to come to the dinner at the main house tonight," Emily says.

"I would love that," I say. My phone vibrates again.

"Maybe you should get that."

"I don't have to."

"It's fine," Emily says, waving me off. "Take care of it, and Olive and I will discuss details."

"Okay." I don't want to, but I walk away to pull my phone out.

Noelle, five missed calls. Twelve text messages from her.

I tap on her number to call her. She answers on the first ring.

"Hi," I say. "What's going on?"

"I'm here."

"What?" I ask. My mouth drops open.

"I'm here. In Goldheart. That's where you are, right?"

"What?" I ask. "Why?"

"Where are you? I'm at this coffee shop. I think it's called Gold Roast?"

What is Noelle doing here? While it's been thirty days and I did miss her, her being here is not great. Pausing, I hear the grinding of coffee in the background, the clanking of plates.

"Max?"

"Okay, I'll come find you." I punch a button to end the call and pull at my collar that now feels too tight.

Walking toward Emily, her face drops. It feels like before, that perfect week, when we didn't have to say anything. We sensed each other's thoughts. It's strange we're right back there.

"You can't make it tonight."

I tap my phone against my palm. "Something came up. I really want to make dinner tonight, but I'm not…"

"It's fine. I understand. Let us know if you can." Her smile is sweet, but I can see the disappointment in her meadow-green eyes.

"My girlfriend is here. In Goldheart," I say.

"Oh." Emily's face drops down to the ground.

"You have a girlfriend, Max?" Olive asks, looking up at me.

"Yes."

"What's her name?"

"Noelle."

"Huh," Olive says, folding her arms, judging me. This kid is perfection.

"You should go take care of that," Emily says. "We can always have a rain check on dinner."

"I'm sorry," I apologize.

"Don't be." Emily smiles but I can see the sadness in her eyes. "Go see your girlfriend."

"Noelle can come if she brings me a present," Olive blurts out.

"Olive Jean Finch." I knew instinctually that her last name might be her mother's, but it still hits me like a sword to the gut.

I kneel in front of my daughter so we're eye to eye. "It was nice to meet you, Olive," I say, outstretching my hand. She looks at my fingers and then back up at me.

"Max, can I have a hug?" Her eyes are wide and pleading.

"Of course," I say. She wraps her arms around my shoulders, and I circle my arm around her back. I can't help but lean into her hair; it's soft against my cheek. A tear wells in my eye, and I sniffle as she pulls away.

In that moment, I want to say all the "I'm sorrys," all the "I'm proud of yous" I missed over the years. Now is not the time, but I hope I can soon, when she knows who I am.

"She doesn't usually hug strangers," Emily says.

"I just felt like it. Max looks like he needed a hug."

She has no idea.

"We'll see you later." Emily pulls Olive close, and our daughter hugs her waist. I see a tear in Emily's eye as well. We hold each other's gaze.

For a moment, I wonder if she wanted me there, raising Olive with her, this entire time. The air crackles between us, like there's a live wire about to spark.

Running my hand through my hair, I drive the short distance from the brewery to Main Street, circling looking for street parking. After I find a space in front of the town square gazebo, I get out with a deep intake of breath.

Noelle loves me, and I love her. However, I wish she would've respected the space I requested. It's been a battle for years, her bamboozling me into looking at engagement rings or sending me cute proposal ideas. She's the one who issued the ultimatum, and now she's here, forcing my hand. This week was about figuring all this out without her breathing down my neck, and now a huge complication has been thrown in.

I want to throw up thinking about telling her.

When I first saw Noelle at a party, I was drawn to her and had to meet her. After we had been dating for a few months, she told me she saw me and wanted me, orchestrating run-ins and laying bait so I would bite.

At first I thought it was cute. As our relationship progressed, I saw it become controlling. I'm a pretty easy-going guy, so I didn't mind bending. At first.

My parents love her. I love her. However, the ultimatum was a long time coming.

Three years, and I *should* be ready to propose. Noelle is perfect, and she could have any guy she wanted, but she picked me. I should feel like a king. Instead I feel like a prisoner.

As I walk from my parking spot, I'm ashamed that I'm thinking about Emily, our hug, how she smelled, how her body felt pressed against mine. It's a piece-of-shit move, and deep down, I know coming here was the shittiest thing I could do to Noelle.

I would've never known about Olive if I didn't come, so when it comes down to it, I don't regret a thing.

I walk into Gold Roast and see my girlfriend, facing the espresso machine. She turns with the bell, and her smile breaks wide open.

Noelle is stunningly beautiful with wide blue eyes and blond hair, and when she stands she looks down on me in her high boots.

"Hi, baby." She kisses me and then wipes lipstick off my

mouth. My eyes flicker to the counter, and Tara, the owner, looks away quickly, like she's been watching this exchange.

"What a nice surprise," I say, sitting down across from her. An espresso cup and saucer sits in front of her, and her phone lays face down.

"Right? I knew you would talk me out of it so I thought I would surprise you." She fans her hands out, like she's on a cruise dinner show.

"I probably would've."

Tara, the owner I met yesterday, drops off a to-go cup. When I look up at her, she says, "On the house."

"Thanks," I say. Tara grimaces at me, and I nod once, turning to my girlfriend. Noelle says nothing but folds her hands in front of her. Mirroring her, I look down. How do I tell her? I really don't want to, but the longer I don't do it, the more dread I'll have.

"Noelle, I have something to tell you."

"What is it?" She sits up straighter, a hopefulness tugging at the corners of her mouth. I know what she's hoping, that I came to my senses, that I've made a deposit on a ring. She won't see Olive coming.

"I came here for a reason. I wanted to be sure. About us."

She nods, her eyes wide and hopeful. Shit.

"I was involved with a woman here."

Noelle's eyes enlarge and her mouth parts, her gasp audible. "Who is she?"

"Her name is Emily. I haven't seen her since I left this town, ten years ago."

"Okay," Noelle says hesitantly. "Did you see her?"

"Yes." I take a scalding sip to break the tension and scan the room to delay. When I look at her, recognition covers her face.

"Oh no, what? What?"

"Um," I say, tracing the table with my finger. "She has a

kid. A nine-year-old daughter." Her gaze hits mine when I look up. "She's mine. I'm a father."

"What?" Noelle shrieks at the same time something crashes behind the bar. We turn, and the owner pops up with her arms splayed.

"I am so sorry," Tara says. "I'm so *clumsy*."

We both turn to each other, and Noelle looks shell-shocked.

"You have a daughter. A real human daughter."

"Yes."

"Do you know if it's yours?"

"She's mine."

"No, do you really know for sure? How long did you know her? Her mother, I mean."

"Emily's not like that." I lace my fingers together and grip.

"Okay, okay." Noelle stares at the table and breathes in and out with her hands circling to mimic the breath. "This will be fine. This will be okay."

"I just found out yesterday. I didn't know. I swear to you."

"How dare she not tell you. What a bitch."

I flinch. The feeling I have, it's just an inkling. She ignored my emails; she kept my daughter from me. But the Emily I knew wouldn't have done that. Maybe I didn't know her all. Still, calling Emily a bitch is crossing a line. "She's not, Noelle. That's not fair."

"Fine." She shakes her head, flustered. "Did you meet her? Your daughter?"

"Yes. Olive. She's wonderful." Turning my head, I catch the owner staring at me and immediately ripping her gaze away.

"Well. Well." Noelle breathes and out.

"Everything is fine," I say, like I wasn't freaking out

twenty-four hours before. "I just need to figure out some things."

"What does that mean for us?" she asks. That makes me pause. I just found out I had a daughter I didn't know about, and Noelle is asking about us as a couple? That doesn't sit right with me either.

Taking a deep breath, I say, "I'm figuring it out."

"Okay, okay," she says. "Does Emily have a boyfriend? A husband?"

"She has a boyfriend." That admission makes me twinge.

Noelle deflates with relief. "That's good."

"Like I said, I just found this out, and it's a lot to process."

"I bet." She leans back with her arms crossed. "I would love to meet Olive. And Emily."

"I want you to," I say and mean it. Although we've had our problems, Noelle is important to me, and I want her to meet my other important people. "There's one thing. Olive doesn't know I'm her dad yet."

"Who did they say you were when you met her?"

"I'm an old friend." I grip my own hands tighter.

"Emily and I should meet each other," Noelle says. "It makes sense."

"How long are you planning to stay?"

"As long as you're planning to stay."

I hide my grimace under my hands. "Where are you going to stay?"

Her eyebrows lower, and her jaw slacks. "With you, of course."

"I'm staying on Emily's property. I'm not sure if she will be okay with it, but I can ask."

Noelle grabs my hands, and I want to tear mine away, but I keep them there. Her being here complicates everything. I should tell her to go home so I can process. But she's already on edge, and asking her to leave would create a catastrophe.

"Okay. If not, I can find somewhere else and you can stay with me." She pauses. "You should call Emily. I would love to meet her. She could bring her boyfriend." Noelle smiles like she just suggested we go to brunch, not meet my long-lost daughter.

"Sure," I say. "Will you excuse me?"

"Of course." Noelle turns her phone over, probably to scroll on Instagram.

I hold out my hand. "Don't tell anyone yet. Before I figure out what to do."

"I won't." She smiles sweetly and focuses on her phone.

When I close the bathroom door, I lean against it to take a deep breath. What do I do? I can't tell Noelle to leave, but it would be easier if she wasn't here. I pull out my phone to see a text from her. A smile crosses my lips.

Emily: Olive has been playing with her Mike toy since we got home.

This whole time, I've been telling myself seeing Olive complicated everything.

That's not entirely the truth.

My feelings for Emily lived in the hollows of my being. Being around her brought them out of the shadows.

No matter how angry I am with her, Emily was my first love. I'm not sure if it's nostalgia or real feelings, but my heart battles with my head. Right now, I'm just very confused.

Emily

.   .   .

"Hi, Tara," I say into my phone when she calls. "Are you dying?" We only text, so her calling me is weird.

"Em, there's this blond guy here who was here yesterday asking about you, but he's with this stunning woman who is *very tall* and they're talking and he mentioned Olive and oh my God did your baby daddy show up?"

"Yes," I squeak out.

Tara shrieks, and then brings it down to a whisper. "Why didn't you tell me? This is crazy. I think it's his girlfriend and he's not happy she's here. I've been trying to listen without getting caught. He looks so much like Olive it's shocking."

"I know. Olive just met him. She doesn't know about his *role*. I am freaking out," I whisper, looking to my living room. Olive sits on the couch with the Mike Wazowski stuffed animal while she reads a First Reader version of *Anne of Green Gables* to him. It makes my heart grow five sizes.

"Did he invite her, do you think?" I ask.

"No, I'm getting the sense she just showed up unannounced. She'd been at the coffee shop for at least two hours before he showed up. They're going to have a hell of a time finding a place to stay. Goldheart Inn is booked, and even crappy Stake the Claim is sold out."

I cringe. If the Stake the Claim Motel is full, there's no rooms within fifteen miles, period. People think Stake the Claim is cute because it looks like the Rosebud Motel from *Schitt's Creek*, but that's where it ends. I've heard of several fungal infections that started at Stake the Claim, and then there was the unfortunate raccoon gang incident.

"Where is he staying?" Tara asks.

"At the tiny house."

"Guuuuurrrrllll," Tara says. "When he finally leaves, I need to know everything. Everything. *Do you understand me?*"

"Understood," I say. My phone buzzes against my ear, and I pull it away to see Max calling. "He's calling."

"He's not at the table. He's calling you from the *bathroom*. This is getting so juicy," Tara aggressively whispers. "I will gather as much intel as I can. Take the call."

"Okay," I say, ending the call and taking Max's.

"Hey," he says. I can hear the stress in his voice.

"Hi," I say. "You should see Olive right now. It's so precious."

"Oh, I wish I could be there."

I wish he was too.

He pauses before he continues. "Noelle is staying for a little bit. Do you know of a place that will be available for us to stay?"

"She can stay at the tiny house with you, if you want," I say. *Be cool, Emily. Be cool.*

"Really? Is that okay? I just thought it was weird."

"It's fine." I can't believe I'm about to say this. "She can come to dinner tonight. I'll invite Burke so it's not awkward. Did you tell her about Olive?"

"I did."

"Good. She knows we're not telling her right away, right?"

"I told her to keep it a secret. Noelle won't say anything."

"Okay, great. Can't wait to meet her," I say, although it feels weird to act okay with this. It would be weird if it was not weird. "Six thirty? Just come to the back door."

"Okay. Looking forward to it."

"Me too," I say.

There's a pause, and I pull my phone away. The call is still active. I can hear Max's breath over the phone.

"Olive is extraordinary. You did a great job. I'm really glad I came," he says. *Tears go away, stay away.* Max pauses again, then says, "We'll see you tonight."

"Great," I say. We say goodbye and hang up the phone. I

walk into the living room, but Olive doesn't look up from her book.

"Honey, Max is coming to dinner tonight with his girl-friend, Noelle. I'm going to ask Burke to come over too, if that's okay."

"Fine, Mom," she says, barely looking up from her book.

"How did you like Max?"

"He's nice," she says. Olive clutches the stuffed animal tighter. At the brewery, she was super excited for him to come to dinner. I'm not sure if she's bummed Burke is coming or Max is.

"Okay, well, what should we have?"

"Spaghetti. With garlic bread."

"Sure," I say, leaning against the wall and folding my arms. "I love you, you know."

"Love you too, Mom." She props the book on her lap and her eyes hone in on the words.

Olive is turning into a little adult before my eyes. I blinked, and she was this big.

For all these years, I thought Max didn't want to be a father. However, the way he looked at her, laughed at her jokes, held her a beat longer when she hugged him gives me small hope that he regrets the decision he made all those years ago.

In my heart, I want to believe he wished he was here from the beginning.

But my heart has been wrong before.

MAX

NINE-AND-A-HALF YEARS AGO

"Where are you? I'm making pot roast for dinner tonight," Mom said on the phone as I drove into Goldheart town limits, through bare trees and wheat-colored fields. Class released for the holidays, and instead of driving south home to San Diego, I drove east, past Sacramento to Goldheart.

I needed to know.

Emily hadn't responded to a single email. As soon as I got to the place we were staying in Costa Rica, I sent her an email about my phone.

My phone is completely dead and getting zero service. I'm not ignoring you, I swear, I wrote, already feeling anxiety. I emailed my parents the same and got an immediate response, so I know the connection at our place worked.

I checked my email religiously, every morning when I got up, and I would get the occasional one from my mom and stores that had my email from when I bought something.

I never saw the email I really wanted to see.

When I got home, I asked my stepdad and mom if she had called, and they said no. She'd disappeared completely. Even the number I have for her was wrong. Turning my room and luggage upside down, I found the scrap of paper in her hand-writing with her number and email. I double-checked the email, and I've been sending it to the right one. I tried her number, but it wasn't working.

A part of me couldn't believe it was over. I wanted to know why. I felt crazy showing up in her town, but once I got my answer I would move on.

I knew the words we said to each other the last night we were together were real. That's why her silence was so goddamn loud. I never dreamed she would disappear without a goodbye.

My phone never recovered. Once my parents picked me up from the airport, I brought it to the store, and all the employee could say was "I'm sorry, man, this phone is done."

"I need to know if someone called. Left a voicemail."

"Nah, man, this phone is completely fried. You'll need a whole new everything."

The phone number I had no longer worked, and I couldn't find her in the USC system when I checked, but I knew she would be home already for Thanksgiving break. I just didn't know where to look. I had been to her parents' house exactly once and didn't remember how to get there. My only hope was that she was in town, walking around with family or friends.

When I got out of my car, I pulled my coat tighter, my breath visible when I exhaled. Small patches of snow littered the ground, and I bounced as I walked to create more warmth. During the summer, Emily had worked part-time at the Goldmine Bakery in town, so that was my only weak lead. I was hesitant to call when I couldn't get ahold of her. What if she honestly didn't want to talk to me?

The bell clanged when I walked in, and a few people stood, waiting for their orders. I said excuse me several times as I weaved in and out before I reached the cashier.

"Hi, I'm looking for Emily Finch," I said. *Please know her. Please tell me where I can find her.*

"She's not here. May I help you?"

"I'm looking for her. Do you know where she might be?"

The employee looked up. "I don't know, home, I guess?"

"This is going to sound weird, but can I get her address?" I asked, cringing as it came out.

"Sorry, we don't give that kind of information out." She looked at me like I was a stalker.

"Thought I'd try." I hesitated and then blurted out, "Is she...happy?"

The employee nodded with a pursed bottom lip. "I think so. Yeah, I think she's doing great."

My falling smile didn't disarm this employee, who became even more alarmed. I ordered a coffee and a donut for the employee's time and watched as customers retrieve their orders and filter out. My eyes scanned everyone who walked by, looking for anyone who might look like Emily or the brother I met once, Cameron.

After my order was called, I left with a cup and a white bag in hand. Where would she be? It felt weird to be hanging out in her town just in case she made an appearance, but that's all I had to go off of. All I wanted to know was if she was happy, and I got that. But I needed to see it, to truly know.

I saw my breath, but I walked to the gazebo, already decorated with garlands and unlit twinkle lights for the holidays, and sat. Slim benches lined the inside of the structure and I sat down, although there was wetness seeping through my pants. After I finished my donut, I watched people walking by.

Did I read our relationship completely wrong?

When we met at the snack bar at the lake, our connection was immediate. I bantered with her over Diet Coke, we created inside jokes deeper than I'd ever had with lifelong friends, and we were finishing each other's sentences by the end of the third day. Whenever I was with her, I couldn't stop touching her—the small of her back, her leg if we were seated next to each other. It was crazy, but I fell and fell hard. Doing a dental medical mission to Costa Rica was my dream, but I should've never gone.

Because I lost her.

Maybe she was never mine to begin with.

Time passed slowly, but I still lost track of it. Shivers ran through me and my teeth chattered as I watched folks walk by. In the distance, I saw a poof of brown curls sticking out from a crème-colored hat. It was a flash, but I stood up, my coffee spilling over the side, creating a steaming brown spot in the snow.

I sprinted from the gazebo, my feet slipping against the melting ice.

It was her. I would know her anywhere.

I reached the corner of Main, and saw that same head, walking next to a tall man. They were bundled up, and she gripped his arm as they walked.

If her happiness was because of someone else, I could accept defeat. However, in that moment, my heart broke again.

I crossed the street so I could walk parallel to catch a glimpse of her face. When I saw the profile and notice the small nose, the cheeks and pink lips I kissed, I knew.

She was covered in a puffy black jacket, sticking out in its thickness. She was laughing and walking with a good-looking man—tall and wearing a gray knit cap. His expression was serious as they walked, as their breath comingled with each other. She looked happy.

I stopped and let them walk away.

She found someone else, and she was happy.

There was my answer.

The last piece of my broken heart shattered.

I pulled my cell phone out and dialed my mother's number. "Sorry, Mom, I'll be late tonight. I'm sorry I'll miss your pot roast."

12

EMILY

"**M**om, why are you dressed like that?" Olive asks, giving me a look up and down like a conservative father. I pulled out a low-cut black dress I wore when I went to Vegas when Olive was two.

"Like what?" I ask. No time like the present to start gaslighting my daughter and give her another topic for therapy. The dress wasn't Vegas-flashy, but it does show off what little cleavage I have and hides the weight around my middle Olive gave me as a parting gift.

"Your boobies are out."

"Yeah, so?" I try to stuff myself into the strapless bra, but it just makes them look bigger. That's not a bad thing.

The way Tara described Max's perfect girlfriend, I need all the help I can get, even if I'm deeply uncomfortable with it.

The doorbell rings, and Olive sprints to the door. Olive's smile evaporates when she opens it to Burke, holding a bottle of wine and a bouquet of flowers.

"It's only Burke," Olive says to me without greeting him. Burke still smiles, looking inside like there might be a camera crew.

"Hi, baby," he says, walking in. "You look so great."

Olive scream-sighs behind me.

"Thanks, baby," I say, walking toward him and kiss him. He grips me tighter, pulling me to him. My daughter makes a gagging sound.

"They're not here yet?"

"Not yet. They're still at the tiny house, so any moment."

"Ah," he says. "Let's open this wine. We'll need it."

"I one-hundred-percent agree." I already dove into my emergency stash of anti-anxiety meds that I keep on hand for situations just like this. It's nice not to be overwhelmed and be somewhat calm.

Burke hands me a glass of wine as the doorbell rings.

Olive runs toward it and rips the door open. "Max!" she screams, launching herself at his mid-section.

Burke grumbles next to me. Olive has never tackle-hugged him.

"It's the genetics," I whisper to him. He pulls me toward him, gripping my hip like I'm a trophy.

A statuesque blond woman stands behind Max. Her skin is flawless. Her teeth are straight and blinding white. She wears a floral sundress effortlessly. She stands an inch or so taller than Max in her wedges, and I feel silly in my cheap Vegas dress.

"Olive, I want you to meet Noelle," Max says, presenting her.

Olive shapeshifts to her shyness as Noelle crouches down so she's eye-level with her.

"Max has told me so much about you. I'm Noelle. Max is my boyfriend."

Noelle gives me a glare, and the blood drains from my face.

Doesn't she know I can't compete with her? I'm just a small-town girl he got pregnant and then dismissed. He can start a new family with her; he can have the big wedding at a winery, and she can bear his tow-headed children that they slather in sunscreen when he takes them to a beach in San Diego. There's no way he could want me when he has her.

Olive runs back to me and circles her arms around my waist, and I drop my hand from Burke. Burke walks to Max and shakes his hand.

"Burke Whitmore, pleasure to meet you." The handshake looks tight.

"Max Sawyer. It's a pleasure to meet you too. This is my girlfriend, Noelle."

Noelle gives Burke the weakest handshake I've ever seen and then slides her arm around Max's waist. Burke retreats back to me and does the same thing to my waist.

"Well, I could use a drink," Burke says, walking into the kitchen. I look back to see Max leading Noelle by the small of the back. A deep ache settles into my gut as I watch him lovingly touch her. There was a time I longed for those touches.

Maybe I still do.

Max looks so handsome in a white polo shirt tucked into slacks, his hair combed in a side part. When he catches me looking at him, the corner of his mouth lifts in a mischievous smirk. I wish I wasn't attracted to him anymore. It would make everything so much easier. If I wasn't, maybe I wouldn't squirm when my boyfriend tried to touch me in front of him.

Walking to the corner where I keep the liquor, I feel someone behind me. I swallow, because I would feel his presence anywhere.

"Is this okay?" Max asks, so close that if I back up, our bodies would press together. "She just showed up. I didn't ask her to come…"

Turning around, I plaster on a smile and say, "It's no

problem. If she's in your life, I want to meet her. Olive should meet her."

"I know, but…" He leans in, and my heart thuds in my chest. "It just doesn't feel right."

I peer over his shoulder to see Noelle and Olive giving coy glances back and forth. "I have white, red, and some of my family's beer. What would you like?" I shout-ask, so loud Max backs up and I can finally take a deep breath.

"I have red open. Baby, you look like you need a top off," Burke offers, stepping next to me, letting his hand brush my hip. No butterflies, no nothing. He pours me some more and I wish I was falling in love with him. It makes so much sense.

What doesn't make sense is that Max stands inches from me with no contact, and my whole body comes alive.

Max shoves his hands into his pockets. "I would love to try your family's beer. Which would you suggest?"

"What kind of beer do you like?"

"Max doesn't like beer," Noelle says with a chuckle. Max stares at her, and mutters something to himself. Noelle's eyes bug. "What?"

"Mom, can I have a root beer?" Olive asks.

"Sure, honey. Give it to Burke to open."

Olive opens the refrigerator and turns. "Max, do you like root beer? It's so much better than real beer. Gross."

Max flicks his eyebrow to me.

"Her family owns a brewery, okay." My cheeks flush. "She may have sipped a very strong IPA by accident once. I think it did some good."

My lovely boyfriend quickly changes the subject. "Max, do you want a root beer?"

"Sure. I can't remember the last time I had one."

"They're great. Uncle Reid finally figured it out. It's called Rory's Root Beer, named after Aunt Shiloh's dog that went over the Rainbow Bridge." Olive brings out two bottles, a new addition to our menu as of March. She hands the two bottles to Max, instead of Burke.

Burke hands Max the bottle opener, and he does the honors.

"Cheers," Olive says, touching her bottle to Max's.

My eyes catch with Max's, and I look away, a tickle in my throat strong enough to clear. I may or may not have taught her to cheers with her sippy cup at fourteen months old.

Mother of the Year here.

"This is delicious," Max says after a hearty sip.

"Can I have one?" Noelle asks, although I doubt she consumes sugar on a regular basis.

"No, they're special," Olive says.

I'm so horrified, it takes a second for my brain to communicate with my mouth. "Olive, that was rude. Get one for Noelle as well, please."

Her shoulders drop, and she audibly sighs as she opens the fridge again, handing the bottle to Burke to open now that it's for Noelle. She treats Burke like the help.

We all watch Noelle take a sip, her face scrunching with the sugar hitting her teeth.

"It's so...sweet," she says.

"That's what makes it good. Duh," Olive says, with an eye roll.

"Olive, one more rude word..." I warn. Olive looks at me with a challenge, and I need another huge gulp of wine.

"Can't wait for the teenage years!" Noelle says. She holds the root beer close to her chest but looks longingly at the red wine.

"Do you want some?" I point to the bottle.

"Please." Her body relaxes as she sets the root beer down. I take it and put in the fridge. We try not to waste in this house, and I'm not concerned about germs. If Olive wants a second one, she can have Noelle's. She seems like a clean person.

I pour Noelle a nice glass and hand it to her. She takes a sip, and the reaction is a complete opposite. She needed the glass as much as I did.

"Well, dinner's ready if you all are ready to sit," I say.

"Mom made spaghetti," Olive says.

"Oh," Noelle says and then smiles. Maybe she's scared of carbs as well. I try not to look at Max. *I swear I didn't make spaghetti to bring back memories.*

Although our last night at La Scarola never really left me.

"Mom's spaghetti is the best, even better than Burke's, and he cooks for a living."

Burke gives me a look, and I laugh. I use jar sauce, and it almost sent Burke into cardiac arrest the first time he saw it.

"I can't compete," Burke says with a laugh. He is a very good-looking man, with his caramel-colored hair, slightly tanned skin, and blinding white smile. Still, my eyes drift to Max, who I catch staring at me. I'm not sure if you would call it a longing gaze, but it sure feels like it.

We walk to my dining room table and I direct everyone to where they should sit.

"I want to sit across from Max. Please," Olive says.

Max smirks. "Sure."

It's like she knows.

I make sure everyone has water and point to the green salad I threw together from a bag for everyone to dig in. Burke helps me bring out the noodles, sauce, and the bread. He's so wonderful. I should think he is wonderful.

The wine is making my head woozy, but I sneak another pour before I sit down. Between my daughter being slightly rude to Max's girlfriend, to my boyfriend being handsy because the father of my child is here, to the father of my child pulling me toward him like a giant good-looking magnet, I will not know peace this dinner. All I can do is survive it.

"How long have you been together?" Noelle asks, flicking a finger between Burke and me. He looks at me, like it's disputed.

"Two months. It's still new," I say, placing the napkin in my lap.

"I'm smitten," Burke says, pecking me on the cheek. I notice Max tensing up across the table.

"Oh, the honeymoon phase. It's like you're *obsessed* with them. When Max and I started dating, we couldn't keep our hands off each other."

My heart sinks. *You have a boyfriend who likes you, a lot, right next to you. Focus!*

I turn my head to kiss Burke quickly, a wet press of lips. There's a sound from Olive, and I turn to see her slumped down, with her arms crossed. When I turn back toward Max and Noelle, Max's face is pale and his eyes are focused on the fake floral arrangement in the middle of the table.

"You?" I ask as I swallow.

"Three years," Noelle says. I watch her hand float down onto Max's thigh. He shifts and coughs into his hand.

"That's wonderful," I say, draining the rest of my wine glass. Olive mirrors my action and tips her bottle to the ceiling, like she just found out the factory she's been working at for thirty-five years laid her off.

"Dig in!" I say. "Don't want it to get cold."

Noelle takes her dinner plate instead of the small side plate and covers it with lettuce, avoiding all the croutons and blue cheese crumbles. Olive looks up at me like, *Can you believe this chick?*

After watching his girlfriend suck the joy from a salad, Max reaches for the noodles, taking a glob of pasta with the tongs and dumping it on his plate. He hands it to Olive, who does the same thing. The hand movements are eerily similar, the flick of the wrist and look of satisfaction. Noelle notices it, and so does Burke.

When my eyes scan to Max, he smiles at me with misty eyes.

We're just one big modern American family.

13

MAX

Noelle grips my thigh like she's testing the sharpness of her nails.

I try to avoid Emily's gaze, to avoid fixating on her. Her creamy neck, the freckles on her chest, the way her green eyes shimmer under the overhead light. That dress she's wearing is torturing me.

When asked about our relationship, Noelle conveniently left out our problems, the ultimatum, the break we took. She's threatened by Emily, and I can tell. Usually, in social settings, we're affectionate, but this is over the top.

Burke is doing the same thing, staking his claim to Emily. He seems like a good guy, but wrapping his arm around her waist irks me.

One wrong move, and we'll have words.

This room feels too hot, and my collar tightens around my neck. Noelle's nails dig in harder, like I will slip away. All of this is too much to handle. A daughter I didn't know about, the mother of my child strumming up old feelings, and a girlfriend demanding a commitment I'm not sure about. The room spins, although I've had two sips of wine and a root beer.

"I need some air." I stand up, and Noelle finally releases me. I walk to the front door, and when I'm finally out of it, I can breathe. My hands on my hips allow for deep inhales and slow exhales. There's footsteps behind me, and I shake my head. Why won't she let me think?

"Noelle, I…" I turn, and it's not her. It's Emily, looking absolutely stunning. My eyes drift up and down her torso as my mouth waters. I look away, although all I want to do is stare at her.

"It was intense in there, huh?" Emily asks. Her smile is hesitant, but my lips curl to mirror hers, and she lets out a one-note chuckle.

"It's so awkward."

"Oh my God, the most awkward." Emily rubs her forehead. "Man, do I know how to kick off my thirties."

"Definitely. You're really killing it."

Her face melts into concern. "Are you okay, though?"

"I'm fine. There's just a lot going on, and there's pressure from all these sides…"

She crosses her arms, and her gaze focuses on the ground. "I'm sorry I added to it."

"No, no." I wave off her comment. "My stepdad is retiring. End of the week, actually. I'm taking over his dental practice."

"Wow, that's finally happening." She looks disappointed. "Is that what you want?"

"Yeah," I say, although it feels odd coming out of my mouth. "Absolutely. It was the plan all along. I mean, it's fine."

"And Noelle?"

I laugh. "That's complicated."

She touches my arm, and I stare at her hand. How are feelings still there? It's been ten years; a lot of life has happened in that time. Still, maybe things that were real never truly go away.

When I look up at her, she rips her hand away and grumbles. "This is a mess."

"Yeah," I say, my gaze drifting to her. "We're fixing it, though."

"Definitely," she says.

"It's just...I wish..." My words trail off, and she looks up.

"You wish what?"

It was ten years ago. It's fine to admit now. "I tried to find you. The Thanksgiving after that summer. I came to Goldheart."

"You did?" Her glossy lips are parted, her eyes wide.

"I just swung by here from San Francisco. Called it a detour."

Her eyes grow wider. "Did you see me?"

"I did. Briefly." I wipe my face, since my nose started running, and I point. "You were with a guy. I talked to an employee at Goldmine, and she said you were happy. I figured you had already moved on."

"Oh," Emily says rubbing her forehead. "That had to be one of my brothers. Probably Jackson. He had just moved to Seattle, and he was home for the holiday. Fuck."

"Really? You weren't dating anyone?"

"No." She crosses her arms again and tucks her hands into her armpits. "Burke is the first guy I've dated since you."

"It's been ten years."

"Yeah, I know," she says. She spins to take a step without looking at me and swings back. "Why did you come to see me this time? If you thought I had moved on?"

"Because..." *Because I was in love with you. Because you smashed my heart into a million tiny pieces. That one week meant everything to me, and I haven't forgotten it. It haunts me to this day.*

"Why didn't you doubt me?" Emily asks. "If you saw me with another guy?"

"Doubt you about what?"

"When I said Olive was yours?"

"I trust you."

"You barely knew me."

"I knew you." Those words hang. Emily's expressions are unreadable as she looks up at me with huge eyes, close to tears. What do I say?

Emily and I stand apart, our arms folded. We're not touching, but the air between us crackles with electricity. Emily still has a piece of me, and a child that is mine, but we're both spoken for and there's the whole "not telling me" issue.

Still, I want to be close to her. I want to pull her in for an embrace. But if I do, I know it will implode my entire life. My perfectly curated future incinerated.

I want it, though. I want to blow it up, but I can't. Too many people depend on me.

"There you are. Dinner is getting cold." We turn to see Noelle stepping across the house's threshold, a hesitant smile on her face.

"We'll be right in," Emily says.

Noelle lingers in the doorframe, refusing to give us privacy. This might be the true end of us, after a slow, painful death. Emily didn't respond to my emails. There was no "Hey, I'm pregnant, what do you think?" or "I love you, come be with me like we discussed." Olive was kept from me. I have to remember that.

"We should go in," Emily says, walking past me. Noelle takes me in for a kiss before I can pass the doorway, and I pull away.

When we reach the table in the dining room, Olive huffs. "Thank goodness you're back."

She mouths *Help me* to her mother, and I stifle a laugh. This child is ten times funnier than I am. Must've gotten it from her mom. Did Noelle try to talk to her? What does Olive think? Is she suspicious?

I'm lost in the scenarios of telling her when I feel a nudge.

"Are you okay?" Noelle asks. Her tone is ten times more accusatory than Emily's.

"Fine. Great. Never been better."

The rest of the meal grows exponentially in awkwardness. Burke sits quietly, but the second he put his hand on Emily's thigh, I notice Emily flinch with a closed-mouth smile. She catches me looking at her, and she looks down at her plate.

She wasn't with anyone back then. This man across from me must be a good guy if he's the first guy she's dated since me.

He better be a good guy.

I don't want to leave; I want to linger. However, Emily mentions that Olive needs to start winding down and do her nightly routine. Emily mentioned Olive has trouble sleeping sometimes, so they do a regimented routine fit for the military.

"We're reading the *Goosebumps* books together," Olive says.

My heart swells.

"Are those scary?" Burke asks. I breathe out a sigh of relief. This guy hasn't gotten to put my daughter to bed before me.

Emily's eyes grab mine. "She didn't get that from me."

She got it from me. Horror is one of the great joys of my life. "You know, I loved those books as a kid."

"Really?" Olive asks. "Which book is your favorite?"

"I like the one where they go to that amusement park."

Olive's eyes widen. Her voice comes out as a whisper. "That's my favorite too."

A huge grin crosses my lips.

Olive points to Emily. "Mom thinks it's weird. She thought I would sleep worse, but I've been fine. Horror calms me."

People who get it, get it.

"They're just really scary," Emily says.

"Mom, life is scary."

I want to pull Olive towards me and kiss her on the head. My girl. Instead, I lace my hands in front of my legs. Eagerness will mess this up for me. If my daughter loves horror, I will be her guide. Flashes of sharing my favorite movies and maybe Stephen King one day? My heart swells thinking of it all.

"You know, Max loves horror. Like, loves it. I can't watch it," Noelle adds.

"Maybe we can start small, find a kid-appropriate horror movie," I say. Once it comes out of my mouth, I laugh.

"Do those exist?" Emily asks.

"Mom, I can handle it." Olive scampers to her mother, leaning into her. Emily smooths down her hair, holding her like I want to.

"We'll see you later," I say, ushering Noelle to the door.

"Wait," Olive says, walking over. "Max, may I please have a hug?"

Noelle's face crinkles in confusion, and Emily adds, "We're an 'asking for consent' family."

"Of course you may have a hug." I drop to a half-squat so Olive can circle her arms around my neck. It lasts less than five seconds, but it's perfect, just like the first one.

What I wouldn't give to pick her up and hold her to me. That's a hug a good father gives. Not one who wasn't around for the first nine years of her life. I get the hug of a distant uncle who only comes over every third Thanksgiving.

Noelle drops down and opens her arms. "May I have one too?"

"No thanks," Olive says, walking away.

"I told Olive it was okay to say no to physical affection. Sorry, Noelle." Emily walks toward her to give her the fakest hug I've ever seen as a consolation prize. I guess Olive hasn't been forced to give pity hugs, which I love.

Burke shakes my hand and offers a small hug to Noelle, who leans into him more than Emily does. When we leave and we're halfway between the tiny house and the main house, Noelle lets out a huff.

"My goodness, I'm so glad to be out of there. You never wanted to leave."

I turn my head to her. She must be joking. "Of course I didn't want to leave."

"That dress. What was Emily thinking? It was a family dinner, not a nightclub."

I bite my cheek to avoid an impulsive response. I unlock the tiny house, opening and stepping to the side so Noelle can enter first. She dumps her purse on the bed with a thud.

I shove my hands in my pockets.

"What did you talk about before I came out there? With Emily?"

I shrug, although there's more to unpack there than my luggage when I went to Costa Rica for two months. "Stuff. We're trying to figure this out."

"You better figure it out soon. You have your dad's retirement party this weekend. He's going to hand you the keys. Literally."

"You know, Olive is a big deal," I say. "You're aware of that, right?"

"Of course I am, baby. You just found out, though. You have a life. In San Diego."

Rage bubbles inside me, but I push it down. "This changes everything. Everything."

"You don't live here. I don't want to live here."

My hands grip my waist and walk the length of the tiny house. I wish this place was bigger so I can escape her, go somewhere to think.

"You wanted a break," I say. "You were willing to walk away if I didn't propose to you, if I wasn't ready."

"I did, but I did some thinking. I love you. I want to be with you. If that means I have to wait a little longer, I understand. Especially with this hiccup." She walks toward me and slides her hands down my chest. Her touch feels like acid. Calling Olive a hiccup rubs me like sandpaper.

"What about Olive? Do you want her too? She's part of the package deal."

"Sure, of course. She can visit in the summers, but she'll live here with her mother. That makes the most sense. They have a life here. One you wouldn't have known about if you hadn't gotten curious. I forgive you, though." She kisses me the tip of my nose.

"I need some air." I open the door and walk out, and Noelle follows me. The one counseling session we went to, I mentioned I want to escape to think about things, and Noelle agreed to let me.

She did the first couple times, but she quickly forgot.

"Why did you come back here, anyway?" she asks.

"You wanted me to explore. Really think about what we are, but you didn't give me any time!" My voice is a little too loud but I don't care.

"I did. I gave you that time."

"No, you didn't." I run my fingers through my hair. I hate the way I'm talking to her, but this ever-present resentment has grown and morphed and lives under my skin.

"You came here without telling *me*!" she shouts.

"I did, and I just found out that I have a nine-year-old daughter who I didn't know existed. You know what my father did to me, and I did it to another person, unknowingly. *You* gave me the ultimatum. *You* are making me choose. It's not fair, Noelle."

Noelle steps back because I've never raised my voice to her, ever. "Fair? You want to talk about fair? Do you know how many weddings I've been to in how many years? How many of my friends have gotten engaged and I've had to act happy when all I wish for is that it's me? That my boyfriend, *who has been with me for three years*, will want me? Instead he runs off to this town in the middle of bumfuck-nowhere to see a girl he had a fling with when he was twenty-five."

I breathe out, my heart beating fast.

"She was more than a fling." My voice is just above a whisper.

"What?"

"She was more than a fling," I bark. Noelle takes a step back, like my words slapped her in the face.

"Excuse me? How long was it?"

"It was a week, but…" My thoughts jumble like items in a junk drawer. It's not possible to love someone more in one week than in three years. That can't be right.

I still drove here. I didn't drive home, to Noelle, even after being apart from her for thirty days.

"I think we need to end this." I look up at her, and her eyes brim over with tears.

"What?" Noelle's lips curl against her perfectly white teeth.

"That's my answer to your ultimatum." My throat constricts as the early days of our relationship flash in front of me. How I fell in love with Noelle without trying and forcing it. How I hadn't felt like that since Emily.

"Do you like her?"

"It's more than that," I lie, although I know the memory of Emily crept in as the pressure to propose mounted. "You deserve someone who can't wait to marry you."

Her face morphs to tear-filled anger. "You're throwing away three years for that woman? Who didn't tell you about your daughter?"

"It's not because of her," I say.

"Be honest, Max. For once in your life." Her mouth stretches over her bared teeth.

"You're right." Nagging thoughts bubble to the surface, and I close my eyes. I'm done being asleep in my own life. Seeing Emily again, meeting Olive, I feel like I'm waking up. My eyes flash open, and I take a deep breath.

"I love you, but it's not enough. Not what you need. Or what I need."

Noelle nods and walks inside. I rub my jaw, prickly from my stubble, and peer inside. There's rustling and thuds, and then she walks out with her weekender bag, overflowing with stuff. I've never seen her pack that fast.

"I'm sorry I gave you the best years of my life." She slings her bag onto her shoulder. I watch her open her car and throw her bag in the backseat. When she gets in and the headlights turn on, she sticks her middle finger out the car door to me.

I watch her pull off, making sure she gets to the main road okay.

When I walk inside and close the door, I lean against it and my shoulders lower a full foot. The last time I felt this relieved, I had just passed the WREB examination, the last thing I needed to get licensed as a dentist. Both times I felt like I'd been under water, unable to breathe, and now I'm finally at the surface, able to take a big gulp of air.

Tuesday

"I think that's it for what we wanted to discuss, does anyone else have anything to add? We'll be back to Wednesdays next week, just FYI," Jackson says, looking up from his notes.

Some version of "I think we're good" comes from every member, as my mother and father stare at me.

"What?" I ask.

"So, is Max still…here?" Mom asks coyly, although she's been studying me like a chimpanzee for the entire meeting.

"That's crazy he just showed up," Annie says. She's so pregnant, but she still insists on sitting in on our meetings, although she's due to have my niece any day now.

I look back, and Olive is giggling, wrapped up in her iPad with her giant headphones that Whitney, my other brother's fiancée, got her for her birthday.

"He's still here." I swallow, although my throat is closing.

"So, does she know?" Mom asks.

"No. I don't know when to bring it up. He and his girl-friend came to dinner last night…"

"His girlfriend?" Annie's mouth drops.

"Burke was there too. It was perfectly normal." Normal as in my daughter acted like Noelle and Burke were radioactive.

"What's his girlfriend like?" Annie asks. While my brothers like to pretend they don't care, I notice all of them move an inch toward the center of the table.

"Tall. Blond. Gorgeous," I say.

"You're gorgeous too," Annie says. I mouth *Thank you* to her.

Cam's mouth straightens to a tense line. "Has he tried anything with you?"

"What? No! They're totally in love. We're just trying to figure things out as parents who want what is best for Olive."

"*Now* he wants to be involved? He needs to earn it." Cam smacks his fist into his hand. He's about as scary as a capybara.

"This all could be a misunderstanding, right?" Dad, always the optimist.

Jackson and Reid shake their heads.

"Is it time to tell Olive?" I lean in, and so does my family.

I can hear a gulp from my mother. "I think so. She deserves to know. I would be so nervous."

"The thought of it makes me want to vomit," Annie says.

"Better you than me," Reid says. He reaches across the table to pat my hand in his own way. "You can do this."

"I have zero idea how she'll react," I say.

"Mom" is loud and directly in my ear. I jump from my chair and land at an angle. Jackson catches me and shifts me back onto my seat. Maybe he can catch my heart when it explodes out of my chest.

"What, honey?" I brush my hair from my face. Please, God, I hope she didn't hear that.

Olive looks around the table, the iPad tucked under her

arm. Her headphones rest around her neck. "What are you talking about?"

"Do you want to invite Max over for dinner again tonight?" I offer my arms, and Olive climbs onto my lap. My body tingles, like it wants to shed my skin.

"Can he come alone? That lady he came with was weird."

"Why was she weird, honey?"

"She didn't eat any croutons. Why? That's the best part."

"It's a fair point," Cam says, turning his hand over.

"Mom, can you stop hugging me so I can watch more of my iPad?"

"Sure." I kiss her cheek, and she wipes it away. Olive climbs off my lap and goes to her corner, placing the headphones back over her ears.

Will she be mad she didn't meet him sooner? Will she be able to forgive me, or will she think I didn't fight hard enough for Max, that I gave up too soon?

"Was his girlfriend being weird?" Cam asks.

"Yes, a little. It was a weird situation. *Is* weird. Olive is a mini Max." I cradle my phone in my hand. "I should call him."

"What is he doing, just hanging out at the tiny house?"

I shrug. "Not sure. Noelle's car was gone this morning. Maybe they went somewhere together."

"Just call him. Be brave," Annie says. Her hand rests on her pulsating bump.

"Okay. I'll do it." I walk away from the table and find his number in my phone. Looking back, I notice my entire family focusing back on the reports instead of watching me. When I put my phone to my ear, it rings a few times and goes to voicemail.

My heart clinches, but I shake it off. His car was still there, right? So what if he's out and about, taking in the sights with Noelle? I have a good phone number, and he seems interested in being in Olive's life. However, the devastation from his first desertion lingers, and I bite my lip.

I turn and hold up my phone. "Voicemail."

"He'll call back," Mom says, standing up. "Let's open."

The rest of my family follows her into the hallway, where our respective offices are. My daughter still sits in the corner, holding the tilted iPad with both hands, unaware that I just called her father. A man she has already met.

The anxiety creeps into the pit of my stomach as I join her at the table.

Max

"Are you having a nice relaxing week? Did you call Noelle?" my mother asks me over the phone.

"She came," I say, then pause. I brace for my mom's reaction. "We broke up."

My mom's shrill "What!" fractures my eardrum. "How did this happen? What happened? I thought you were going to propose to her!"

"What made you think that?"

"Noelle was so sure. We talked about it when we got lunch a week or two ago…"

A headache manifests in the middle of my forehead. Somehow, my mother and Noelle clicked and saw each other regularly without me. I've had to pick them up from one too many boozy brunches they went to while my dad and I watched football.

"We're not on the same page," I say.

"Maxwell, you are thirty-five years old. It's time to settle down. The community will respect you if you have a beautiful wife by your side. Why are you dragging your feet?

Noelle is perfect. I'm sure you can get her back, tell her you changed your mind…"

I grumble. The "community" she's speaking of is the La Jolla elite, full of thrice-divorced older men who chase after twenty-year-olds and women so unhappy with their marriages they complain to the dental hygienists all day.

"Your father and I have discussed this and—"

I'm taking over the family business, and now they want me to marry someone I shouldn't?

"No, Mom, I'm not going to do that."

"I'm just…" A sob interrupts her words. It makes my chest tight, hearing my mother disappointed. I've spent my entire life trying to make her and my stepfather proud, and now it's like I'm kicking it all down.

It doesn't feel right to tell her now about Olive. I'll deliver one blow per phone call. I've never been more terrified of her reaction. Noelle will be a distant memory once I tell my mom about them.

"You're not yourself right now, that's all. Escaping without telling me. Taking an unplanned vacation. Throwing away the best relationship you've ever had…"

That makes me pause. I enjoyed my time with Noelle, but our relationship wasn't the best. Not by a longshot. My relationship with Emily was. Even after she ghosted me.

"Where are you, anyway?" Mom asks.

Might as well tell her so she can stop wondering. "Goldheart. Remember, the place we went to the lake house Dad's golfing buddy was giving up?"

"Oh," she says. "Wasn't that where you had that fling with that cute local girl? Emma?"

"Emily," I say. *I got her pregnant. I have a beautiful daughter named Olive. I made you a grandmother, just like you always wanted. I can't wait for you to meet her. She's so clever and beautiful.*

"Are you there to see her, is that it? I remember I had a mini-crisis when I turned thirty-five…"

"No, no," I lie. "I just remember that was the last time I was truly not stressed at all. I'm just recharging before Dad retires."

I'm trying to not be the shitty dad I was so scared of becoming.

"I understand that, Button, but don't go changing your whole life because you got some time to think. Breaking up with Noelle…you're worrying me."

"Don't worry, Mom, I'm fine."

"I know you are, but…" There's a quiver in her voice.

My phone beeps with an incoming call. It's Emily.

"Mom, I have to go. Someone is calling me."

"Sweetie, I just really want you to think before making any more decisions. You are always welcome to talk to me."

"Got it, Mom."

"I just love you so much." A low sob vibrates through the phone. I fidget, knowing I'm not getting to Emily's call in time. "Are you sure you're not seeing that girl?"

"No, I'm not," I lie again.

"Did you find her?"

I swallow and look down. My phone stops its beeping. "No. Like I said, I'm just here to relax."

"Okay." I can hear the relief in her voice. "I love you."

"I love you, Mom."

"Rethink Noelle, Button. You're not going to get much better than that woman. Stop dragging your feet already."

"Okay, Mom. I have to get going."

"Bye. Be a good boy," she says and the line finally goes silent.

There's one missed call on my screen, with a voicemail. I grind my teeth. I don't lie to my mother, ever. I've always done what is expected of me, I should be allowed to have this one thing before my world changes forever. Figure out Olive.

Figure out Emily. Figure out how this town plays into my life.

I click the voicemail and hold it to my ear. *Hi, it's Emily. I think we should tell Olive. Tonight.*

After I listened to the voicemail, I called her right back and agreed. She asked Noelle not to come, and I confirmed she wouldn't. I didn't mention she was on her way back to San Diego and we were no longer a couple.

Now, I bounce on my feet, the nervous energy making my body feel like a live wire.

"Hi," I say as Emily opens the door wider and I walk through, rubbing my hands together. I catch a whiff of her floral perfume, and I huff a breath.

I want to hug her, but she's flicking her hands. She's as nervous as I am.

"Where is she?"

"She's reading." Emily's breath is shallow as she slides her hands into the back pockets of her shorts. Her voice shakes. "What is Noelle up to tonight?"

I shrug. "I don't know."

There's a flash of a smile on her face, and I swallow. I shouldn't be ogling her, mesmerized by her green eyes, the way her smile is contagious. Her hair is down today, curling around her shoulders. Goddamn, she's beautiful. The energy crackles between us, but the deception makes me stand away from her. I'm close to forgiving everything.

"Are you nervous?" Emily asks.

I nod. My heart thumps rapidly. "Terrified."

"I think we should be vague about why you were gone," Emily says, her eyes wide.

"Agreed." Although I'm so nervous I could vomit, I'm glad we're not hashing out everything tonight. I'm sure there will be questions. I never got to have this conversation with my biological father, but I have a few ideas about what she might ask.

Why didn't you want me?

Why weren't you around?

Did you ever love my mother?

Emily's crossed arms and nervous shaking makes me want to wrap my arm around her, comfort her, tell her everything will be alright. Once it's over, we'll feel so much better.

She holds out her hand, offering it to me. I raise my hand to clasp hers, and calmness flows through me. She smiles and says, "We can do this. I'm so excited. And nervous. I can't believe it's happening. I've been dreaming about this day for a while."

"You have?" My hand grips hers tighter.

"Yes." She looks up the stairs, our hands still linked. Her hand feels so good in mine.

In that moment, everything that happened falls away. We're two parents, telling our daughter part of the truth. Maybe it will lead to the full truth one day. That I would've run back to her the moment I knew.

Emily's head turns to me, and I don't look away, I just let myself get wrapped up in her. "Let's go tell our daughter who you are."

Her hand lets go so she can climb the stairs first, and I pause before taking a step.

This is it.

We find Olive on her bed, her head tilted to read a book in her lap. She doesn't acknowledge us as we stand there, watching her. My heart is in my throat.

"Olive, honey," Emily says, walking toward our daughter. Olive looks up and sees me, a hesitant smile on her lips.

"Hi Max." She shifts to sit up, crossing her legs, putting her book to the side. Emily drops a knee to sit across from her. Do I walk in? Do I stand here? I'm sure if I get any closer, they will hear the thunder in my chest.

Emily touches Olive's hand and they look at each other and my chest tightens.

"Honey, we have something to tell you."

Olive's eyes flick to me and back to her mother. "What?"

"Max isn't just my friend." Emily takes a deep breath, and my heart stops. "Max is your dad."

Olive doesn't react for what feels like eternity. She sits there, playing with a tassel on her bedspread. I exhale, but my body is still on edge. When she looks up, she looks at me, and then her mom.

"He is?" Olive asks, and then she looks at me. Really looks at me.

I'm not sure if she can see my shame or the deep regret I have, but it's there, gnawing at my heart.

Olive must sense it. She's so, so smart.

She still stares at me, like she's seeing me for the first time. The absentee dad. The guy who left her mother pregnant. A piece of shit, here to make amends.

Olive's eyes narrow. "Where were you? Why weren't you here?"

I swallow and my throat closes and I sniffle. We decided on vague, but what I really want to say is *I would've been here the second I knew, sweetheart*. I can't throw her mother under the bus, that she didn't return my emails, that she didn't take my calls. Now is not the right time to change Olive's view of her mother. I can't make Emily the villain here, so I can be the hero.

All that comes out is "I'm so sorry."

I stand still, and Emily's face turns. Her eyebrows crinkle as she studies me.

Olive crosses her arms and settles into the pillows on her bed, and her gaze focuses past Emily.

"I would like to be alone," Olive says.

"Sure, honey. We'll be downstairs."

"Okay," she says. We close the door and look at each other. Emily just walks past me and continues down the stairs.

15

EMILY

"We deserve a drink," I say, walking into the kitchen. I grab for a bottle of wine and open the cabinet for two glasses. When I turn, Max stares at my kitchen table, his hands in his pockets. Showing him the glasses, I ask, "Do you want one?"

"Absolutely," he says, sitting down. I pour us two hefty glasses, and when I turn around, his elbows are on the table, his hands in his hair.

"Are you okay?" I set a glass in front of him. When the rich oak and berry taste hit my throat, it calms my nerves.

Max takes his glass. "That was rough. I didn't know what I expected, but…"

"Well, let's hope this wine helps." I hold up my glass and he raises his as well, clinking it.

"Will she ever warm up to the idea?"

"Give her some time." Another sip, and I say, "She likes to process things by herself."

"She does?" Max asks. He tilts his head. "She gets that from me."

"Me too." I take another drink. "When she was littler, she did ask about you."

"What did you tell her about me?"

"That I loved you. Not much else." The wine must be getting to me already because my tongue is loose, and heat floods my cheeks. I trace the base of my wine glass.

"You did?" he asks.

"Yes, but it was silly. Who falls in love with someone after only a week? An inexperienced girl, that's who."

"It wasn't silly." He takes a gulp, but his gaze stays on my cheap kitchen table. "I fell in love with you too."

My body instantly tenses, but I let out a laugh. "Sure."

"What?" he asks, finally looking at me. "I did. I told you."

"Okay." I walk to the couch and tuck one leg underneath my butt. He follows me, sitting one cushion apart. He drapes his arm over the back, his hand inches from my shoulder. Why did you leave me then? I could panic at any moment, so I swallow my curiosity down.

"She'll come around." I tap his hand with my finger, then quickly pull it away. "I'm sure of it."

"I hope she can forgive me," he says.

Forgive him for what? I'm not in the mood to fight; I'm emotionally drained from the last few days. All I want is this glass of wine and to finally sleep a full night.

"So, your dad is retiring?"

Max nods. "Dr. Fred Sawyer, DDS, is finally retiring. We never thought we'd see the day."

"Is your mom excited?"

"Ecstatic. She has three cruises planned. They leave for Texas to hop on one next week."

"That's exciting," I say, although my one interaction with Fred still turns my stomach.

I pause and look at my wine. "Have you told them yet?"

Max shakes his head. I hope he doesn't hear the huge exhale I've made. He takes a sip of wine. "My mom will be excited. Dad, though, phew."

He takes another sip of wine.

"He won't be happy?" I ask.

"I'm not sure how he'll take it. He wasn't thrilled when I said I wanted to continue seeing you when I got back from Costa Rica."

My heart speeds up, and my stomach churns. He wanted to see me? Thoughts swirl in my mind, and I can't grasp a coherent one.

Best to change the subject. Break my heart a little more slowly. "Gosh, that was so long ago. In some ways, it feels like yesterday, but I also found another gray hair this morning."

"I have some coming in on my sideburns." He touches them.

"I showed Olive my gray hair. Told her it was from the time she let in Darryl the raccoon and it attacked one of our employees."

Max covers his mouth as he convulses with laughter. "I tried to hold it together when she told that story, but that is so funny. Our daughter is something else."

My heart floods with warmth. "Yes, *our* daughter is something else. Thank God she's moved on from the raccoons."

"Did Olive get punished?" Max asks, taking a sip.

"Oh yeah. I took away the iPad for a week. It really was as much of a punishment for me as it was for her."

Max's eyes bore into my insides. "I'm sorry."

"For what?" I take another sip.

"For not being here."

"You're here now." Because I touch people when I'm nervous, I pat the top of his hand. A blaze of heat crawls up my arm as I pull it away and take another sip. Hopefully, this wine makes whatever I'm feeling go away.

He has a girlfriend. A serious one. I have a boyfriend too.

Not to mention the ten years of indifference. Though, I'm

starting to question if everything I've thought for the last ten years was a lie. The way he looks at Olive. How I saw tears in his eyes the first time he met her. A man who didn't want her wouldn't act like that.

Nausea crawls up my throat, so I swallow.

Max balances his glass on his knee. "Noelle went home last night."

"Oh?" *I want to know everything. Give me a play-by-play of everything that was said.*

"We're not together anymore."

On the outside, I'm calm and collected. On the inside, I'm clapping like my best friend won an Oscar. I deserve the Oscar for the subdued performance I'm giving. I can't be excited for this. There is no way Max and I can be a thing again. For so many reasons.

"What happened?"

"We wanted different things. We were on a break anyways, so her coming here was the final nail on the coffin of our relationship." He turns his head to me.

"Why did you go on the break?" I always want to know everyone's business, but the wine makes me extra nosy. Especially when it comes to this handsome man who gave me the most delightful child ever.

Max lets out a long exhale. "She wanted to get married, and I wasn't proposing. There was something holding me back." His gaze is hesitant, but it falls on me. I tip my glass to get a big swig. He admits, "I just realized I didn't see forever with her."

Why is he looking at me like that? Another huge mouthful of wine.

What about you?" Max asks.

"What about me?" I stare into my glass instead of his eyes.

"Burke." His mouth says the K like it offends him.

"Oh," I say. "We've been dating a couple months. He's nice."

"Nice." Max hangs his head like the wine is taking over. "Just nice?"

"He's nice. What more can I say?"

"Um, a lot of things." Max takes another sip. "Is he treating you well?"

"Yes! He made me a full brunch for my birthday. That you crashed."

"Sorry about that." He smiles, and I can't help but smile back.

"Any girl would be so lucky to have him." Why am I rubbing this in?

"Do *you* like him, Emily?"

"Yes." I hope it's convincing. I take a pregnant pause. "It takes time to build a relationship, right? Like, two months is not nearly enough time to fall in love."

We both sit in silence, knowing a lightning bolt hit us, that our week together was so cosmic, we got a child out of it. It couldn't have been love. If it was, these ten years wouldn't have gone by for us to be strangers.

"I really, really like him. We have so much fun together, and he's perfect."

Max drains his glass.

"Another glass?"

"Please," Max says, handing it to me. Our fingertips brush, and there's that spark again. Dammit. He's single now. It's okay. I'm not, though.

I pour some more, filling my huge wine glasses halfway. I'm asking for trouble. The more I drink, the more my filter evaporates. I may say something unhinged. I may spill all of my thoughts about him not being man enough to face me. Tell me he didn't want to be with me. That whatever this would make up for the ten years I wondered why we weren't good enough.

My mind grows more and more fuzzy, heaviness tugging at my eyes.

"Will Olive hide up there all night?"

"Probably not. She likes to eat. Any moment now she'll come looking for food."

"Will this be okay?"

"I think so."

The sadness on his face breaks my heart. Ten years of what I thought I knew comes crashing down around me, like the walls are caving in.

Blood drains from my face. I fucked up.

My dumbass twenty-year-old self trusted a man Max put on a pedestal.

I try to smile, but I'm sure my face contorts strangely. "Excuse me, Max."

"Sure," he says.

I don't remember my walk to the bedroom. I push my hands through my hair and pace across the carpet.

"Oh my God, oh my God." I slide down my closed door into a ball on the floor.

16

EMILY

TEN YEARS AGO

"Emily, someone's here to talk to you," my boss Bethany said through the door. I was face down in a questionably clean toilet bowl, puking up my breakfast. Morning sickness had started with a vengeance a couple days ago, and I couldn't keep anything down but popsicles.

"Okay, be right out." I flushed and stood up, looking in the mirror. My skin was pale, and tiny frizzies framed my face. I'd looked better.

When I walked out to the front of Goldmine Bakery, I found a tall man with thinning hair standing there. Bethany pointed to him, and I nodded.

"Emily Finch?"

"Yes?" It didn't feel right to shake his hand although I washed them vigorously, so I hid my hands in the pockets of my shorts.

"Fred Sawyer," he said.

"Oh my God, you're Max's dad! Hi!"

The man in Max's words was larger than life and it was so strange to see him. I never expected to meet him like this. A twinge in my gut told me this wasn't a friendly visit, but I still spread my lips into a huge smile.

"Can we talk?" Dr. Sawyer asks, gesturing to the door.

Bethany nodded when I looked to her for permission. He opened the door for me, and I walked out. The heat hit me and turned my stomach. I could not barf in front of this man. I'd just met him.

"We got your message," Dr. Sawyer said.

My face lit up. I'd left a message last week on their answering machine, explaining who I was and that I wanted to talk to Max but his phone wasn't working. I had made sure my message was upbeat and cheery, but I had cringed when I hung up.

"Did you get ahold of Max? I tried his phone, but I couldn't get a hold of him or leave a message."

"What do you want?" Dr. Sawyer's tone and gaze made me squirm. Instead of looking at him, I stared at the ground.

"I want to talk to him. His phone is not working." I paused before I said, "I have something to tell him."

"What is it?"

"It's private." My hand instinctually grazed my stomach, and I froze. Dammit, I gave it away.

"Are you pregnant, Emily?" Dr. Sawyer asked.

I choked down a wave of nausea. "Yes."

"And you're sure the baby is Max's?"

"Yes." Shame covered me, and when I looked up, I saw Miriam Oliver, Goldheart's town busybody watching us with a mouth agape. I wished I could move my feet, but they were stuck to the sidewalk.

Dr. Sawyer pulled something out of his pocket and dabbed his forehead with it. "Well, this is just great."

My mother had cried and held me when I told her. We spent a few days discussing all of my options, and I decided, blurry from tears and overwhelm, that I wanted to keep the baby. When I thought about terminating the pregnancy, my heart dropped, like a thud in my stomach. In the end, I knew I couldn't do it.

When I told my mom I wanted to keep it, she had assured me everything was alright and how thrilled she was. My dad had been just as excited and never expressed any of the disappointment I was so scared of.

Then, they helped me with a game plan. They helped me withdraw from school and smoothed my hair back as I cried. "You can always go back when the baby is older," she said, wiping my tears away with her thumb. We both knew that probably wasn't going to happen.

All of my brothers were supportive and promised to be there for me and the baby. "If that asshole doesn't step up, I will," Cameron said after he gave me a big, tear-filled hug.

Dr. Sawyer was the first person expressing disappointment in me, and it made me more nauseous than these pregnancy hormones. Miriam wandered away, thank God. The last thing I needed was her knowing my private business.

Dr. Sawyer said nothing as he wiped his head with his handkerchief. I was trying not to puke in the bushes.

"Do you know how to get in touch with him? I want to tell him myself."

"He's very busy, but I'll try to get ahold of him," Dr. Sawyer reassured. "Give me an hour. When do you get off?"

"At four."

"I'll come back then. I'll get in touch with him so you can tell him."

"Thank you," I said, breathing out a sigh of relief. I had never been to Costa Rica, but it sounded remote and difficult to get in touch with someone there, especially a tourist. I was sure Dr. Sawyer will figure it out. Max probably had about a week or so before he'd be back.

I kept busy the rest of my shift, excited to talk to Max soon. It had been almost two months since I'd heard his voice, and I hadn't gotten a single email from him like he'd promised. I worried he had my email wrong, or something was wrong with his phone. No way someone would act like that on the last night of us together and then disappear on me.

Max loved me. He had told me he would come back to me.

Now, he would know and come back to me and our baby. Our little miracle.

At four o'clock, Dr. Sawyer arrived again, as promised. He stood outside instead of coming in, although the day had grown considerably hotter and his face was the color of the cherry popsicles I've been living off of. I took off my apron and shoved it in my locker, before taking my purse and walking outside. Was Max on his way here? I smiled a stupid wide grin at the thought.

"Ms. Finch."

"Dr. Sawyer."

"I got in touch with Max. It wasn't easy, but I talked to him."

"Great." I'd get to talk to hear his voice soon, and he would tell me everything would be okay. That he would come back to me. "How can I get in touch with him? Did his phone die? Did he get a new number?"

"I told him."

"You what?" I wanted to tell him. My chin quivered, but I took a deep breath. I could be strong. Being weak wouldn't serve me.

"I told him that you're pregnant. He asked me to tell you that he wants the pregnancy terminated."

"What?" I said. My hand touched to my abdomen, my baby. A baby I wanted. The world stopped around me as I stared at a crack in the ground.

That wasn't him. Max would never want that. He had told me that last night all he wanted was to be a dad.

"How many weeks are you?"

"Six or seven, I think."

Dr. Sawyer looked relieved. "Great. You can still get the procedure."

Shaking my head, my voice cracked as I said, "I want to discuss this with Max. If you will tell me how to get a hold of him…"

"Not to be crass, Ms. Finch, but I always believe in telling the truth. Maxwell has a bright future ahead of him, and this will only damper that. You're young, aren't you? How old are you?"

"Twenty," I whispered. My birthday had been the day before.

"Do you go to college, or is this bakery your only aspiration?"

That was an asshole thing to say, but I just answered his question. "I go to college. I'm a junior at USC." I stared him down.

"You sound like you have a bright future too. Why throw it all away for a little accident? You're young. You have all the time in the world to have children."

My mind spun. I didn't believe Max would want this. He would respect me enough to have a discussion so we could decide what was best for us. I supported women choosing the path that's best for them, and I knew I didn't want an abortion.

My choice was to have this baby.

"Tell me how to get a hold of Max. I should be discussing this with him," I said.

"He doesn't want to talk to you. He was very angry when I told him. He asked me to take care of it for you."

My eyebrows crinkled together. When we were together,

Max was nothing but sweet and gentle. Our time together felt like a fairy tale. There's no way he would be angry. He was there when the condom slipped. He was worried, just like me.

Max had also told me his stepfather was an honest man, an honorable man. A man who took a single mother's son as his own would not be a manipulator.

"With distance, he saw this as a summer romance. You should too."

It was more than that, but this man sounded truthful. I wanted to cower and hide, but I looked up at him. "I want to hear it from him. He told me he wanted to be a father…"

"He meant *someday*, Ms. Finch. He asked me to pass along the message that he doesn't want to talk to you. He asked that you stop contacting him. He has changed his mind about you." Dr. Sawyer paused. "We understand this wasn't one hundred percent your fault. We can help you. I'm sure USC isn't cheap."

Money, this was all this was about. Swallowing back tears, I said, "I want to hear it from Max. Please. If I can hear this from him, I will let it go. I will never reach out again. Please, Dr. Sawyer. Please."

"It's over, Ms. Finch," Dr. Sawyer said. My shoulders slumped, and I crossed my arms tightly around me. He twisted the knife further. "I didn't want to say this, because you seem like a nice, smart girl. I love my son, but he has a history of doing this. You're not the first."

I shook my head. "No, no, no, that's not true."

"It is. He talks about his feelings and gets these girls all excited, just to lose interest. He means it when he says it. He's a very focused man, but when it comes to ladies, well —" Dr. Sawyer shook his head. "I love him as if he's my own flesh and blood. However, he has some of his biological father in him that I'm trying so hard to fight. He makes all these promises, tells the girl how she's different, but it turns out she's just like the rest. You're not the first, and you probably won't be the last."

My legs grew weak, and I braced myself against a wall. Here was this man Max idolized, telling me things I was blind to, because I fell in love with him. I was so stupid, falling in love after a week. Giving that guy my virginity. Believing every word he said.

It was just going to be my baby and me. If Max wasn't going to be here, I needed to look out for us.

I hated myself for asking, "How much?"

"Would five thousand be enough?"

I tilted my head towards him in silence. My mom always taught me never to take the first offer.

He countered with "Seven?"

"Fifteen," I said. "And I sign nothing."

Dr. Sawyer stared at me for a moment before stretching out his hand. "You drive a hard bargain. You have a deal, Ms. Finch."

I shook his hand. He applied uncomfortable pressure around my fingers as I tried to pull away.

"You will terminate your little issue?"

"Yes, of course," I lied as I ripped my hand away. He pulled out a checkbook and a Mont Blanc pen, ready to write me a check.

This man could go fuck himself. Max could go fuck himself.

A wave of nausea crept up my throat, and I stood up. "I would prefer a cashier's check. You can drop it off tomorrow. I work open to noon. Excuse me."

I walked behind the building and hurled up the contents of my stomach. When I stood straight, my eyes filled with tears. I pulled out my phone, a device I'd watched for a month, waiting for a call, some response. It felt like a molten rock in my hand.

I would take their money, and I would live so well without them. My baby will be better off without this family in his or her life.

Without thinking, I drove to Tin Lake as the sun set, golden hour casting a sheen over the beaches and the tourists packing up.

With a scream, I tossed my phone into the water.

I plopped to the ground, sand spraying around my backside. I cradled my stomach.

"I promise I'll love you enough for the both of us. I will make us a life so beautiful you won't miss him. He's going to be so sorry he missed out on you. I already love you so much, it feels infinite."

17

MAX

NOW

Emily is still in the other room when I hear footsteps come down the stairs.

Olive steps down in robot pajamas, looking around with crossed arms.

"Where's my mom?"

I put my wine glass down because my hands shake. "She went in the other room. Do you need something?"

"No," she says, walking to the recliner and sitting down. She stares at her knees. When she looks up, my chest clenches. "So, you're my dad."

"Yeah."

"Do I have any other brothers or sisters?"

I shake my head.

"Are you going to marry Noelle?"

I shake my head again. "Noelle and I are no longer boyfriend-girlfriend."

"Oh," she says. I see a glimmer of a smile on her face. When she looks up, she says, "Where do you live?"

"San Diego," I say.

She nods again. When she looks at me, I see an expression I wish I could take away. A cocktail of hurt and confusion infuses my daughter's face, and I wish I could get rid of it. Forever.

"Why now?" she asks.

It's implicating her primary parent if I tell her the truth. I didn't know. Emily never returned my emails. If I had known Emily was pregnant, I would've moved heaven and earth to be here. For everything.

"Well…" Footsteps pull Olive's attention to the hallway where Emily emerges with a smile so strained, I wonder what happened.

Emily looks at Olive and then at me. "Everything going okay?"

"Mom, what's for dinner?"

"How about pizza?" Emily asks and turns to me. "Do you want pizza, Max?"

"I love pizza," I say.

"I do too," Olive whispers.

"Do you like olives on your pizza? Because of your name?" I ask.

Her nose crinkles, and she shakes her head back and forth.

"It's the great irony of my child," Emily says. She immediately realizes her mistake and corrects herself. "Our child."

Olive squirms and avoids looking at me.

After forty minutes of small talk and awkward silences, the pizza comes, and we dig in.

"Real cheese," Olive hums as she takes a bite. "We usually get fake cheese."

Emily smiles because she asked me before she ordered if I ate dairy. When I said yes, I noticed Olive give a fist pump.

I hope her stomach will be okay. This looks like a lethal

amount of dairy.

My daughter takes another bite of pizza, so overcome with real cheese, she closes her eyes. Then, she drops her slice dramatically. "Are you lactose-intolerant, Max?"

I shake my head. "Nope. I'm fortunate. Are you going to be okay, Emily?"

Emily takes a hesitant bite. "I took a whole sleeve of Lactaid. We'll see."

"Max, do you like ranch with your pizza?" Olive asks.

"I *love* ranch on my pizza."

She hands me a tiny cup. "Mom always orders extra because I love it." Olive swirls her pizza point in a glop of white on her plate and puts it in her mouth. I do the same, and she smiles.

My heart hurts that I missed out on nine years of pizza nights.

My phone buzzes in my pocket, and I pull it out. It's my mom. I click my button to power my phone down. Nothing will interrupt this moment. Olive knows I'm her dad. We're eating together as a family.

I shouldn't look at Olive's mother across the table, but I can't help it.

She looks so beautiful eating the crust first.

"What, it's my favorite part. I can't get too full before I eat my favorite part." Her mouth is full of bread.

"Mom is so weird. Who does that?" Olive asks.

"I mean, really. The weirdest." We laugh together, and my heart grows five sizes.

Emily looks at both of us and shakes her head. "Are you two ganging up on me already?"

Olive and I nod at each other.

A half smile crosses Emily's mouth as she looks down at her plate, picking up a stray piece of pepperoni.

"Mom, can Max stay for *Goosebumps* tonight?"

"Sure, if he wants."

I nod and try to contain my excitement. Sharing what I love with my kids was one of the things I was looking forward to most as a dad, and now I get to.

"Mom gets so scared when we read *Goosebumps*," Olive says. "You'll see."

"I can't wait," I say.

"You should hear Mom's scary doll voice. It's so silly."

Turning towards Emily, I motion to her. "Proceed."

"No, not now."

"Come on," Olive eggs on. "Mom, do the voice."

Emily takes another drink of wine and clears her throat. *"Maxwell, do you want more wine?"*

Her voice is high-pitched and squeaky and ridiculous, but I grab my chest like I saw an apparition.

"I was so scared," I say over Olive's chuckles.

"You wonder why there's no dolls in this house," Emily says. She points to Olive.

"They're just dolls, Mom." Olive props her elbow on the table and flaps her hand, like she's explaining a mutual fund to me. "I really want this one doll, but Mom won't let me."

"That doll will come to life, I know it. It's the creepiest thing I've ever seen, and it will *not* live with us." Emily grabs for her phone and shows it to me. The skin of the doll is a grayish white, dressed in a period dress, with black holes where the eyes would be.

All I need is for that doll to end up at the foot of my bed in the middle of the night.

"Your mother is right. Very creepy."

"Mom," Olive whines. "You never let me live my dreams!"

"Get used to it."

"She won't even let me watch *M3GAN*. It's not even rated R."

"It's too scary for you," Emily says.

Olive swivels her head to mine. "Max, can I watch it?"

Emily's pizza falls from her hand. "Why are you asking him?"

"Well," Olive says, flaring out her hands, "Kenzie's parents are divorced, so when her mom says no, her dad usually says yes."

A guffaw leaves my mouth, and then I'm laughing so hard, tears fall from my eyes as I wipe them away. "Sure, you can watch it."

"Max!" Emily says out loud.

"You let her watch *Thelma and Louise*."

Emily huffs and leans back with folded arms. I hold out my hand, and Olive smacks it.

"I want to watch it first," Emily says.

"Mom will have her eyes covered most of the time," Olive says. I feel eyes on me, and when I turn, Olive stares at me, her pizza slice mid-raise.

"Max, are you going to live here now?" Olive asks.

"Um…"

"We have a lot of things to figure out," Emily says. "Just know, your father and I both want what is best for you. That's our goal."

My heart clenches. She called me a father. A smile crosses my lips.

"Okay," Olive says. She places her pizza slice on her plate. I continue to eat, but I feel eyes on me again. Turning, I see Olive's blue eyes, the ones she got from me, studying me, like I'm a painting in a museum.

"Olive, it's not polite to stare."

"Sorry." She picks her pizza up again and nibbles. "This is just weird. He came out of nowhere."

I cough into my hand. "If it makes you feel better, this is weird for me too. In the best way," I add. After I take a swig of wine, I lean in and say, "Just a little secret. I've never had a daughter before so I don't know exactly how to act."

"Because you don't have any other kids."

"Correct," I say, sitting up.

Emily holds her wine in front of her chest, staring at me. "You never have any close calls?"

I shake my head. "My friends in college made fun of me for always...looking both ways before I crossed the street."

Olive ate her pizza without a flinch.

"So, you never...got hit by another car?" Emily asks.

I shake my head. "Just your car."

"Mom, you hit him with a car?" Olive asks, snapping up.

"Kind of." Emily's eyelashes flutter as she takes a sip. Her expression is what I'd imagine if the creepy doll appeared at the end of her bed.

"Mom, can we show Max the wishing well?" Olive asks. "Tomorrow?"

"If he wants to," Emily says. "You'll be around tomorrow, Max?"

"Absolutely. Where is this wishing well?"

"Goldheart's best-kept secret." Olive turns to her mother. "It's okay to tell him, right?"

"Right." Emily's green eyes arrest me. "Goldheart doesn't want the tourists to know. It's this wishing well behind the indie bookstore. It's a tradition for us to go on our birthdays."

"You have to see it, Max. You have to."

"I would love to." I take a bite of pizza and grin so hard, my cheeks ache.

"Also, we *must* have a dance party tonight," Olive insists.

"No," Emily says with a shake of her head.

"Come on, Mom. Max has to see your sprinkler move."

～

After a vigorous dance party (I did see the sprinkler, and it was glorious), we put Olive to bed. She requested I read to her tonight.

She snuggled into the crook of my arm, and I had to hold back the emotion creeping up my throat as I read. We made it through twenty-three pages before Olive yawned next to me. She leaned into my chest, and I rested my head on top of hers, savoring this moment and loving every second.

Olive stretched her mouth one last time, and Emily stood from her lean in the doorway.

"Ms. Olive Jean, it's time for bed."

"Okay," she says and rolls from my embrace and curves her arm around her pillow.

I switch with Emily as she leans over and kisses our daughter's head. "Good night. I love you."

"I love you too, Mom." We're walking to the door when Olive asks, "Max?"

Emily motions for me to approach, and I walk towards her hesitantly. She's on her side so I lean my knuckles into the bed, kissing my daughter's temple. In that moment, I don't care if it's too soon. "Good night. I love you." My voice creaks on those words.

She says nothing as she hugs the pillow harder. I think I hear her say "So weird" before settling into her spot.

Emily switches off the light, and a small nightlight paints stars on the ceiling. We walk down the hall, and Emily's arms encircle her torso.

"Thank you for letting me...you know," I say, giving her distance. If she didn't have a boyfriend, I would pull her towards me, maybe kiss her hair. Instead, we walk side-by-side. There's so much to discuss between us—now that I know about Olive, I'm not disappearing. I will show up every day so she knows I will never run around away again, even if I didn't know.

Emily bites her lip as she grabs her glass of wine. "Do you want some more?"

I really shouldn't, but I want to stay in this house as long as she'll let me. "Sure."

She says nothing as she pours us some more. She walks to the couch and I follow her, sinking into the doughy cushions. We both pull a knee into the seam of the couch, to face each other, and I can smell the flowers on her skin.

I offer my glass for a toast. "To what we made." Emily's eyebrows raise, and her lips downturn. I smile, since I'm not sure what that expression is. "What?"

"It's… That's sweet." She clinks our glasses together, and we both take a sip.

"I need to leave Thursday. To get back in time for my dad's party."

Emily nods. "Have you mentioned this to your parents yet?"

"No, I want to wait." I shrug a shoulder. "I'm enjoying our little bubble. It's nice to pretend. You know."

"Pretend, what?"

"That we don't have a million things to figure out." I swallow, as the anxiety rises in my chest. When we're together as a family, I can forget we had ten years apart, that she made a deliberate choice to keep me from Olive, although she seems open to me being involved now. The wine has loosened my tongue, so I say, "It's nice to be together. I wished we could've done this the whole time."

Her eyebrows raise again. "Really?"

I nod. "I would've dropped…everything. I wanted to…."

"Really?" she repeats.

I study her and narrow my eyes. "Did I miss something?"

Emily shakes her head. "No, no. I agree with you. Maybe don't tell your parents just yet."

"I'll tell them after his retirement party," I say. "Once the dust settles."

"That sounds like a good plan." She smiles, like that alleviated some nervousness. "Do you think they'll be mad?"

Why would they be mad? I shake my head, jutting out my bottom lip. "I don't think so. Surprised, maybe."

She smiles and takes another sip. "Good."

"Good." My body leans in, pulled to her like a magnet, my chest leaning into hers. Our gaze locks. Rolling my lips together, I can't stop looking at Emily.

Her phone on the counter buzzes, breaking the spell between us. She stands up and checks it. "It's Burke."

"Does Burke know I'm over here?"

Emily shakes her head.

"Why didn't you date more? You must be beating them off with a stick. Was Olive deploying the raccoons on them?"

Emily covers her mouth since she lets out a deep belly laugh. "I was busy with raising Olive and growing my jewelry business. I always said I would when she went to school. Then, my dad decided to open the brewery, and dating kept getting pushed out and pushed out. I went on a date here or there, but nothing stuck. Burke asked me to dinner, and that was that. I finally felt ready."

An odd cocktail of emotions swirls in my gut. Burke seems like a nice guy, but I hate him. Maybe she didn't want to have a relationship, and that's why she cut me off. Still, this magnetism I feel between us can't be a coincidence. She must feel it too.

Once I felt that with Emily, I knew I needed to break it off with Noelle. I've just been lying to myself for years. It's obvious Emily doesn't feel the same, and that's fine. If it's not Emily, I will work like hell to gain Olive's trust and love and spend the rest of my life trying to find a woman who makes me feel the way Emily makes me feel.

Chuckling, I sip my wine. Maybe it was all in my head. "We were so dumb back then."

"Yeah," Emily says. "Who knows if we would've worked out."

"Yeah, totally," I say, laughing so I don't spill my soul to this woman who doesn't care. "I mean, you were nineteen, I was twenty-five..."

"Totally, I was so dumb."

"*I* was dumb," I say, putting my hand on my chest. "Remember when we skinny-dipped in the lake and got caught by that group of old ladies?"

"What would soon become the Bad Biddies Club," Emily says. "Miriam Oliver is my nemesis."

"What?"

"She was in that group that night. She overheard something..." Emily's words trailed off and she rubs her eyes. "I'm really tired. We'll see you tomorrow at the wishing well? Maybe ten? I'll text you the address of where to park. I have a couple errands to run before."

I stand up slowly, wishing I could stay longer. "That sounds wonderful."

"Okay, good night." We stand, staring at each other, and she offers a friendly arm for a hug. I hold my breath when I take her in so I don't get lost in her scent and wish things were different. Here's another place I want to stay forever.

She walks me to the door and flicks on the porch light. I step onto her porch and turn.

"Watch me in case the raccoons get me?"

A smile crosses Emily's face. "Of course."

I shove my hands in my pockets as I walk across the field to the tiny house. Looking back, I see Emily, her hand on the doorframe, watching me.

Damn, what I wouldn't do to time travel back ten years and try like hell to stay in her life.

18

EMILY

When I hear the slam of the tiny house's door, I close the door and slide down it, hitting the floor with a thud.

His stepdad orchestrated everything, and Max didn't have a clue.

Max was exactly who I thought he was. The what-ifs rattle in my mind as I realize I wasn't going crazy. I didn't imagine it or was wrong. Max was kind, sweet, unbelievably handsome, and he wanted me. If he'd known about the baby, he would've been here in a second.

Instead, his stepdad intercepted my news and bamboozled me into taking money, made me think Max was a douchebag who only left broken promises for women to clean up.

I wring my hands and push them into my hair. A thousand invisible pins stick my body. It's almost nine o'clock, and I want to call someone, but I'm not sure who. My mother would find Fred Sawyer within the hour if I told her. Caroline is probably fast asleep. There's only one person who is probably still up, gives great advice, and wouldn't immediately find Fred Sawyer and pummel him.

"Hi, Emily, what's going on?" Shiloh's bright voice asks

me when she picks up.

"Hey, Shiloh, do you have a second?"

"For you, of course! What's up?"

I pause, trying to find the words. Instead, I burst into tears.

When you try not to cry for ten years, sometimes the tears come out of nowhere.

"You need me there," Shiloh says. "I'll be right over."

The line goes dead before I can object.

When Shiloh knocks on my porch door fifteen minutes later, my face is streaked with tears and mascara.

Shiloh says nothing but takes me in for a hug. "What's going on, Em? Sit."

I sit down, and Shiloh scootches a chair directly in front of me. Her tiny hands take mine.

"I realized something," I say, through tears and hiccups. "I think Max's stepdad interfered. Back when I was first pregnant."

"Okay." Shiloh's face doesn't change expression. "Tell me more."

"Max left for a dental mission immediately after we met. We talked about trying a long-distance relationship when he got back because he was going to dental school in San Francisco. While he was gone, I found out I was pregnant. His phone wasn't taking messages, so I called his stepdad's dental practice. He showed up and gave me this story that Max had a pattern of doing this to other women. His stepdad offered me money."

"Okay." Shiloh's hands gripped me tighter.

"He wanted me to 'take care of it.' I knew I wasn't going to do that, but I still took the money." My head drops to my hands. A warm, comforting hand rests on my back.

"You were right to take his money," Shiloh says. "Gosh, that man is evil. Evil."

I sniffle and wipe my nose with my hand. "What do I do? Max thinks that I ghosted him and kept Olive from him. If he knew his stepdad, the man he *idolized*, did this, I…"

"You don't have to do anything now," Shiloh says. She breathes in and out. "He needs to know, but not now."

"You think so? We told Olive tonight who he is."

"Does Max treat Olive differently because of what he thinks happened, do you think?"

Shaking my head, I feel a swell of tears build behind my eyes. "The way he was with her, he's so sweet. I missed out on that because I was stupid and naïve…"

"Hey, hey." Her thin arm circles my shoulders and pulls me in. Shiloh always smells like cupcakes. "This is not your fault. You were how old? Twenty?"

"Yes."

"You were so young. A man you were told was honorable and good lied to you. It's not your fault for trusting him." Shiloh pauses and pulls me tighter. "Folks take advantage of trusting people. Trusting, young people."

"Thank you." I take Shiloh into a proper hug, her petite body fitting into mine as I sob quietly against her shoulder.

"Give it a few more days, and then tell him. Enjoy being together as a family." Shiloh is quiet as she continues to hug me, rubbing my back. "I'm jealous. What I wouldn't give to have my dad come back like Max did. Not sure he's as good of a guy as Max is, but a girl can dream. Even if it's not the best idea."

I pull away and wipe my face. "I didn't expect Max to ever show up again."

"We never do. But we secretly watch the door, just in case today a miracle happens."

Tears cover the back of my hand when I wipe them away. I did my best to stop wishing. However, Max returning has brought closure I didn't know I needed. It's filling a missing piece in my life. If we never end up together, if he never forgives me for taking his dad's money and letting him go so easily, this is enough.

In my bones I know he won't abandon Olive now that he knows about her.

When I think about Max reading to her, with Olive tucked into his arm, I can't help but cry. "I feel so bad. My daughter missed out. Because of me."

Shiloh kisses my forehead. "Not because of you. Max is here now. He wants to be here. There's not much more you can ask for. You don't have a time machine."

I roll my lips together before I say, "I think I have feelings for him again."

Shiloh sits back and crosses her arms. "Oh, that is a pickle."

"I tried with Burke. So hard," I say. "He's nice, but…"

"You're not in love with him. I get it."

"What should I do?"

Shiloh shrugs one shoulder. "It might be time to cut Burke loose. See what happens with Max. Didn't he have a girlfriend?"

"She showed up here, and he broke up with her. She gave him an ultimatum, and I guess that was the final straw."

"Oh," Shiloh says. "Maybe old feelings are coming back for him too."

I shake my head vigorously. "No, I don't think so. He thinks I kept Olive from him. He still hates me."

"Well, maybe he's doubting what happened," Shiloh offers.

I tilt my head up to dry the tears. "So, the plan is to wait a little longer to tell him about his stepdad and enjoy the moment. And think about breaking up with Burke."

"Sounds like a plan," Shiloh says, hugging me again.

I already really liked Shiloh before my big brother fell in

19

EMILY

Wednesday

"He's here," I say to Olive in the backseat as we pull into the parking lot in front of the path to the wishing well.

"Hi, Max," Olive yells through her window with a wave. Max mirrors it, leaning against his car, looking so freaking cute, I can't handle it.

"You can do this," I say under my breath.

"Yes, you can, Mom. Wait, what can you do?"

My heart clenches. "Nothing, sweetie." I turn off the car, and Olive explodes out before the car even turned off. She plows into Max, caging him in with her arms around his waist.

Max is still staying at the tiny house, but I used a fake excuse to meet him here. I told Olive I needed something from the brewery, but it was an opportunity to silently freak out in my siblings' joint office. My mother sensed it so she hovered until I acknowledged her.

She offered to babysit tonight so Max and I can be alone. That dialed my anxiety from a solid eight point five to an eleven.

Now, he's standing there, with his blond hair combed back, his bright blue eyes somewhat happy to see me, and his broad shoulders covered by a short-sleeved white button-down. He looks like he's ready to hop on a yacht owned by a billionaire, not about to see a run-down wishing well with his love child and his baby mama.

"Hi, Emily," Max says, leaning in and kissing my cheek. I shiver from his touch. "You look beautiful."

"Thank you," I say, looking down at my simple T-shirt dress and white sneakers. My cheeks warm as I walk ahead so Olive doesn't comment on my blush.

"It's this way," I say. The path is so worn it's easy to follow as nature envelops us. The forest is a few degrees cooler, and when you look up, you see a sliver of sky between the trees.

"It feels so magical," Olive says from behind me. When I turn back, I see Max and Olive chatting animatedly, their hands moving with their words. They're mirrors of each other, and my ovaries cry at the sight.

Olive's voice hits me from behind. "What, Mom?"

"Nothing," I say, quickening my pace. We turn a corner to see the wishing well in the middle of a clearing. A beam of sunlight illuminates it like we're in a fairy tale cartoon, specks of dust floating within it like glitter. When I stop in front of it, Max joins me, his body too close for me to be normal.

"Wow," Max says. "This is really special."

"Yeah," I agree. Olive squeezes between us, and she slips her hand into mine. Out of the corner of my eye, I see her slip her other hand into Max's.

I can't handle this. It's too precious.

"Max, since it's your first time, you have to make a wish."

"Do I throw a coin in, or...?"

"Yes. A penny. It has to be a penny."

Max slips his hand into his pocket, fumbling for change and pulls out a shiny coin.

"Close your eyes, Max."

Max's blond eyelashes flutter as he mouths something. Then he flicks the penny, and it spins into the darkness of the well, never to be seen again.

"Congratulations, Max. You just made your first wish at the Goldheart's very own wishing well."

"Have anyone's dreams come true that you know of?" Max asks.

I feel a tug on my sleeve. Olive motions for me to kneel down, and I do, her hand cupping my ear. "Mom, my wish came true. Can I tell Max?"

"Sure, you can tell him," I whisper back.

She spins around. "Max, *my* wish came true."

"What was that?" He puts his hands on his hips.

"I wished for my dad to come back." Olive then grabs Max again and links our hands together so his hand is in mine.

"Olive, what are you doing?" I say. Max doesn't let go of my hand as we stand there, our daughter snickering behind her fists.

"You're holding hands."

Turning, I see a lump in Max's throat as he swallows. We're still holding hands, but I lean in. "How long do we need to hold hands?"

"I'll hold it forever," he says. Heat floods my cheeks and he swallows and looks down at the wishing well.

His thumb rubs my knuckle as he holds it, and the contact makes me involuntarily smile as Olive hugs me around my middle. I want to bottle this moment, remember every second, every breath, so I can replay it for years to come.

In this moment, we weren't robbed of ten years together, and Olive had Max the whole time. We're a family, and when I look at Max, I know what I need to do.

"Olive, do you want to get a milkshake with Max at Ice Dream? Have some alone time? It's almost eleven so they'll be open soon."

My daughter, who begs for milkshakes almost daily, lights up. I know it sucks having a lactose-intolerant mom. It sucks being lactose-intolerant. I miss regular ice cream.

Olive splays her fingers to Max like she's in showbiz. "Max, you're going to love them. They have this cookies-and-cream one that's so good…"

Max lets go of my hand, and I miss it immediately. Max grabs Olive's, and I trail behind, watching my daughter create a core memory with her father.

A man who touches me, and my body feels like it's a live wire.

It's time to do what I need to do.

Stop pretending.

"I can't be with you anymore," I tell Burke when I find him at the restaurant. Bistro 530 is about to open for lunch, but I texted him and he met me at the back door.

Burke is stoic, running his hand down his face as he turns away from me. When he turns around, he can't look me in the eye.

"It's Olive's dad, isn't it?"

I don't admit it, but it is. It's funny how three days can make me so sure I have feelings for someone, when I spent two months hoping feelings for Burke would develop.

"I didn't expect him to come back." I swallow down a thick lump in my throat. "It's just very confusing."

He nods once. I feel like absolute shit. "He's the reason, right? Why you never let your guard down with me?"

There were so many things he did to try to break me open, just for me to clam up. Burke is a casualty of an impossible situation. My chin bobs slightly.

"Well, he's a lucky man," Burke says. His gaze pierces me. "Tell him one thing for me. If he breaks your or Olive's heart, I will punch him in the fucking throat."

I chuckle. "I'm not sure it's like that."

"I saw the way he looked at you at dinner. I was hoping it wasn't true, because I really, really like you. But I get it." Burke rests his hands on his hips.

Lifting onto the balls of my feet, I kiss his cheek, and he leans into it. Why couldn't I feel this way about Burke, an uncomplicated man who is easy to be around and cares about me and my daughter?

"I got to go. Take care, Emily." He opens the heavy door to his restaurant and disappears.

I expected to feel heavy after breaking it off with Burke, but I feel the opposite. I feel light, like I could fly. It feels like helium filled my veins and I could crawl out of my skin. In a good way.

Bistro 530 is a couple storefronts down from Ice Dream, and I stop in front of the window, looking on the dreamy parlor, full of white-wire furniture and cartoons of smiling ice cream cones. Max sits there, across from our daughter's ponytail, as her little hands flail as she tells a story. Max laughs with his whole body as she tells it.

He catches me in the window, and his eyelids crinkle as he stares at me. Olive touches his arm, so he refocuses on our daughter as he pumps his straw into his milkshake. Heat curls low in my belly as his gaze sears me. I'm a free woman, he's a free man, but my knowledge presses on me like a weighted blanket. He wanted me, would've wanted *us*. When he told me the other night he fell in love with me, I now finally believe him.

Seeing him with our daughter does something to me. A long-dormant desire whispers to me, making me want to jump his bones. What happened with his stepdad holds me back.

"I'll be right back," I mouth to him, pointing with my thumbs.

"Okay," he mouths back, his face so wide in a grin.

When I open the door to Woody Finch Brewery, my mother clocks me instantly.

"I thought I gave you the day off." She folds her arms across her.

"Max is having some alone time with Olive. They're drinking milkshakes."

"That's sweet."

"Yes," I say, walking to the office I share with my siblings. Mom follows me and stands inside as I sit down at the computer. "I just broke up with Burke."

"I'm not surprised."

I swivel in my chair. "What?"

"I knew you and he had an expiration date."

"Mom, really?" I ask. "Why didn't you say anything?"

"I learned a long time ago that voicing opinions on my children's partners was a bad idea. I said something once about Callie."

"Callie was the absolute worst. Did Reid get defensive?"

"He did. Dated her another year, though. I always thought it was out of spite, but you know your brother."

Reid had dated a single mom for three years. About six months in, it became clear Callie was using him as a glorified babysitter. While Reid got close to her son and still hangs out with him, it was never a good relationship with his mom. Thank God he found Whitney. She's so much better for him.

"Don't get me wrong, Burke is a nice guy," my mom says. "Just something wasn't right for you."

"He's so nice."

Mom walks over and perches on the desk. "Is Max nice?"

My core tightens, thinking about holding his hand, how handsome he is. We only had one night, but it changed the course of my life, and I will never forget the tenderness he showed me, how he gave me my first orgasm before we had sex. How caring he was. It was the perfect first time, even if I got pregnant from it.

"Max is very nice," I say. "I think his stepdad interfered in our relationship."

My mother freezes, her arms tightening around her rib cage. "How?"

"I think he lied about talking to Max, that time he came to Goldheart."

"What makes you think that?"

"Max said something that indicated to me he didn't know at all." I drop my head into my hands. "He's about to take over his stepdad's dentist practice. He's retiring this week."

"Has Max told his parents about Olive yet?"

"No. He's waiting." I run my fingers through my hair. "I really didn't want to deal with this this week."

"You need to tell him," Mom says. "He needs to know. The longer you wait, the more he's going to resent you."

"You think so?"

"Yes. Trust me, you don't want to let this go on too long." Mom slaps the desk with her palm. "Olive will sleep over tonight, and you and Max can have some alone time to figure some stuff out. You can tell him about his stepdad and about your breakup with Burke, and then you can move forward, whatever that looks like. He said he was leaving tomorrow, right?"

"Right." My stomach roils as I think about how tonight might go. Will he look at me differently once I tell him about his stepdad? Will he kiss me when I tell him I broke up with Burke? Do I want him to?

I definitely want him to. I want his hands on me, his lips on mine. Whenever I'm around him, I feel this crackling energy, this unspoken heat that we tried to forget about for ten years. The memories never faded for me, and I'm not sure they did for Max either, although he thought I was horrible for keeping it from him.

"Thanks, Mom. That would be great."

Mom pauses, her mouth straightening to a line. "Are you on something?"

Heat blooms in my cheeks. "What?"

"Birth control."

"I got an IUD a couple months ago."

"Good," Mom says. "But if you do sleep with him, use a condom, even though they didn't work so well the first time. You don't want a sibling for Olive just yet."

Although I'm thirty and know this, I swallow any response. Heat floods my cheeks, thinking about sex with Max. "Sure thing, Mom."

She kisses me on my head, like she's done since I was a kid. "I love you. I just want you and Olive to be happy."

"Thanks, Mom. I want that for us too."

"Good." She moves to the door and turns. "It's been one of the great joys of my life to see you be a mother. You're so, so good at it."

My chest feels like it'll split open. "Even if I let my daughter watch *Thelma and Louise* and she lets in raccoons because of it?"

"Especially because of that. I'm sure you'll figure out

what to do and it will be the right decision for you and Olive."

After my mother leaves, I arrange things on my desk just to move them to their original spot. I promised Max an hour to spend alone with Olive, which we decided would be a good amount of time to start.

When I have ten minutes until I have to be back, I walk out of the brewery, after saying hello to Shiloh and Ramon behind the bar. I'm barely out the door before I'm stopped by Miriam Oliver.

"Hello, dear," she says, blocking my exit from my family's business.

My body cringes at her use of "dear." She may be sweet-looking, with short hair and her recently acquired turquoise frames, but she is the devil incarnate, and the devil loves petty gossip. This woman is the bane of my existence.

Miriam has a sliding scale of meddling in my family's affairs. After I screamed at her after she outed me in front of the whole town on Labor Day weekend for revealing I was pregnant before I was ready to announce it, she keeps a wide berth.

Once and awhile, Miriam forgets. I have the sneaking suspicion it's because I'm a girl.

Miriam refuses to move. She knows I won't plow through an old lady, no matter how much I hate her.

"Leland and I were enjoying a nice mid-day beer, and I saw you out and about. It was your birthday recently, correct?"

"Yes."

"How old are you now, my dear?"

I'm too young to get mad with someone asking my age. "Thirty."

"Oh, thirty. Such an important milestone. You know, we

just passed by Ice Dream, and we saw Olive there with a young man. Dressed very nicely."

Her thin fuchsia-colored lips press together, waiting for me to answer. I just fold my arms.

"I vaguely remember a summer where you were seeing a boy. I saw you once at the lake together."

I do not answer, dwelling in the uncomfortable silence.

"Olive sure looks like him."

I'm not sure how she knows because Max's features are barely visible from the window, but okay. I wouldn't put it past Miriam to make an excuse to go to the bathroom to scope out the situation. My daughter has never really interacted with Miriam, so she wouldn't recognize her.

I love this town, but everyone is so goddamn nosy.

"Miriam, just spit out your question. I have somewhere to be."

Miriam grabs her chest like I'm the rude one. "Is that *him?*"

"It's none of your business, Miriam." I walk around her, but she grabs my arm, digging her nails into my flesh.

My eyes widen as I look down at her.

"I just wanted to say that if he is back in town, I think that's wonderful. I—" Her voice cracks, and she looks down. She cowers, and her lips quiver.

"Miriam, I have to go."

Whatever she wanted to say, I don't want to hear. If she wants to apologize, she's about ten years too late. Finally, she lets go of my arm.

"I just wish you and Olive the best of luck. That's all."

I mutter "Thank you" as I walk out the door.

"So, does your mom *like* Burke?" Playing it off, I stare at my milkshake. My daughter sits across from me with a smaller version, sucking it dry.

"I think so."

"And he's a good guy, right?"

"That we know of." Olive slurps the bottom, hitting the end of her drink. She looks up, tilting her head. "Why do you ask?"

"Nothing." Fidgeting, I look down.

"Max."

"Olive."

"Do you *like* Mom?"

"Of course I like your mom." *Every time I see her, I want to kiss her, if that's what you mean.*

"No, like *like* Mom."

"Your mother is very nice. And pretty."

"I know that." Olive rolls her eyes and tries for more milkshake. I hand her mine, so she can finish it. I've already developed a killer sugar headache. "I mean, do you want to be her lover?"

I cough against my hand as Olive sucks the milkshake,

making loud straw noises, oblivious that I'm turning eight shades of red.

A hand rests on my shoulder, and Olive doesn't react. Turning back, I see Emily, smiling, as her hand lingers on my shoulder, traveling to the middle of my back. It creates shivers in my limbs.

She can touch me all she wants.

"Thanks for taking care of Olive while I ran some errands," Emily says. Her hand rubs my back as I adjust in my seat, because my pants tighten around me. This is awkward. I might need to sit here for a minute.

"Did you get what you needed done?"

Emily nods, and her hand leaves my back. My phone vibrates again in my pocket, and I ignore it. My mom called me this morning and didn't leave a message. It might be her again.

"Mom, these milkshakes are so good."

"I bet," I say.

"Mom once had a milkshake on a road trip with me, and she accidentally knocked down a teenager on a skateboard because she had a poopmergency—"

"Olive," she says firmly. Chuckling, I stand up.

"I can take her for milkshakes. It can become our thing," I say.

"I'm glad she got that lactose-tolerant gene from you." There's her hand again, tapping on the middle of my back. What is with the touching?

I'm not complaining. It just went from zero to a hundred, and I'm so curious why.

"Olive, you're going to stay at Grandma's tonight. Max and I need to discuss some things."

We do have so much to discuss, but a night alone with Emily may make me forget everything I'm fighting against.

I'm so close to kissing those beautiful lips and laying her

out on her bed, saying "screw it" to everything that happened and making up for lost time. This morning, I thought about her too much—her hair, her eyes, her ass in those tiny shorts she wears. I painted the shower wall after a few strokes of my cock, a roiling fantasy of her on top of me, my hands on her breasts.

I felt instantly guilty. She has a boyfriend. We have a history that changed the whole course of my life. My resolve this morning to never think about her that way again dropped the minute Olive put Emily's hands in mine. Now I'll be alone with her while Olive stays with Emily's mom? That's all sorts of temptation there. Not to mention, I'm leaving tomorrow.

"Yes!" Olive says, stretching her arms above her head in victory.

"Grandma spoils Olive more than any grandparent has ever spoiled a grandchild," Emily whispers.

"Wait until my mom gets wind of this. She might give your mother a run for her money."

"You should tell her. Maybe before the party," Emily blurts out.

"Really?" I've thought about telling her, but I wasn't sure what Emily wanted. We've had enough time, I think, and my heart pumps fast every time I talk to my mom and don't mention a huge nine-year-old secret.

"As soon as possible," Emily says. Her face is stoic without a hint of her thoughts.

"I will," I promise and pull out my phone. Another missed call from Mom. I show Emily. "That's her now."

"Great. Olive and I will meet you at home."

They walk towards Emily's car as I open my phone and walk outside to a small bench facing the street. I tap on my mother's contact and hold it to my ear as I watch Emily and Olive cross the street, hand in hand.

"Maxwell?" Mom asks, the second the call is answered.

"Hi, Mom."

"Are you still in Goldheart?" Her voice sounds uneasy.

"Yes, Mom, is everything okay?"

"I talked to Noelle."

All blood drains from my face. "Oh?"

"She told me something truly shocking. Did you have a baby with that girl you saw ten years ago?"

Goddamn Noelle. "Yes," I answer.

"Maxwell, I...I..." Quiet sobs echo through the phone. My heart squelches as I listen.

"I didn't know," I tell her. "Honestly. I don't know why Emily kept it from me, but she did."

"Noelle says she met her on Monday. You knew for three days and didn't tell us?"

I lean forward on my thighs. "I wanted to get to know her first."

"It's a girl?"

"Yes. Her name is Olive. She's so beautiful and so smart. So funny." That makes my throat swell, difficult to swallow.

"Oh, Max. That's wonderful, sweetheart. But are you sure that child is yours?"

My brows furrow, and I grind my loafer into the ground before standing up. Walking into an alcove between storefronts, I say, "Emily was a virgin when...we, you know."

"Oh," Mom says as we devolve into silence. I check my phone to make sure the call is still active. My mom breaks our pause. "What are you going to do?"

"I don't know."

"Please think this through, Max. Please. Are you back together with the girl?"

"No" feels strange coming out of my mouth.

"All I say is don't throw away all of your future plans. You already broke up with Noelle. I just don't like where this is going. At all."

"Mom, we'll talk about it on Saturday."

"Oh good, you're still coming to the party."

"Of course I am. I wouldn't miss it for the world." I roll my lips together. "Are you going to tell Dad?"

"I can, if you want."

"Please," I say. We say goodbye and hang up.

My dad was never thrilled about Emily. One night I came home, high as the clouds from my time with her. My smile must've looked insane, as I floated from room to room, drunk from our kisses and hand-holding and soul-baring. We had kissed for the first time, and I had never felt that sensation of ember sparks like I had with her.

My dad stared at me throughout dinner and leaned over when my mom walked away to prepare dessert.

"Don't let this girl get in your head. You're so young. You have your whole life ahead of you."

I remember looking down at the table and then looking my father in the eye, something that made my skin crawl and stomach churn. "I think I'm in love with her."

"You've known her for four days."

"I know that," I said. I pounded my chest. "My intuition tells me that she's the one. I feel it in my bones."

My dad gave me a patronizing head nod. "You think you do. You just want to sleep with her. There's a difference."

It was always more than that, but I closed my mouth. "We talked about me seeing her when I get back from Costa Rica. San Francisco isn't that far from LA. She goes to USC. She's smart, Dad. We will be smart about this."

"I hope so. I'm counting on you," he said.

Out of the view of my parents, I texted Emily, *I miss you.*

My phone lit up instantly. *I miss you too. :heart emoji:*

Everything pointed to her. I felt pulled to her by the universe.

That's why everything that happened felt so off.

In that moment, I knew she was the one. I thought she didn't feel the same way.

But sometimes Emily looks at me over our daughter's head, and I'm transported right back to that week.

When I fell in love with her after four days and she fell in love with me.

21

EMILY

After I dropped Olive off at my parents' house and a couple hours of pacing, I furiously type my talking points into my Notes app. Every few minutes, I glance at the tiny house. We discussed him coming over at four, so five minutes before, I covertly watch Max walk the distance from the tiny house to my back porch. The way his arms swing, the way his shoe hits the ground reminds me too much of Darcy walking the field in the best version of *Pride and Prejudice*.

Talking points. That's what I should focus on. Not how sexy my baby daddy walks.

When he mentioned that he told his mother but didn't talk to his dad, a deep whoosh of breath left my lips. It would happen eventually, but at least the shit won't hit the fan...yet.

That he won't hear that the small-town dumb bitch his son slept with actually took his money and had the baby, no matter what he wanted.

I would have to face him eventually, but I secretly hoped I would never have to. Maybe I should head to the wishing well with a penny of my own. Maybe a whole roll.

First talking point—visitation. How many times a month? Will Max come up and see her? Will Olive go visit him in San Diego? How busy will he be when she's there? I know nothing about dental practices and how taxing they are on your personal life, but I intend to find out.

Second talking point—I will casually mention that I broke up with Burke. It has nothing to do with Max whatsoever. It's a simple coincidence. It has nothing to do with Max's sexy walk or his eyes that burn imaginary holes into my skin.

A knock rattles my back door, and I smooth down my tank top and adjust my shorts. My outfit is cute but not trying too hard. There's no way I'm trying to look sexy for Max. Why are my hands shaking? Huffing out a breath, I open the door. How does he do that, looking up like he's in a cologne ad? How does he know what to do to make me question everything?

"Hi," he says, walking in and looking around. "This kitchen is so quiet without Olive."

I close the door and press against it. "I know. It's wonderful."

"I'm glad we get to do this."

"We have a lot of stuff to talk about." I grab a fresh pad of paper and slap it on the table. "Where do you want to start?"

My butt is halfway to a chair when Max points to the door. "I'm hungry. Are you hungry? I can't discuss the big life stuff without sustenance."

My three pieces of turkey jerky and a granola bar wasn't enough for lunch, but my nerves were shot. Now that he's here and it's normal, my stomach is calm enough to accept a full meal.

I ache to spend time with him.

"Sure. What did you have in mind?"

"There's a diner I saw…"

"Moe's? We love Moe's."

"Or I think there's a café or something?"

"Betty's Café. That's risky."

"How so?"

"That's where the gossips hang out. However, they're more of a lunch crowd."

"Let them talk." Max offers his arm, like he's a prince. I laugh as I rest my hand on his arm. He pulls me to him, covering my hand with his. I'm not sure if he feels the electrical charge I feel as we press our sides together, walking to the door.

When we arrive, a quick scan of the restaurant tells me we're good. None of Miriam's bad biddies are there in the corner. Carly, a teenager I've seen around here or there, is at the hostess stand, but her parents keep to themselves. We're as safe here as I anticipate anywhere else.

"Do you see any of the gossipers?" Max asks, leaning in. God, he smells good. Why is he standing so close?

"No, thankfully," I say. Max pulls my chair out and pushes me in. His fingers brush against my bare skin as he walks to his chair, unaware that he just made my whole body shiver.

He opens the plastic flap of the menu. "What's good here?"

"I like their soup and salad. Or they do a half sandwich too."

"Isn't it too hot for soup?"

The air quivers outside against the blacktop of the road, but soup is one of my big love languages. "I love soup. Soup is welcome year-round."

"Fair enough." He closes the menu and leans forward. "Did we come here that one time?"

I shake my head. "No, we just went to La Scarola the last night. The place we went where I told you…"

"Oh yes, that's right." He reopens the menu and continues to peruse. He stares at his menu. "It's been bothering me, so I have to ask. Did you ever get my emails?"

"Emails?" I ask.

"Yes," he says, his eyes still glued to the menu. "I sent you an email almost daily when I was in Costa Rica."

My face melts. "You did?"

He looks up, nodding. "Did you get them?"

I shake my head, biting my lip.

He looks down at the table. "That explains a lot."

"Yeah," I say. His forlorn expression makes my heart drop. "What did they say?"

Max doesn't respond; instead, he pulls out his phone and scrolls, tapping the screen a couple times. He sniffles as he reads it over, pushing his phone toward me.

The date was two weeks after he left. It was also around when I checked my underwear constantly for my period that never came. EmilyFinch0717 instead of EmilyFinch0711. I remember writing it down for him on a slip of paper.

"You're one number off. It's 0711 instead of 0717. I didn't have your email." His expression gives nothing away, his eyes ice-cold. Looking back down, I see what I hoped I would see in my email, every time I opened it that period after he left.

Hey Martini. Are you getting my emails? I haven't heard from you and I'm dying to know everything. Did things get better with your job? Have you been able to see Caroline? What have you been up to? I want to know anything and everything.

I miss you. I think about you all day whenever I have a free moment (and even when I'm busy). I know we talked about long distance and how hard it is, but I want to try with you. We'll both be done with school in a couple years and then we can move somewhere together. My dad wants me to take over the dental practice and I love San Diego, but I would only do it if you wanted to live there. If you want to move to that big city like you always talked about, let's do it. People need dentists everywhere.

I know it was only a week, but I've never felt for anyone the way I feel about you. I think we have something special. Please tell me we have something special. Please write back. Please.

All my love,

Max

When I look up, water leaks from my eyes and I wipe my nose. "I would've *loved* to get an email like this back then. Do you have any more?"

"Sure." He swipes through his phone and shows me another. And another. All had similar themes. He loved me. He wanted to be with me. His messages were contrary to everything his dad told me that day he came to see me.

My chest could split open on how much time we wasted. How we missed our chance. I was going to tell him, but now I'm not sure if I *should* throw his stepdad under the bus. He's the only father figure he's ever known; he took his name and is about to take over his business. I'm just some girl he met one week and got pregnant. Maybe it's easier if he resents me.

It's just too sad otherwise.

Max laces his fingers in front of him, looking up at me from behind his lashes. "I thought you weren't replying to me because you changed your mind."

"No," I say, shaking my head. My voice cracks. "I tried calling you."

"I always wondered about that."

"It wasn't taking my calls, and I couldn't leave a message. My friend thought you had blocked me."

"No, my phone was getting zero service in Costa Rica. I should've tried harder. Come earlier to see you. Just my dad…" His brows furrow as he stares at his hands. He's so close to the truth, he could grasp it. My spine straightens as I wait for the lightning bolt of realization to hit him.

"Your dad what?"

"When I came home and tried to call you, your number changed, and I was so torn up. He told me to forget you. I knew something was wrong, but I listened to him. I shouldn't have."

Without thinking, I grab his hands. He grips them and really holds them, looking at me from the across the table. The truth makes my tongue feel like a boulder. In that moment, fear seizes me and I can't say it.

He emailed me. He wanted to be with me. And I believed his asshole stepfather. The true villain here is me.

"Max, I changed my phone number—" I start.

"Don't," he stops me. "Let's talk about something else. Anything else. It's my last night before the boom drops, and I —I just want to enjoy this night. With you."

"Okay," I slap a smile on my face although guilt chews at my gut. "You know what we're going to do? We're going to order the house wine, eat dinner, and have fun tonight. I don't get kid-free nights often," I tell him. "Then, we can go over my talking points."

"Yeah, but let's worry about it later." A small smile crests his lips. We pull our hands away when the serves stands by our table, taking our drink and food orders. Kim, our server, is friendly with my mom, but she doesn't spread gossip. The way she lingers, I know she senses this man is special, but she doesn't pry.

When Kim leaves to put in our order, Max says, "So, you mentioned you have a jewelry line."

I nod. "I wanted a specific necklace with an initial so I could put an O on it. I didn't see anything I liked so I decided to create it instead."

"Has it been successful?"

I nod. "I think so. I was profitable in year two. My house is paid off."

"Wow, that's great. What does the jewelry look like?"

I pull out my white gold chain with a dainty O hanging from it. We lean in, and Max takes the pendant in his hands, his fingertips swiping my collarbone, delicately, and my nipples harden. I cross my arms.

"Wow, did you make this?"

"Kind of. I worked with a designer, and I have them manufactured and sent to me."

He looks up, his gaze on me, making me squirm. We're so close, he could lean in and kiss me.

I kinda wish he would.

"This is beautiful."

"Thank you." I pull away and rest my elbows on the table. "I've gotten a lot of pressure to expand, but I want to keep it simple. Initial necklaces in three different styles, three different metals. I've only seen steady growth. Do you know the country singer Savannah Watson? She wore one of my necklaces, and it changed everything for me."

"That's incredible. How do you find the time?" He stretches his arm across the table, his hand so close to my forearm. "Between being the best mother to our daughter and best daughter to your family's business?"

"I'm very organized. Not a day or hour is wasted. This week has been...challenging."

"Sorry about that."

"It's okay," I say, although I have a mountain of orders and haven't posted to social media in a week. "What is your house like?"

"I own a condo downtown, but it's definitely not paid off."

"Did you live with Noelle?" My heart squeezes waiting for the answer.

He shakes his head. "She didn't want to live together until we were engaged. I started looking at starter homes down there, and none of them felt like home. I go with my gut on big decisions."

His stare makes me wonder if he means me. I shake it off.

"I'm like that too. When I walked into my house, I looked around for fifteen seconds and I knew." I swipe my arms above me, like I'm picturing my perfect life in the air. "It hit me hard. I saw an older Olive playing in the living room, and it was done. I looked at the rest of the house, of course, but I put in an offer before I even left."

Max presses his lips together. "Did you ever imagine more kids? Or a husband?"

"I don't think that far ahead." I study my fingers tracing the patterns in the tablecloth instead of looking at the handsome man across from me. "I didn't want to hope for something that's out of my control. Small-town dating is tough, and the pool is so small. All I wanted out of life was Olive to grow up being loved and happy. Everything else was a pipe dream."

Max leans back in his chair and crosses his arms. "Huh."

"Was it your dream? To be a dentist?"

"That was never my dream. I love it now, but I wasn't a boy asking for a play dentist drill when I was a kid. It's just— I like helping people. I knew I wanted to be a dad, so that is a dream come true."

Max clams up, and I wait for the question I know is coming. We've danced around it like we're at a Regency-era ball, but we're not confronting it. Why I didn't get in touch with him. Why the email was changed when I knew that I wrote mine down correctly.

I want to tell him that it's Fred. He lied to my face; I highly suspect he changed my email address. However, he's still a god in Max's eyes. I can't destroy that image to save my own.

Maybe Fred will finally be decent and come clean.

"I'm glad I came to Goldheart. It might've been nine years too late…" His words drift off into the air.

"I'm glad you came too. Better late than never."

"I just wonder…" I want to know every thought he has. Does he wonder about his dad too? Does he even question it, or am I still evil in his eyes?

I take a sip of wine because I know the answer to my question will break me. "I just wonder if I hadn't shown up, how long would I not have known about Olive?"

"Probably until she was eighteen. She has asked about you. I think she would've tried to find you."

"Did you ever wonder about me?" he asks.

A lump develops at the back of my throat and I swallow. No more tears tonight. None at all.

"Every day," I whisper.

Max doesn't respond, just takes a drink.

22

MAX

Something doesn't add up.

Emily's posture tells me something is wrong.

She loved me. It seems like she wanted me around. Emily already confirmed she didn't receive the emails and didn't read the words I poured over. I used to look forward to checking my email and writing her emails, even if I was bone-tired from providing dental services all day to folks who had never had a dental exam their entire life. She may have thought I didn't want her, but I hoped she questioned it. She just didn't shrug her shoulders and think, "Well, I guess I'm raising this baby on my own."

Everyone in my life expects so much out of me. The one person who should expect everything is sitting across from me, expecting nothing. She owns a beautiful home, runs a successful business, and helps with her family's business. She and Olive are doing just fine without me, but I want to be here to support her, however I can.

Being close to her is not making it easy to keep this professional.

It's more than the light freckles across her nose or her legs from those shorts she's wearing that's driving me mad.

When I stand close to her, I smell her perfume, light and clean, and I have to stop my sinful thoughts from seeping in.

If I let myself, I can fall back into the magic of our first week.

She has a boyfriend. I can't.

When we're finished with our meals, I pay the bill to Emily's objections. We stand up and after we walk out of the restaurant, I say, "We should go to the lake. I haven't seen it since I came back."

"Really?"

"Yeah. Since we're kid-free and all." Without thinking, I wrap my arm around her shoulders. She lets me pull her toward me, and I kiss her head, without a thought. Just a friendly side-hug between two old friends. Although if I were Burke, I would be pissed to see someone like me doing this.

It's a short drive from Betty's Café to Tin Lake, the parking lot overflowing with cars and campers. Chatter from lake-goers and sounds of glee float towards us as we close Emily's SUV's doors.

"It hasn't changed a bit. Holy shit, the snack bar."

A rush of memories hits me. Glancing down the beach, I spot the vacation rental we stayed at. It looks more worn than I remember, the blue faded to a dingy gray. It was the first time I remember no tension between my mother and father. Everyone was relaxed, happy. I had finally convinced Dad to let me go on a dental mission, something I'd wanted to do since I heard about them. We had spent the first day, lounging, reading, just talking and being together.

It was the most perfect day, because that was the day I met Emily.

The afternoon of the first day, I slammed the door to the beach house and came down to the beach, just to realize I didn't have money to get a Diet Coke.

A bright voice offered me money, and the rest is history.

"Thanks for the dollar, by the way," I say, nudging her with my elbow.

Emily giggles and crosses her arms. "You looked like you were about to cry when you realized you didn't have any money on you."

"It was just an excuse to get you to talk to me." I had noticed her behind me and psyched myself out. It was only when I got to the front of the line and thought to myself, *I can't be a broke loser in front of this gorgeous girl.*

"Well, I'm glad you didn't have any money," Emily says. "For lots of reasons."

"Me too."

I pat for my wallet and pull it out, just to double-check I had a few dollars. "How about I finally pay you back?"

"You got me that Diet Coke for my birthday."

"It only counts as payback if I get it from the snack bar."

"Okay," she says as we walk to the line behind a kid buying candy.

"Gosh, this brings back memories."

"It does." She looks melancholy as we stand there. I try to grab her stare as she looks at the rocky sand. "What are you thinking about?"

"Oh, nothing. Actually—" She punches a finger in the air. "It feels like no time has passed. Like obviously a lot of time has passed, but it also feels like it's always been like this?"

"It does." I press my lips together, wondering if I should say it. Screw it. "It's always been easy. Being with you."

"I agree."

"I think we have this co-parenting thing down. I mean, I like you."

"You do?" Emily asks.

"I do. You know," I say, "I was so mad at you for not reaching out, but my phone wasn't working, and I had your email wrong. This was my fault."

"No, Max—"

"No, Em, it was." Before I called her Martini, I called her Em. My use of her nickname parts her lips, and it makes me wants to push her against the snack bar's wall and devour her mouth.

"What can I get you?" the teenage employee asks, interrupting our conversation. I order two Diet Cokes, then hand a sweating can to Emily. Anything to break this tension.

"To being kid-free," I say, knocking our cans together.

"To being kid-free," she says, her face growing sadder. She pauses, and I drink my soda, the liquid cool on my hot throat. It's warm out today, with the highs in the nineties. Emily's hair is wild around her face, and I want to push it away and lay one on her.

She's quiet until she blurts out, "I broke up with Burke."

"You did? Why?" I'm trying not to let a smile creep onto my face.

"I just didn't feel...enough for him."

I shove my hands in my shorts. *You can't smile at this.*

"That's too bad."

"It is. Burke is a nice guy. Hopefully, he finds someone who, you know, can make him happy."

I kick a rock with my shoe and take a drink.

Emily elbows me. "Why do you look so smug?"

"I'm not being smug."

"That's a smug face." She swirls her finger around my nose.

"It's just...you've always felt like mine, even if you weren't."

"Oh, really," Emily says, reaching out to tickle my side.

"Not fair, Em."

"Good to see you're still ticklish." I wiggle out of her grasp, her fingers feeling like ants on my skin.

Two kids run between us, and a little bit of soda spills out onto Emily's arm. Dark brown liquid runs down her bicep onto her forearm. I consider offering my tongue to lick it off. She's a free woman; I'm a free man.

But I'll wait for crystal-clear signals that she's interested again.

"I can go get some napkins," I offer.

"It's fine." She licks her hand, and I imagine her licking my cock, making my shorts tight with the thought. I cough into my hand and turn away.

"What?" she asks.

"Nothing" comes out a little too high. Even though she said she didn't want some, I jog to the snack bar to grab a stack of small napkins. It's just the kind of break I need to calm down. I return with a stack and hand them to her.

"Thanks, Max." She wipes her arm down, and I take the crumpled balls of paper back.

"Let's take a walk." We walk between blankets and clusters of chairs as we watch kids and adults play in the lake, splashing water on each other.

"Do you and Olive come out here often?"

"Once in a while." Emily points to a house coming up. "My parents own this house. My brother Reid and his fiancée Whitney live there."

"Reid was the brother I saw you with that one time, right?"

"It was Jackson."

"Oh, that's right. I should've said hi."

"I should've—"

"What?" I ask, although my heart stops in my chest, waiting for her to finish.

"It's just sad, is all. We could've…I don't know. Maybe we had a real shot back then, but at least we would've had a chance. Rather than a silly, honest mistake."

"Give you a chance to be annoyed with my dental hygiene routine?"

"I'm sure I could learn a thing or two from you."

"I can't wait to teach Olive how to properly brush her teeth."

Emily scoffs and lightly slaps me on the arm. I want her to do it again. "Hey, I'll have you know I did a great job. Look how delightful our daughter is."

"So delightful," I agree. "That's all you."

"You had something to do with it. She is half you, after all." Emily crosses her arms and bumps intentionally into me.

I bump her right back. "Are you open to more kids?" I ask.

"With the right person. You?" Emily asks.

We can get pregnant tonight runs through my head, and I shudder because it's an asshole thing to think. However, I don't know how I would've handled Emily pregnant with my baby. She wouldn't have been able to get me off of her.

The wind picks up her curls, sweeping them across her face. Emily is still the most beautiful woman I've ever seen. I shove my hands in my pockets so I don't grab her hand.

"Are you sad you never got a chance to be a big shot in a big city and have martinis at night?"

"No," she says.

"Not even a little bit?"

She shakes her head fervently. "Not at all. You want to know how I came up with Olive? She became my new dream. If I couldn't have a martini with an olive after a long day in the big city, I would have a daughter named Olive. I just didn't expect my brother to start calling her Martini out of nowhere one day. Every time he called her that, I thought of you."

"Aww," I say. We still walk, the invisible elephant in the room walking with us.

"However, I should've really thought her middle name through. For her initials."

"Jean?"

"You remembered my middle name?"

"I remember a lot about you." Unspoken truths hang over our heads, so I change the subject back. "Olive Jean, OJ? Yeah, that's unfortunate. But I like it though. We'll just pretend she's named after a juice."

Our arms brush against each other's, and we flinch. We both create more space, but within a few steps, we accidentally brush our hands together again.

"Sorry," she croaks.

"No, it was my fault." I shove my hands in my pockets again. Out of the corner of my eye, I see Emily looking at me with parted lips, and I look forward, so I don't do something I regret.

Light music drifts up from a cluster of people, and I recognize the song immediately.

I've always considered it our song.

Ten years ago, we went to the Swift, the local dive bar, even though Emily was underage. Carl, the owner, knew her father, and he told me he wanted to keep me where he could see me and that's why she could stay. She drank sodas while I drank beer, and she slid a quarter into the jukebox the second she saw her song.

"'Wonderwall'," she told me, the fluorescent light reflecting on her eyes.

"Ugh, that song is terrible," I said.

"Shh, dance with me."

And there we danced when no one else was, a group of bikers watching. Two bargoers pulled me aside when Emily went to the bathroom.

One of them said, "I don't look like much, but I know tae kwon do, and if you hurt her, I will roundhouse kick you."

"I promise I won't." I meant it, and then I broke that promise.

Now, the song appears again, and I don't think it's a coincidence.

"It's our song!" Emily screech-whispers, holding my arm in her hands. "Do you still hate it?"

"Oh, absolutely," I lie. I don't tell her that I bought the song and listened to it every morning I was in Costa Rica. How much hearing this song brings back the visceral pain of how much I missed her.

"Let's dance," she says. She's still holding my arm. My eyes roll as she pulls me to a wooded area off of the beach, partially hidden by the bathrooms. It masks my utter excitement that I might get to touch her. I offer my arms like a prince in a fairy tale, and she curtsies, before stepping into my arms.

I wrap my arm around her waist, my senses firing at rapid speed. Her breath is hot on my cheek as I pull her closer, taking her hand out in a waltz pose. I can smell her perfume, musky with a hint of floral. Holding my breath, we start to move. If I give in and inhale her scent, I'll be in big trouble.

Now that I have every way to get ahold of her, I don't think Emily can keep Olive from me. But what if we make a real, honest go of it, and she decimates my heart again? Decides one day she doesn't want me and puts me back at square one? Destined to be a stranger for the rest of her life?

I can't have that. She feels so good under my hands.

"What are you thinking about?"

I shake my head, burying my thoughts deep inside the recesses of my brain. "Nothing. Just memories, I guess."

"That's all this week has been for me." We continue to

move in a circle, her head on my chest. "It's weird how normal it is."

"Right, I was thinking the same thing."

"Like the last few years didn't happen."

"Absolutely." She nuzzles into me further, resting her head into my chest. "This is so nice."

"It is." If she looks at me, I will kiss her. Burke is no longer a factor, but I can't think I was the reason. Sometimes things run its course. If she did it because of me, that makes everything more complicated.

The song ends, and we step apart, looking around. We had a couple audience members, including a middle-aged woman with dark sunglasses smiling goofily at us.

"We're cheesy motherfuckers," Emily says.

"We bring the gouda, cheddar, and Swiss," I say. "Man, I'm already making dad jokes."

Emily snort-laughs, dropping her head onto my shoulder. Without thinking, I take her under my arm. "I happen to love dad jokes."

"Oh, good. I've been waiting my whole life to make them."

I wish I could say the moment floated away from us and we were just two people, figuring out to co-parent. However, in that instant, it didn't matter what happened or who didn't reach out to whom.

All the feelings were rushing back faster than I knew how to process them.

I 'm having too much fun.

Max is too handsome.

I'm too in my own head.

Back when I met Max, I was nineteen and stupid. I thought everything would work out perfectly and I had the found the person I would spend the rest of my life with, just for him to disappear with a few words from his stepdad and a check.

Now, he's back, I'm in his arms dancing to a song I've listened to with bittersweet memories, and it's not just okay.

It's euphoric.

It's more than my feelings I have to keep in check. It's also my daughter's. Her long-lost father is back with the best of intentions, and while I know his stepdad set him up, ninety-nine percent sure of it, there's still a small part of me that's jaded and devastated from being abandoned ten years ago.

"Just breathe," I whisper under my breath, and Max hears.

"What?" he asks.

"Nothing." I cross my arms so I'm not tempted to reach

for his hand. We're standing in front of the beach house his family rented, the place I lost my virginity, where we made Olive. Typically when I come to the lake with her, I avoid this place.

Max smiles like he does when he talks about Costa Rica. "The house looks a little rough, but mostly still the same."

"Yeah, the new owners haven't kept it up as much. It's a shame."

"Things change with time, I guess." When I turn my head, I see him looking at me, his eyelids heavy, his mouth relaxed. I walk past him. He cannot kiss me, not here.

We continue walking again. Max gazes over the lake, the water dotted with boats and the jet skis getting one last run in before the sun sets. It's golden hour, my favorite time at Tin Lake. It's when the lake looks like it's wrapped in glitter and gold.

"This is so pretty. Almost beats being a city girl, with martinis and a nice apartment overlooking a park amongst skyscrapers."

I shrug one shoulder. "It's absolutely fine. You want to hear a secret?"

Max leans in and it feels like flirting. "What?"

"I don't like martinis."

"Shut up." Max laughs behind his fingers, and I have to look away because he looks too good and the area between my thighs aches.

"Yep. I tried one on my twenty-second birthday, and they're just…so gross."

"Vermouth is a love-it-or-leave-it type of thing."

"Seriously." We walk a few more steps before I continue my confession. "You know, I actually went to Chicago with a friend when Olive was six. I fell in love with this Airbnb online because it looked exactly like what I imagined in my fantasies when I was a kid. We got there, and it was…fine.

Don't get me wrong, it was cool, but the buildings were too tall, too claustrophobic. Everyone was in a hurry, and I was just this small-town girl, in everyone's way. After that trip, I came home, snuggled with Olive on my porch where I could see my land and the whole sky, and I just knew my life went exactly the way it was supposed to."

"I'm glad. I've felt a little guilty about this."

"You didn't know. I'm perfectly happy."

Max presses his lips together, looking ahead at the folks packing up their beach bags and chairs to head back to their rentals or into town to Betty's Café or even our brewery. Tilting my head towards him, I ask, "Are you happy?"

"I don't know," he says. Wind picks up, kicking up dust into our eyes and mouths, causing us to gag. I think the topic is done before Max says, "Sometimes I feel like I don't have any control over my life. Like, do I live in San Diego because I love it, or is it because I grew up there? Am I a dentist because of my stepdad, or would I have chosen it? Even Noelle. We finally broke up, but I tried to break up with her once and she refused."

I laugh, thinking how easy it was to break up with Burke. It's like he knew I wasn't one-hundred-percent committed. It's tough to date someone who had their heart broken in a devastating way. We're tougher to get through.

"Why did you try to break up with her?"

"She started pulling me toward jewelry stores every time we went to the mall, telling what kind of diamonds she liked and the type of settings. I wasn't ready to get married, and I never knew if I could ever be ready to get down on one knee for her one day."

"Oh."

"Yeah, so I tried to break up with her after dinner one night. She kept coming over and eased up on the marriage conversation. Then, a year passed, and the marriage talk started up again, even worse than the first round. She finally gave me an ultimatum, and we took a break so I could figure out that she was the one." Max doesn't look at me, and thank God, because my face must be beet-red.

"I was so single before I met Burke. I had zero interest in dating. I had my house, I had my daughter, I had my business, my family's business. I was good. Burke came to town and would keep showing up at the brewery, asking my brothers about me. Cam was the one who convinced me to give him a chance. He said he didn't find Burke 'that terrible' and said I should go for it."

"'Not that terrible,'" Max says with a laugh, and I chuckle too. That's not how you start a love story. Max tilts his head to one side and purses his lips. "At least Burke got his approval. Cam looked at me like he wanted to murder me. I doubt I'll ever get the go-ahead from your brother, so you're safe."

"Thank God," I say sarcastically. Max glares at me for a split second then smiles. I nudge him and say, "It never felt right with Burke."

"Hence, why you dumped him."

"Exactly." I bite my lip. Does Max feel something? I feel like he's flirting. Is he flirting? I'm so out of practice. "So, what are we going to do?"

"I think that's a tomorrow problem," Max says.

"You're leaving tomorrow."

My heart sinks. I may never see him again, no matter what he tells me. Max senses my thoughts and touches my arms.

"Don't worry, I'll be back. Hey, hey, come here." He pulls me to his chest, and I melt into him, pressing my hands into his strong upper back. Max gives the best hugs.

"I'll book your ticket."

"I can book my own ticket, but I plan to buy one immediately once I have an idea of my schedule. I will have serious Olive withdrawals."

"That is totally a thing. I get those." I pull myself away from his grasp, and Max's arms are still outstretched, like my body is still against his.

"She's the best. I hope she wants to talk to me every night because we'll have FaceTime dates."

"She'll love that. Just wait until she's back in school. Her stories about the most mundane things are classic. She's a gossip, and once you get her going, there's hand gestures and everything."

"I can't wait," Max says. "I'm really sad I haven't seen the raccoons."

"Ever since I got rid of the free cat food, they don't come around very often. I see them from time to time. It's like a nice surprise."

"That's one of Goldheart's attractions, right? The raccoons?"

"If you're lucky. Or unfortunate, if you get on their bad side. If you have food, though."

"Maybe I'll see them before I leave. Or when I come back to visit."

We're quiet as we reach the snack bar near my car. Max takes one last sweeping look over the lake and then looks back to me. We must look like a cinematic shot, my hair blowing all over the place and the wind billowing Max's shirt.

I don't want this night to end. If I invite him into the main house, it doesn't mean anything, right? We can be two people catching up. Not talking about what really needs to be talked about. The truth about his stepdad sits in the pit of my stomach like a boulder.

"Hey, I have an idea," I say. "I have some Woody Finch root beer stashed, and I have photo albums. How about you come into the main house, and I can show you Olive's baby photos? That is, if you want to."

Max looks away in thought. Are guys into baby photos? I mean, Olive *is* his kid.

"Sure. That sounds like fun. And I like actual beer."

"Great," I say. I can't help the huge grin on my face.

When we get back to my property, I drop Max off at the tiny house so he can charge his phone. I walk into my own house and my breath shallows, like I'm on the brink of a panic attack.

Today was strange. It was strange how normal it felt.

When I was around Max, my ping-ponging thoughts slowed and I could be present, without thinking five steps ahead. We could just talk without thinking about my work or Olive's general well-being. My thoughts didn't quiet with Burke. They got worse.

Now, I'll be alone with Max, sitting close to each other, drinking some beer. We did that the other night, but Olive was our little chaperone.

Olive being at Grandma's house changes things.

"Get it together, woman," I tell myself as I pace my living room, shaking out my hands. I peek behind the curtains in the kitchen to see Max walking across the field, looking like a stupidly handsome model again. He looks to the side, like only hot men crossing the street do, and I dart away from the window the second I'm caught.

He knocks on the door, and I jump in place a couple times, trying to loosen my limbs and alleviate the ache between my legs to no avail. I am so screwed. Why did I invite him in again? This will complicate everything.

But I really, really want to.

When I open the door, he smiles instantly. "Hello again."

"Hi. Come on in." I open the door wider and I shiver as he walks past me, although it's hot as hell outside. Beers. I can get beers.

"What kind of beer do you like?"

Max juts out his bottom lip. "Which one do you recommend?"

"I like Gold Dust. It's an IPA."

"Sure, that sounds good." Max wanders as I pull two cans of Gold Dust out and two pint glasses with our brewery logo on it. I pour both the way I was taught.

"Wow, great pour," Max says when I hand it to him.

"I'm a professional." We touch glasses and drink. He takes a sip, and I want to lick the suds off his lips.

I've made it awkward. Max has no idea so it's one-sided. I wonder what will happen if I straddle him. Why do I feel like a floozy seducing my daughter's father?

"That's good. Really good." He holds it up to study the clarity and the bubbles rising to the top.

"It's my favorite."

"It might be my new favorite too." Max stares at me for a second too long, his expression curious. Does he want to leave? Make out? Learn the truth about his stepdad?

"Let me get the photo albums." After I place the beer down on the kitchen table, I run to our side table, where the photo albums are stashed. I did not put them together; Olive's first few years were and still are a blur. My mom took photos and gifted me a photo album every Christmas, with Olive's big milestones and the more mundane, adorable, everyday moments.

When I turn around, Max is seated at the table, so I hand him the oldest one and he smiles when he opens the front page.

The first page is me holding Olive in the hospital. She's in a pink blanket, and my face is puffy from pregnancy hormones and crying. My throat thickens as I look at it. How scared I was. How deliriously in love I was. My whole pregnancy I questioned whether I was doing the right thing, but when the nurses handed her to me, I sobbed with happiness.

Max stares at it, his head down. His fingers trace the photo. Olive was so tiny, so perfect.

"Man," he says, wiping his nose. Is he getting emotional? "Can I get a copy of this?" Red rims his eyes, his eyes glassy from emotion. It hits me straight in the heart that he wants this memory although he wasn't present to see it.

"Sure, of course. I think I have an extra one around somewhere."

"Great." He turns the thick page to our first days at home. My parents holding her, each of my brothers taking turns. Me looking so young, with fuller cheeks and freckles, my hair bone-straight because I hated my curls then. If I could go back and tell past me everything would be okay and hug her, I would.

He looks through more memories. Naked, smiley Olive covered in cake and frosting at her first birthday. Olive dressed as a koala when she didn't have a say in what she wanted for her first Halloween. My family is in every other photo, whether it's my mom or dad or my brothers. It makes my eyes leak thinking how full of love and family my daughter's life was, even if her dad wasn't around for most of it.

"I missed so much," he says. "I wish I was there."

"You're here now. That's all that matters." I pause before I say what I've been wondering this whole time. "Did anything prompt you to come to Goldheart? Did anyone say anything?"

Max looks up. "My best friend when I lived in San Francisco mentioned Goldheart. His wife is from here."

My forehead tenses. "Who's his wife?"

"Raegan Mansfield."

My eyes widen. "Raegan Stewart?"

"I think that was her name?" Max asks.

"Raegan is Annie's little sister. Annie is my sister-in-law. Holy shit."

"They're moving to France."

"I know, Annie is so proud of her. Raegan has always wanted to live there."

"Wow," he says. "Small world."

"Yeah, small world." I take another drink. Raegan has only been with Henry for a little over a year, but it's another reminder of how close we were without knowing it. How we were kept apart by circumstance, but a small conversation with a mutual acquaintance steered him back to me.

"It's always been nagging at me, though. My intuition just wouldn't let go."

"Really?" I ask. I can't help but smile.

"Really." His gaze makes my chest expand, because it says so much. The truth, that no one else felt right for us. No matter how logical we are, something illogical happened to us ten years ago.

I hold his stare, shifting on my feet. Do I tell him? Do I let him know?

"This is great, thank you," he says, raising the beer and nodding to the photo album.

The magic is gone.

"I thought you might enjoy it. Olive was a really cute baby."

"She looked like me as a baby. I should have my mom find my baby photos, and we can do a side-by-side comparison."

"They say when the baby is first born, they look like the dad so the dad will claim them as his own. That he can't deny paternity."

"She is definitely my kid. I was that blond when I was little."

He points to a picture of Olive at three, bright blond hair in two baby ponytails held together with bows, holding a sparkler on the Fourth of July. As he continues to flip, I lean closer so I can look at them. I try not to look at them because I'll just cry at how little she is and how I blinked and she grew up, but it's so nice to do this with her father.

"Oh." He points to a picture. Olive is about two, in my arms. While her little arms are outreached in joy, my lips are turned down, and my body jerks, like it remembers.

"Were you sad there?"

I nod. "Cam found me sobbing on the floor one night, after Olive refused to go down. He moved in and kinda never left. He built the tiny house himself. I bought it off of him when he moved into town with his wife. Thought about turning it into an Airbnb."

"I'm sorry that happened. That you felt like that." His gaze is serious, and I look away and he does too. "I'm glad you had such a great family who was there for you."

"Me too."

I must've been hovering too much because Max points to the album.

"Do you want to look too?" He moves his chair so he can be facing half of the album and I can squeeze beside him. I pull up my chair so we're so close and my hand comes down, grazing his thigh. He freezes, his jaw flexing. When he looks at me, I hold my breath.

"Sorry," I say.

"Don't be." He pats my own leg, sending firebolts up my thigh. I cross my legs to alleviate the pulsing between them. Being this close to Max is not helping.

"Remember when we got caught making out in the library?"

I laugh, covering my mouth. "I think you had a hand up my shirt."

"I probably did." He laughs. "You remember that night at La Scarola? The last night we were together?"

"How could I forget? That was the night you got me pregnant."

"The very one." He holds my gaze again.

"You know, that was the last time I had sex."

God, Emily, why did you say that?

Max's ears immediately turn red. "Really?"

"This is why I shouldn't have alcohol around you."

"What about Burke?"

I nod. "I never wanted to."

"Oh," he says. He studies a picture of Olive and me, with my parents on Easter.

"It doesn't mean anything," I say. "I've just been busy. I'm a mom. I don't have time for dick."

I turn my head and mouth *Oh my God* because I can't believe I just said that.

Max nods. "Good to know."

Maybe I have time for your dick.

No, Emily. Knock it off.

We reach the end of the photo album, and when he closes it, I knocks it with my knuckles. "There's more from where that came from. My mom went through a scrapbooking phase."

"She did a great job."

"Do you want to discuss what we're going to do now?" If we discuss co-parenting, I'm not going to think about kissing him. I'm not going to think about taking his clothes off.

"I just want to talk, if that's okay. We can figure out the co-parenting stuff later."

"Okay." He walks to my couch and I follow, plopping down next to him. It feels like he's inching closer.

24

MAX

I'm not sure if it's the alcohol or Emily's proximity, but my head spins. Her accidental graze of my thigh made my dick go on alert, sent me into a deep spiral of shame.

How could I want her as badly as I do if I made her miserable?

Those photos will haunt me forever.

It was fun to see my daughter grow up, how she looked just like me as a baby, the blond hair a tell-tell sign that she's mine. Never mind the mannerisms I've noticed she didn't learn anywhere else. However, studying Emily's slumped shoulders, the dark circles under her eyes, the hairs sticking out on end in the pictures—it didn't look easy doing it by herself.

We were supposed to talk about the future, what will happen, and we haven't, really. Over the last couple days, I've been secretly researching Goldheart dental practices and seeing if there's a demand, driving around to get a feel of the town. Goldheart is completely different to La Jolla in vibe and atmosphere. I'm giving up the beach for a lake, something I wouldn't mind doing.

Goldheart also has this pretty woman in front of me, who gave me the most perfect child. A child I want to see every day.

Emily's tan leg is bent, resting on the cushion, and I want to reach out to touch her skin. Her lips press to the corner of her pint glass, and I wish I could taste her. The closer we get, the more I want to say "Fuck it" and bring her lips to mine.

However, I'm the bad guy here, and it feels like I'm taking advantage that I was the only guy she has ever slept with. I should've tried harder. I shouldn't have waited until Thanksgiving. The second I stepped off that plane and her phone wasn't working, I should've driven to Goldheart and taken her in my arms.

It's too late. Too much pain has happened.

"How's the beer?" Emily asks.

"Great, actually. Your dad is really talented."

"It's more Reid nowadays. My dad is a big-picture kind of guy."

"What do you do for them?"

"Social media. I run the Instagram and Facebook, and I started a TikTok that I make my brothers be in. We got a viral video the other day."

"Nice," I say, taking another sip. Brains and beauty.

Emily might be the best thing to ever happen to me, and I blew it.

"It's funny how many things can change in a year. They're all coupled up now. Cameron is having a baby, and he married his wife a couple months ago. Reid just proposed to Whitney. It's coming for Jackson and his girlfriend, Shiloh. That just leaves me."

"Leaves you?"

"I'm the single one. The celibate one."

We could change that.

No, shut up, Max.

"Maybe you'll find another guy. Just because Burke wasn't it..." That hurt coming out of my mouth. Because I'm starting to want it to be me. "You're too good of a woman, Emily."

"Why, thank you. You're not too bad, yourself." Emily pauses and looks down at her glass, tracing the edge. "Max, what are we going to do?"

I rest my elbow on the back of the couch and my head on my hand. "I don't know."

"You don't live here."

"I'm fully aware of that."

"You're taking over Fred's practice."

I flinch. Emily never met my stepdad, so why is she using his first name? "First-name basis with him?"

"I've heard you say it, I think." She takes a nervous drink of her beer. "Have you heard from your mom since you told her?"

"No. I told her I would see them on Saturday. We'll discuss more then, I'm sure." I really stare at her. "Why do you keep asking?"

She pauses and shakes her head. "Nothing. I'm just curious how they're taking it, that's all."

"Let's just...hang out. Who knows the next time we'll be alone."

"Okay." She settles into the cushions, and she's inching closer to me. All I have to do is reach out and I can brush her shoulder. "Best thing to happen in the last ten years?"

"My dental missions. To Costa Rica."

"You went on more?"

I nod. "I wish I could go for longer. I love my hometown, but Costa Rica is my happy place. The people are so kind and giving. They need good dental care, but in those rural areas, they don't have a lot of access. Whenever I get on the plane to come home, I'm itching to go back. I couldn't go the last couple years."

"Why not?"

I shrug one shoulder. "We've been really busy, getting ready for the handover. It was important that Noelle and I went away together, so with that, I couldn't go last year."

"So, this is kinda your first vacation in a while. If you can call it that."

"It is absolutely a vacation. I get to hang out with you and this really cool kid. Never thought I'd stay at a tiny house. Got to see more of this town that holds so many memories."

"Aww," Emily coos, taking a drink of beer. "I am pretty awesome."

"Look at you. You have this awesome house, an awesome kid, the most awesome baby daddy."

"I'm the complete package."

"Totally," I say. "It's just—"

"What?" Emily asks, her eyes wide.

"It wasn't over. Not for me. I hope you know that." Balancing my glass on the back of the couch, I look everywhere but at her.

"It wasn't for me either." Emily mirrors my body language, balancing the pint glass near mine.

"I'm not going anywhere. I promise." My throat tightens.

"We'll see." She stares at a spot of the couch for moments. All I can do is prove to her that I will be here. I will come back. "If you did come here, I know you could set up a dental practice easily. One that allows you to do your charity work. You could see us all the time and go to Olive's sports and dance."

"That would be nice. It's just my dad's practice…"

"Yeah," she says, quickly. I know staring at the couch spot feels safer, so I look away as well. "Is that something you want?"

That makes me pause. "Huh. No one has really ever asked me that."

"Really?"

"Really," I say. "It was always assumed I would take over. I mean, my dad has done so much for me that I want to continue his legacy. He helped my mom when she was a broke single mother, and that's the least I can do."

"You don't *have* to take it. You don't owe him anything," she says. "Dreams change."

That line hits me in the gut. Emily's whole world changed because of me. Her new dream is to make a good life for our daughter, for her to be happy. I admire the hell out of that.

Emily touches my knee. "Just think about what you want. Is your stepdad worthy of a legacy?"

I freeze and grind my jaw. "He is. He's the best man I know."

"Okay," she says. "I'm just making sure."

"I appreciate your concern, but yes. My dad deserves the world."

She smiles sadly and looks at her beer.

"Hey," I say, tilting her chin up. "You're not alone in this anymore. Even if I live five hundred miles away."

"I know that," she says. Her eyelashes flutter as she looks at me, her lips pressed together in a line. God, she's so beautiful. My focus goes to those plump pink lips, and she rubs them together, with a flicker of her tongue to moisten them.

"Hey, Emily," I say, my fingers still bent under her chin.

She looks at me, deep inside my soul.

"What do you want, Emily?"

"A time machine," she says.

My hand travels to her jaw, my fingers threading through her hair.

"This is not a good idea," I say.

"The worst."

"You just got out of a relationship. I just got out of one."

"And we have to think about Olive…"

"Yeah, we do." My thumb rubs her cheek and her eyelashes flutter close and her lips part.

"This is not a good idea."

"You already said that." A tiny moan leaves her mouth as my fingers curl around the back of her neck.

Leaning in, our lips touch, and my fingers curl around the back of her neck, pulling her in. It feels like coming home. I taste the citrus from the beer on her lips. She tastes better than I remember. I scoot across the cushions to be closer.

Our kiss is not how I remembered.

It's better.

The tension of the last week breaks as I pull her to me, our heads tilting from side to side as I taste her, over and over again. My tongue tests the seam of her lips, and then I break through, tasting her deeper. Her hand fists my shirt as she kisses me, ten years of longing manifesting into this kiss.

My dick rumbles to attention, bucking against my shorts. Every nerve ending remembers her and how she made me feel. How she makes me feel now.

She pulls away first, breathless and strained. She stands up, walking to the kitchen. Then the pacing starts.

"Are you okay? Was that okay?" I ask, crossing my legs so she can't see the bulge in my shorts.

"No, it's fine. It's just a lot to process."

"Okay—"

"Is it too fast? We just saw each other again a few days ago… It just feels too fast," she says, pushing her hair off her forehead.

"Maybe. Maybe not."

"Why are you so sure?"

Emily is spiraling, so I stand up. Pointing to the door, I say, "I'm going back to the tiny house."

"Why?"

I rest my hands on the soft skin of her arms, looking her in the eye. "If I don't leave right now, I'll lay you out on the couch, spread your legs wide, and make you come again and again until your hands are in my hair and you say my name over and over."

Her chest heaves high and lowers as she folds her arms. I notice she's squeezing her legs together.

"What else? Would you do, I mean?" Her gaze is full of fire, and I smirk. I would love to give her more to think about, but it'll probably end with me taking a shower I don't need so I could beat off to thoughts of her.

"I probably shouldn't. Have a good night, Em."

Emily stands frozen as I rinse my glass and stick it in the dishwasher. I reach the back door and look back.

"If you asked me to, I'd drop everything. My dad can figure it out. He may be my family, but you are now too. My feelings never went away, Em. It's always been you. I see that now."

Her mouth creaks open, but no sound comes out. I knock the door frame as I walk through it and close the door.

25

EMILY

It's one o'clock, and my house is too quiet as I punch my pillow again. I crawled into bed shortly after Max left, and I've been wide awake ever since.

I've traced my mouth where he kissed me, trying to remember every head dip, every tongue swipe.

That kiss was a bolt of lightning. I knew it would be good if we ever got physical again, but I was unprepared for the jolt to my system. How my body remembered how it felt to be kissed by Max.

The lie by omission eats away at me. Should I tell him? Should I force Fred to tell him? I don't know.

All I can wish for is that Fred owns up to what he did. But Max will know I lied when that *does* happen. I've made him believe I'm the villain to save his image of the man who raised him. Maybe I am the villain now.

When I stand from my bed and walk to my window, I see the light on at the tiny house. It glows against the inky sky, so bright it looks like a painting. I wonder what Max is thinking. His words before he left shook me. Why can't I let myself go?

The secret eats away at me, but even with Max believing I

kept Olive from him, our connection transcends the cosmos pulling us together, like we're inevitable.

The devil on my shoulder wants to go to him and see what happens.

The angel is more logical, suggesting at least four more conversations about the status of our relationship. Figure out the unsexy stuff first, and *then* jump on him like a spider monkey.

However, that kiss. That *kiss*.

It was impulsive. It was dangerous. It was…hot.

Part of me wants to be reckless right now.

I pace again, double-checking the light is still on at the tiny house.

Fuck it.

Without thinking, I slip my feet into slippers and wrap a robe around the tank top and boy shorts I sleep in. I rifle through my nightstand for the item I need and slip out of my house. The air is balmy but warm against my skin as my feet crunch the grass. It feels like years before I reach Max's door. It feels like I'm walking to my funeral.

I raise my fist but stop myself before I can knock.

Don't knock. This is a bad idea. You will regret it.

Breathing in and out, I swallow down. I shouldn't be here.

Then I feel the ghost of his lips on me again, how I hadn't felt that alive, how it took me back to nineteen when I never felt heartache, only intense, overpowering love for him.

I want to feel that again.

Before the world crowds in on us, I want to feel him again. In my bones, I know Fred Sawyer will tear Max away from me for the second time.

Going to Max will be the most selfish thing I've done in years. It's for me. No matter what I did, what money I took, I want to be wild. It feels so wrong, it's right.

I knock on the door, the piece of wood rattling in the

frame. I hear footsteps, and I swallow down my fear. I throw my shoulders back to fake confidence, although I'm more scared than I have ever been.

When he opens the door, he's in a black shirt that hugs his lean frame and basketball shorts hanging low on his hips. He lets me in without a word. I drop the foil packet on the bar. Max stares at it and then looks down at me.

"Em." His voice slides over me like silk.

I say nothing as I bunch the material of his shirt and coax his arms over his head. He moves closer to me as the shirt falls from his wrist. Max just stares as I take off my robe, exposing my see-through tank top, my nipples erect and visible. Lust dances in his eyes. He wants to touch me, but he just watches.

Every part of me screams to run, but I ignore it. There's dampness between my legs, and my core begs for release. Last time, sex was painful but beautiful. This time will be for us, burning and messy and crazy.

I pull down on his shorts, revealing black boxer briefs and an impressive bulge, solid because of me. Cupping him, I hear a groan near my ear. My panties dampen more, as I feel him in my hand, so full and hard.

He remains quiet as he kisses my neck to my ear, his mouth flicking against my earring, and my legs quiver. My vision is hazy.

Without warning, he picks me up by the bottom and slams me against the door, and I lower my head to fuse my lips to his. It turns from sweet to ravenous quickly. His tongue sweeps inside my mouth, and I press his face between my hands, kissing him deeper. I can feel his cock against my center, and my mouth opens in pleasure. I pull my tank top over my head, and now we're down to our underwear. All terror gets cast aside.

One hand clutches my ass while his other hand palms my

breast, pressing himself into me. His cock hits my clit at the perfect angle.

I screech as he keeps rubbing against me. My sounds get louder. His lips tickle my ear.

"Let go, Em. It'll be the first of many tonight. We need to make up for lost time."

His growly words make me build higher. His hardness against the most sensitive part of me is relentless. I'm so close, teetering on the edge.

He carries me to the small couch, laying me out. He rips my underwear from my body and pushes my legs apart, like he promised. He doesn't say anything, but dives in, licking, covering my clit with delicate suction until I see stars.

My hands ruffle his hair as he drags his tongue up my seam, landing on the spot that matters. He takes his time, like I'm delicious. He sinks one finger into me, and I'm done. My back arches and everything goes bright as I cry out. He moves with the jerks of my body. I grip his hair until my legs relax, floppy on the cushions.

After a few quiet moments, he pulls me to standing by my arm, kissing me, letting me taste myself.

I cup him again, and he's only gotten harder.

"Are you on something?" he asks, between gasps of air.

"I have an IUD," I say. "I brought a condom as backup."

"How many do you have?"

"A whole, brand-new box at the house. I just brought one, though. I didn't want to be presumptuous."

"I want your presumptuousness all over me." We both laugh as I tilt my chin to meet his halfway. The kisses are sweet, tickling my skin so I scrunch my nose.

"You have no business being this fucking cute and sexy all at once," he says.

"It's a talent," I say. Reaching into his boxer briefs, I work him down and up. Max drops his underwear at a pool around his ankles. We kiss again, building to our previous fervor, devouring each other's gasps of air.

He finds the condom and rips the packet. His hands shake as he rolls it on, spending a little extra time to make sure it was secure.

"Knowing us, we have to be extra careful."

I giggle behind my hand. He takes me in his arms again.

We fall together onto the couch, him on top of me, kissing every part of me—my neck, my breasts, my stomach. Under the overhead light, he can see everything, and he stops at my tiger stripes on my stomach.

"These are from when you were pregnant from Olive?" he asks. His hands are like feathers along my skin, creating a trail of goosebumps.

"Yes," I say.

"They're beautiful," he says, tracing one finger over a gray rivulet down my abdomen as he kisses me. Max takes a moment to stare at me before he kisses me with more passion, more attention.

Lining myself up on his cock, I take a deep breath. If this is painful, I am ready to feel everything to be connected to him.

Max eases into me, and I feel so full. We exhale at the same time. "Are you okay?"

"It feels… good."

"Perfect," he says, withdrawing and thrusting into me again. It's slow and steady at first, and he kisses me, his breath mingling with mine. His pace intensifies, but I can tell he's being gentle and holding back. I dig my fingernails into his ass, locking him into me.

"Faster," I squeak out. That unleashes something primal in him as he quickens his pace and slips his hand between us, his thumb on my clit. It feels different than the last time. I cry out as he thrusts into me, hard and fast.

"Flip over," he demands.

"Okay," I say, unsure what to expect. He slips out of me as I reposition on my knees. He drags his hand down my back, grabbing my bare ass as he leans in, licking me where his cock just was. My clit is sensitive again, and the flick of his tongue from this angle is dizzying.

"Oh fuck" comes out of my mouth as his tongue destroys me. Gripping the afghan on the comforter, I don't know what to think, what to process. He lifts his head from under me and lines up his cock, rocking into me, and I cry out. He hits a spot I've never been aware of, and he pulls out and back in, teasing it.

He reaches around and finds my clit again and everything around me spins.

"Come again for me, pretty girl," he says, rubbing in a way that makes me delirious, creating moaning from the back of my throat. From then on, he's not gentle. He pounds into me as I hold onto the couch. Our flesh smacks together as I cry out, another orgasm deep inside of me, so guttural, it pulsates my limbs and my core.

Max's groans grow in urgency as he takes my neck and pulls me up, turning my head so he can kiss me before he gently lowers me down to my forearms and he lets out a groan so deep, it means he's coming.

"Oh fuck," he says, letting it all go, and his body is on my back, kissing my sweaty neck. His arm wraps around my waist, like he's giving me a hug.

"Hi," I say.

"Hi." He kisses between my shoulder blades. We stay like that for precious moments as he softens inside of me. After he anchors the condom, he pulls out and I feel instantly empty. We become a sweaty, naked heap on top of each other. He smooths my damp hair from my forehead and kisses me.

"The condom *did not* slip this time."

"High five," I say, holding up a limp hand. He obliges me with ragged breath.

"So, you have a whole box, huh?"

"I do," I say.

"And it's not here."

"Correct," I say. Inside, I'm face-palming. I should've just slammed the whole box down instead of one packet. Didn't really think that one through.

"I can go get it. Just give me a moment," Max says.

"No, I'll get it. My property is pretty private, but all we need is someone seeing a naked man run through my field."

"Hey, I would put clothes on."

"I may never let you put clothes on."

"We do have a kid, Em."

"That is true," I say. "Thanks for poking holes in my plan."

"You're welcome."

Our skin sticks together as I peel myself away to look at him. His blue eyes study me as his fingertips run up and down my arm. His fingers drift to my nipple, padding it.

"I think we need some snacks."

"I like that idea. Something tells me we're about to pull an all-nighter." He kisses me, deep and sensual. "Is your mom okay with watching Olive?"

"Olive loves going over to my parents. Especially now that they have a dog."

"Good, because I will not get enough of you moaning like that, and I don't think we want Olive hearing that."

"Noooo." I shake my head with a laugh.

"We'll have time. I want you to see Costa Rica. We could rent a place on the beach and just lay in the sun and make love all day long."

"That sounds nice." Snuggling closer to him, I kiss the crook of his neck.

There he goes, making future promises again. No matter what happened in the past, I want to believe him. Will he want to, though, if his dad confesses? I was selfish coming here today, without that out in the open. Because I wanted to feel something, I wanted us to have a moment together, before the world crashed in, where we could be just Emily and Max.

"If you're going to keep lying naked like that on top of me, I might say fuck it and put another baby in you."

"Not if Connie has anything to say about it."

"Connie?"

"My IUD. I named it. Since I got the copper one, Connie sounded cute. My gynecologist thought I was crazy."

"I love it." He kisses my forehead like he wants to eat me.

"Do I have to get up?"

"Offer is still on the table. You can get the town's tongues wagging by having a naked blond man streak across your field."

"It would be a nice change from all those women Cam told to leave. No, I'll do it."

"We could always go to the main house too. I can escort you like a bodyguard."

"No, I kinda like this being a sex shack."

I wriggle away from him, laughing as I walk across the tiny house floor to my discarded robe. There that hunk of a man lies, looking at me with hooded eyes and a half-mast erection.

"Hurry back," Max says. "I hope you weren't planning on getting a good night's sleep."

My arms are full of snacks, and the pockets of my robe are filled with strips of condoms. I was ambitious grabbing ten, but you know, dream big. After I lock my door and turn around in my porch light, two furry creatures appear in front of me.

"Oh shit," I breathe out. It's Thelma and Louise.

I had put out food for them for ages and finally stopped after Darryl the raccoon attacked Shiloh at the brewery. Now, they're back, stalking toward me, completely unafraid because that's the precedent I've set. They know I have snacks.

"Hey ladies," I say, although I've never been certain of their gender. "Long time no see."

They are eye-fucking the shit out of my chips.

"I mean no harm," I say, looking at the pile in my hand. They're all snacks I love. Puff Cheetos, Dot's pretzels, an unopened bag of Sour Punch strawberry straws I was keeping for a special occasion. I love all of them, so I really don't want to sacrifice any of it.

However, I would really, *really* like to get laid again and not end up at the urgent care to get a series of rabies shots, like Shiloh had to.

Which snack do I sacrifice?

No matter how much it pains me, these girls always loved Cheetos. It's why they tipped my trash can.

"I come in peace." I set down the bag and inch away, sweeping an arm out like I'm presenting a new car on *The Price is Right*.

"Here you go," I say. I really should've smuggled Max into the house so I wouldn't be stuck in this mess.

My heart hammers a thousand beats per minute as the bigger raccoon scurries to the Cheetos and snatches it, turning back and bolting into the darkness of the night. I let out a robust exhale as I look around.

Max's face peers out of the side window, his face a big grin. I drop down into a curtsy, my robe billowing with my triumphant gesture. I look down to see my boob, completely out of my robe. He crooks his finger towards me, and a huge smile crosses my lips as I pull out a strip of condoms, warning him that I will do my damnedest to use them all.

He saw the raccoons. He's getting laid repeatedly. I gave him a child.

I'm making all his dreams come true.

Thursday

I've been awake for fifteen minutes, but I can't bear to wake her. Emily lays on my bare chest, naked under this sheet, her hair tickling my nostrils. Bending an elbow, I tuck my hand under my head, looking at the wood panels on the ceiling, breathing out in satisfaction.

If I could, I would live in this moment forever.

When Emily and I had sex ten years ago, it was mind-blowing for me, but I knew it wasn't good for Emily, since it was her first time. I tried my best, warming her up with my tongue and fingers, giving her first orgasm, but penetration was still uncomfortable for her. She promised me it was good, the best first time she could ask for.

However, I always carried the weight that she might've been fibbing to save face.

This time was our redo. My chance to redeem it for us, and it was fucking incredible.

I've never come some hard, been shook to my core so

much so that it rearranged everything I knew about how intense sex could be, how obsessed I could be with a woman. It was more than attraction and lust. Seeing her with our daughter, how she nailed motherhood, how she negotiated with raccoons by offering them Cheetos, I almost dropped to one knee when she reached the tiny house's door.

Instead, I took her in my arms and fucked her with abandon.

We fed each other pretzels like lovesick weirdos and fell asleep in an exhausted heap in the wee hours of the night. Her soft snoring soothed me, and I slept like the dead with her in my arms.

Now, the crack between the curtains and the window frame lets in a sliver of light, illuminating her face. In that moment, my dad's dental practice be damned. My hometown be damned. All I want to do is stay here, in this bed, with her.

"Hey," she whispers, smacking her lips and looking up at me with hooded eyes. "Oh, good, it wasn't a dream."

"No, all of that really happened."

"Thank God," she says. "Do you care about morning breath?"

"Absolutely not."

She scrunches her nose in a cute as hell way and kisses me, our breath through our noses in sync. The kiss deepens, and our tongues pass each other's. My nails trail down her bare back, and she shivers. The sheet drops as she climbs on top of me, her nipples erect and close to my face. I take one in my mouth and let it go with a pop as she whimpers. Her pussy grinds against my erection, and I better sheathe myself soon before we make another baby.

Even with an IUD, knowing us, we would find a way to create another human before we figured all our stuff out.

"You've got to stop grinding on me," I say.

"Well, get a condom on." She lowers her lips to my neck, kissing up to my ear, licking my lobe.

"Yes, ma'am," I say, standing up naked, walking to the strip of condoms we obliterated last night, a small pile of ripped foil building.

"Damn," Emily says from behind me.

Turning, I ask, "What?"

"Just this view. It's a shame I live with a nine-year-old. I would demand you be naked all the time. Your butt is too cute."

Emily's head is propped on her hand, her elbow digging into the couch. I chuckle as I roll a condom onto my swollen cock. "Good thing our daughter likes your mother. My mother will help too. So we can have proper adult naked time regularly."

"Oh, you know exactly how to get me aroused, Max. Babysitting."

"Anything to make you titillated, babe." Dropping a knee on the couch, I kiss her, picking up right where we left off. Last night, she really enjoyed being on top, so I spun her, sinking her onto my aching erection, letting her ride me. It's slow at first, lazy, and then she picks up the pace. Her hands plant on my chest as my hands roaming to her breasts, to her hips, to her ass. My thumb strums her clit as she rides me, her moans beautiful and long. She comes and then I do, and she drops on top of me.

"You're spoiling me."

"I'm glad it could finally be good for you."

"My first time was perfect. This is also perfect, in a different way." I play with her nipple as she lays on my chest, our skin sticking from our mutual sweat. Emily lifts her head to look at me. "I don't want to go back to real life. I want to live in this sex bubble with you forever."

"I know. I don't want to go home today."

She sits up, looking around.

"What's wrong?"

"My clothes. Do you see them?"

She swings a leg to the floor, and I stop her. "Hey, hey. I will come back, Em. We will figure this out."

"I know, it's just…" She runs her hand down her face. "There's just…I don't know."

"What?" I ask.

Emily grabs her phone, and her eyes pop out of her head. She swipes her thumb to read through the alerts. When she puts her phone to her ear, she covers her mouth.

"Tara, what's going on?"

I hear muttering from the phone and I can't make out what Tara is saying. My forehead creases as I look around for my own phone. When I open it, I see fourteen missed calls, thirteen from my mother, and one from my father.

"Maxwell, this is your father" is his usual voicemail message starter to me, but his voice is firm, stern. It cools my blood to a block of ice. "Son, your mother and I are in Gold-heart. We're at this coffee place since we don't know where you're staying. It's imperative you call us back as soon as possible. Your mother tells me you have lots to discuss."

Emily and I lower our phones at the same time and stare at each other.

"Your parents, they're at—"

"Gold Roast." I point to my phone. "That was my dad."

"Max," she says, her face turning to anguish, her eyebrows knitting together, tears slipping from those beautiful green eyes.

"It'll be okay," I say, cupping her cheek. "We will be a family. I promise you that."

"Okay." Emily doesn't look convinced.

"I want you to come with me to the party," I say. "As my girlfriend. As the mother of our incredible child."

"Okay." She sniffles back her tears. "I should really put some clothes on."

"Me too." I kiss her, and her lips press into mine like I'm giving her sustenance. It's strange, but it reminds me of our last kiss before I left Goldheart to go home and then to Costa Rica the next day.

Like it's final. It's a kiss of goodbye.

However, there's nothing that could happen that would make me say goodbye to her.

"Shit, fuck, shit." My hands tremor as I move hangers, looking for the best outfit to meet the man I lied to and took his money. The hoochie dresses were out, and sometimes sundresses looked too slutty. I need to look harmless and young.

"This will have to do," I tell myself as I pull a striped T-shirt dress from the rack and drop it over my most boring panty and bra set. Slipping my feet into sneakers, I step in front of my full-length mirror. I look cute, I feel confident. Still, my heart thumps in my chest at a rapid rhythm.

I should've told him. Why didn't I tell him? It could've solved so many problems telling him earlier, but now, the truth will come out. Maybe it would've been better coming from me, not his father.

This man who will pull Max aside and tell lies about me so he has a precious legacy to a practice he spent decades building and the investment he put into his son, just for him to throw it away on some small town nobody who tried to trap him in a pregnancy.

"I have value. I take up space because it is my birthright," I say into the mirror as I pull my wild hair from my face and

slick on mascara, getting more on my eyelid than my
eyelashes. More mantras spill out, phrases I haven't uttered
in years. "I am worthy of love. I am a good person. I bring
value and creativity to the world around me."

The words do nothing because I sit on my bed and my
eyes scrunch together, bringing tears. What if I lose him?
What if I introduced Olive to her father just for him to leave
and never come back once he knows the truth? I took money
from his father. I made a deal with him. I was nineteen and
stupid and didn't question it hard enough.

The reason we were apart so long is my fault.

"Hey. Are you okay?"

Max leans against the doorframe, looking so handsome.
"It'll be okay, Em. I promise."

"I hope so," I say, standing up. He offers his hand, and I
tuck mine into his, his fingers interlacing with mine. He
kisses my hair as we walk out of my house, into my car, to
face…everything.

Time has not been kind to Fred Sawyer.

When we reach the front door for Gold Roast, I see Fred
looking down at his hands, the top of his head shiny and
bald. It was thinning when I saw him last. Spots pepper his
skin, and his clothes hang off of him. A woman sits to his
right, and I would know her anywhere. Her hair is dyed
blond and sits above her shoulders, but her cheeks, her nose
—they're the ones I kiss on my daughter. My heart swells
because Max's mom is the last bit of my daughter I'm not
familiar with.

We open the door with a clang, and Tara appears from the
back, her eyes large.

Are you okay? Tara mouths to me.

I give a thumbs-up, although my stomach twists and folds into itself.

Max grips my hand tightly as we walk in, like a united front.

"You must be Emily," Fred says, outstretching his hand. He pretends like he didn't intimidate me ten years ago.

I take it, gripping it with all my strength. "Fred."

He flinches at that, and I try not to smile. I bet he corrects people with "doctor" when they call him Mr. Sawyer. It must grind his gears that some small-town hussy called him by his first name.

"Son," Fred says, taking Max in a half hug, but Max still holds my hand.

"Max," his mom says, hugging him as well. She looks at me, really looks at me. "It's such a pleasure to finally meet you."

I let Max's hand go. Her perfume reminds me of a rose garden, and she hugs me like she already cares about me. "I'm Molly Sawyer."

"It's a pleasure to meet you," I say and mean it.

Fred motions for us to sit, and Tara lurks behind the pastry case, watching us. I shoo her away without trying to get caught, I hold my thumb and pinkie to the side of my face, pantomiming I'll call her. She nods once and turns to her coffee machine, pretending to clean it.

"So, you reconnected," Fred says, staring at me with each word.

Max turns to me, like he's asking for permission. "Yes, I actually walked in on her birthday party." He laughs nervously, resting his arm along the back of my chair. I lean into him, needing to gather all the warmth I can before it all comes crashing down.

"And there's a child?"

"Yes." Max's thumb brushes against my skin. *Everything will be fine*, it says.

"She's nine years old. Her name is Olive Jean. Jean is my middle name, and it was my late grandmother's name," I say, my voice cracking.

No matter how nervous I am, I smile because my daughter makes me happy. Everything about her makes me proud.

"Olive," Molly says, practically melting into her chair. "Where is she now?"

"With her grandmother." Molly flinches, and I clarify, "My mother."

"I can't wait to meet her. May I…I would love to see a picture, if you have one."

"Of course." I pull out my phone from my purse and swipe to my photos. There's so many options, but I pick the one from my twenty-ninth birthday in my Favorites folder. Olive is sitting on my lap in front of my cake. Her face is turned, laughing at something, probably her Uncle Cam. We both look so full of joy.

Molly crumples in her chair, letting out a soft "Ooh," touching the screen.

"And you've met this this little girl?" Fred asks, his glare zeroed in on his stepson.

"Yes, and she knows who I am." Max looks down at the table before he knocks it. "I know the timing of this is shitty, but I think we need to reconsider the practice coming to me."

"Are you two…romantic?" Fred asks. He stares at me like I single-handedly ruined all his plans.

"I would like to see," Max says. "Plus, now that I know Olive exists, I want to be in her life. I don't want to miss another moment. Like my dad did with me."

He swallows, and I see the way his cheek flexes, trying to hold in the emotion. Fred's skin has reddened to the shade of beets, his gaze like laser beams on my skin. He's furious.

"Emily, may I speak with you a moment?" Fred asks. Max freezes and looks at me. Here we go.

I stand but say nothing. I smooth down my dress and follow Fred outside of the coffee shop. Looking back, I see Tara bobbing behind the counter, unsure if she should intervene.

What she doesn't know is I have ten years of fantasies saved up for what I would say to Fred Sawyer. How I would've insisted harder to get Max on the phone. That I would've never promised anything in regard to an abortion.

That I would've told Fred to go fuck himself.

He ruined Max's chance to be in Olive's life from the beginning. Fred robbed any chance we had to see if we could work. There could've been children that will never exist because Fred intervened.

Fuck this man. Fuck him.

Once we're clear of the door, he grabs my arm.

"Emily, I am very disappointed you didn't keep our agreement," Fred says. I rip my arm away and grind my jaw. Shoulders back, chin up. I stare him down as he continues, "I paid you fifteen thousand dollars to take care of it. We shook on it."

Calling my daughter *It*, well…

"I owe you nothing. You lied to me. You never told Max. You never got him on the phone like you said you did."

Fred gives away nothing. He has the gall to look me in the eye.

"Do you realize how you ruined his life? How—"

Fred holds up a hand to interrupt me. "*I* ruined his life?" Fred asks. He looks at me like he's so furious, he could explode. "You got your hooks into him after a week and tried to trap my accomplished, driven son. *You* ruined his life. He's thinking about walking away from something we've built together, and you have no remorse. None. I gave that boy everything, when his loser sperm donor couldn't. I'm not the villain here. I was protecting him."

Taking a deep breath, I formulate my response. Fred Sawyer is just a sad man who cares more about protecting his legacy than the son he adopted. Nineteen-year-old Emily deserved so much more, and I'm doing this for her.

"Protecting him from what?" I flap my hands down. "I am a good person, Fred. This was an accident. An honest mistake. I never expected my life to go this way. I didn't chose this."

"You took my money!" he yells.

"Fuck you, Fred. I would do it again!" I yell back.

Turning back to the building, I see Max, standing in the doorway, his face pale. He swallows, looking at me and then at his stepfather.

He heard everything. I breathe in and out, and calmness takes over my body. It's all out in the open.

"You took money from him?" Max asks, looking at only me. His face is what I was avoiding. He's crestfallen.

"I did," I say calmly. "He wanted me to 'take care of it.' I lied and said I would."

"Fred," Max asks, looking at him. "Did Emily call the business because she hadn't heard from me?"

Fred coughs against his hand. "She did, yes."

"Why didn't you call me?" Max asks, looking at him, his mouth agape.

Fred shoves his hands into his shorts, staring at the ground. He can't tell him the reason because it's selfish and too awful for words.

"He told me you wanted nothing to do with us. That you've been in this position before with other women…"

"And you believed that?" Max looks at me, like I'm the one who betrayed him.

My nods are hesitant and small. Molly comes to his side,

looking at Fred and then at me.

"Fred, what did you do?" she pleads, walking toward us with crossed arms. Pedestrians weave around us, looking back like we're a five-car wreck. I don't blame them. I was always good fodder for town gossip.

"I protected our family," he says, so sure of himself.

"Did you lie to this poor girl?" Molly asks, pointing to me. "How old were you, dear?"

"I was twenty. Barely twenty," I say.

"Frederick, really?" She folds her arms.

Fred says nothing. He walks past me, and I feel the breeze from his movement. Molly says from behind me, "We need to go home."

"Yes, we do," Fred says. Frozen in my spot, I hear the door to Gold Roast open and close. Max still stands against the brick, staring at me. I feel hands on my arms.

It's Max's mom, the regret etched in her face.

In that moment, I know she had nothing to do with it. That Max got his heart of gold from her.

"I'm so sorry, dear." She hugs me, hard, and I melt into her arms. Her hand pats down my hair as I struggle to keep the tears away. I glance at Max, who hasn't moved.

"Today is not the day, but I would love to meet my grand-baby one day, if that's okay with you," she says when she pulls away, grabbing my hands.

"She would love that," I say.

She lets go of my hands and walks back inside. Max still stands there, his iciness palpable. Bracing myself, I walk toward him.

"Why didn't you tell me?"

Breathing in and out, I still feel my heart drop. "I wanted to tell you, but I—I didn't want you to think less of him."

"He kept me from you, from our daughter."

"I know." Looking down, I say, "He told me you didn't

want anything to do with me."

"You believed him? And you took his money?"

I nod, holding my head up.

"Did you figure it out? That he lied to you?"

Nodding, I bite my lip.

"When?" he asks. His voice drops to a whisper. "When, Em?"

"Tuesday," I say.

That truth hunches Max's shoulders, and he can't look at me. He leans in so I can hear his whisper. "Really? You made love to me, *knowing* my dad lied to you?"

"Max," I say, tears dropping down my cheek, "I didn't expect it to go as far as it did. It would be easier for you to hate me than him. I wanted to tell you…"

"When?" Max asks. He runs his hand over his mouth while he stares at a gray car parked on the street. "I need to go home."

I nod, and the tears finally come. "Max, can you look at me?"

When he does, my heart breaks even further. He looks at me like I was the betrayal. I was the reason we were apart. "Max, I'm so sorry. I had the week of my life with you, and I didn't want it to end. I spent ten years dreaming about this moment. Yes, I took the money. Yes, I didn't question it further when your dad told me you didn't want to see me anymore. That you wanted me to…" I swallow because I can't say it.

He nods, his gaze back to the ground.

"Okay," I say, smiling through my tears. We stand there while pedestrians walk between us. I'm not sure how much time passes, until I say, "Well, you have my number."

"I do," he says. "Emily, I—this week meant a lot to me. I just need some time."

"I understand." The words I want to say most linger on

my breath. Then, they tumble out, before I can really think on how to say it. "Just, please, don't punish Olive for this."

"Punish her?" His forehead creases and his mouth parts. "I thought you knew me better than that."

My focus lands on Miriam Oliver, lurking between the building and the florist next door, looking at me with pity. Lashing out won't do anyone good. Swallowing down my pride, I turn.

"I'll call you. Do you need a ride back to the house?" he asks.

We took his car to meet his parents. "No, I'm fine."

"I'll talk to you later, Em. I have some stuff I have to figure out. I just..." I wait for more words, but it doesn't come.

I smile through my tears. "Okay" is all I can muster. I walk away and turn.

Miriam watches me as I walk away. I wipe my nose and my cheeks as I keep my head down.

"Dear, do you need a ride?"

"I'm fine, Miriam."

"Emily, let me help—"

"Miriam," I say, a little too firm. "You've done enough. Let me have a broken heart in private for once."

"Emily, this is not your fault."

"I know." There's a swirl of anger, hurt, and remorse within me as we walk, side by side. While I wish she would leave me alone, it's comforting to have her there.

My phone in my purse pulses, and I scramble for it. When I look up, Miriam is gone.

Tara: Are you okay?

I type back, *I've been better.*

The bubble with the three flickering dots appear and then her message: *I'll report back whatever I hear.*

My heart sinks as I type *Thanks.*

She sends me back a smiling face. I try to smile, but it hurts.

I dial my mother. "Hi, honey. I'm at the brewery dear with Olive. Are you with Max?"

I squeak out a sound, and my mom says, "Come to the brewery. Where are you?"

"I'll be there in five." I end the call.

The walk is warm and humid as I make my way down the dirt driveway to the brewery. It's still early, two hours before we open, so I unlock the employee entrance with my key and walk in. The sounds of Taylor Swift echo throughout the brewery. Olive has been playing "Bejeweled" nonstop since it came out last year.

When I arrive at my parents' office, Olive is strutting, swiping her arm from one direction from another, something she learned from the drag queen brunch I took her to. I can't help but smile, although my heart is shattered and I'm about shatter hers. Max will leave without saying goodbye.

"Mom, I missed you!" She collides with my stomach, and I let out an "oomph" with her impact. I smooth down her hair and kiss her part, cradling her to me.

"Is he gone?" my mother whispers. I nod over Olive's head.

I sit down in my dad's chair and wheel towards Olive. "Baby, come here."

Olive turns with attitude, and when she sees my face, her cheeks drop. "What is it, Mom?"

I rub my lips together, and I taste the salt from my tears. "Max had to go home to take care of some stuff, but he said he would call you as soon as possible."

Her forehead creases. "Max is gone?"

"Yes, baby." My heart breaks into smaller pieces as I watch her process it.

Olive nods once and looks at me with determination.

"He'll come back."

I grab my heart. Dear God, I hope she's right.

"Yes, he will," I say, taking her into my arms, although I'm not sure. Sometimes, I have to lie as a mother. It's better than breaking her heart.

"Max is a good guy," my daughter says, sounding older than nine.

"He is," I say.

Her tiny arms go around my ribcage, pressing into my back like she's the one comforting me.

"My sweet girl," I say against her hair as she sniffles against my chest.

My phone pulses in my pocket, and my eyes bulge when I pull it out.

It's Max.

"Hi," I say, my voice hopeful.

"Can I talk to Olive?" Max asks.

"Of course." I hand the phone to Olive. "It's Max."

She smiles widely as she take the phone and holds it to her ear. "Hello?"

I can't hear a word Max is saying on the other end, I just watch Olive's head nodding as she listens. "I will" is all she says.

After a few more minutes, she says "Bye" and hands the phone back to me.

"What did he say, Olive?" my mom asks before I can.

"I can't tell," Olive says. Her face is serene and peaceful as she walks past us, turning, and looking up at me. "Mom, can I use the iPad?"

28

MAX

My shirt sticks to my back and the heat is oppressive on my skin, making it difficult to breathe.

I have no idea how long I've sat here on this bench in the town's gazebo. Fifteen minutes, an hour?

Fred tried to talk to me, right after the revelation but I held up one hand. "Not now," I said, my teeth gritted so I didn't say something I regretted. Usually, my stepfather loves to defend himself, but he retreated.

Leaning my elbows on my knees, I wring my hands. She lied to me. My stepfather tried to buy her off, to will our daughter out of existence, and she knew and she didn't say anything. She let me meet Olive, made love to me, all while keeping this information from me.

I'm not sure if this is anger I feel or deep, deep hurt. Maybe a combo of both.

"May I sit down?" a crinkly female voice asks. When I look up, there's a woman who looks vaguely familiar, wearing turquoise-rimmed glasses with a gold chain attached. Her hand braces on the railing of the gazebo as her arm shakes.

"Please," I say, and I offer my arm for support. The woman sits down across from where I was sitting.

"You're a nice boy, thank you," she says. She looks up at me, her fuchsia-painted lips curling to a smile. "So, you're Olive Finch's father."

My mouth dries up, and I cough against my hand. I didn't know it was common knowledge yet. "Yes, ma'am. And you are?"

"Miriam Oliver." She holds out a wrinkled hand, and I take it. Her hand is soft and small in mine.

"Max Sawyer," I say.

"Max, that's a nice name." The woman shifts on the bench. "My, this bench is as uncomfortable as I remember."

"May I help you with something?" I ask.

The old woman doesn't skip a beat. "You know, I'm a fifth-generation Goldheart resident. My ancestors founded this town. I've lived here a long time. Same as my husband. I've known Kit Finch since she was a baby."

Kit Finch is Emily's mom. I lean closer.

"That was your father and mother, correct? The ones I saw with you outside Gold Roast just now?"

"Stepfather. He's my stepfather," I correct.

Miriam shifts again, pressing her palms into the seat to help her move. "That makes sense. You're way too handsome to come from *that*."

I laugh because I've heard similar sentiments since Fred came into our life.

"Back to the Finches. I've watched those kids grow up, and while the family has never really liked me, I always kept my eye on them. Made sure no one hurt them. That's why when your stepfather came to talk to Emily ten years ago, I kept close, just in case."

Leaning closer, I stare at the ground. "Mrs. Oliver, this is none of your bus—"

She interrupts me. "Emily was always the smart one. Everyone says her older brother Reid is the smart one, but I disagree. It's a heated topic amongst my friends."

A little messed up, but okay.

"Emily graduated valedictorian, you know. She got a full-ride to USC. She was going to make something of herself."

Regret still lingers in my bones. I knew this, but it twists my nerves to hear it from a third party. Reminds me again that I ruined Emily's life and my stepfather rubbed salt into the wound.

"Then she met you. I saw you two once, ten years ago or so. I've never seen her so happy. She didn't look like that when she achieved what she achieved. That girl was always chasing something to make herself feel important. However, she wasn't truly happy until she got to have some *fun*."

A smile creeps through my cheeks. "Miriam, I…"

She cuts me off. "I heard that conversation between your stepfather and Emily. Your stepfather strong-armed that poor girl. I saw it. It's not Emily's fault. You need to take up any issue you have with her with the man who raised you. He's the villain in all of this."

I nod. "She figured it out sooner than this and didn't tell me."

"So what?" Miriam asks. "Emily is a smart cookie. She knew this would crush whatever relationship you had with your stepfather. Frankly, it should've been him to tell you what he did. Because he kept you from making your own decisions and whether you wanted to be in their lives or not. And trust me, I've watched it from afar, and it's a beautiful life, the one she created for herself and your daughter. Emily turned lemons into lemonade, cookies, and pie. That little girl is odd, but she is a bright little thing and will be something one day. At the very least, she'll be *happy*. Strange but happy."

"Hey, you're talking about my kid," I say, straightening my spine.

Miriam holds up her hands. "I mean no offense. Sometimes I say the wrong thing." She braces herself to stand up. She walks to the staircase to leave the gazebo and turns back. She slips a folded piece of paper into my hands. "There's my number if you need anything. I put my email as well."

I crumble the paper in my hands. "Thanks, but I—"

Miriam waves at me. "I'm just making a gesture. But I'll say one final thing. You won't find a woman better than Emily Finch. Yes, she kept something from you, but it came from a good place. Her heart was always made of gold, that one. You seem like a smart guy. I know that because that little girl is one half of you. I already think highly of you, and I don't even know you. Don't disappoint me. Also, make sure you call Olive if you're leaving town. It's the least you could do."

I watch the old woman shuffle across the lawn of the town square as I mull over what she said to me. When I look up, I see my parents hovering by their car, and my mom waving me over.

Holding up one hand, I grab for my phone with the other.

Emily's voice is hopeful when I answer. Then, she gives the phone to Olive, and I tell her I love her and I have some things to take care of. That I love her mother and we'll figure it out. I ask her not to say anything.

When the call ends, I stand from the gazebo to join my parents, clear on what I need to do.

29

EMILY

Friday

S eated at the desk I share with Cam and Reid, I'm lost in a trance when I hear a knock at my door. I told my mom I wanted to be alone, and she ushered Olive away. An hour could've passed, fifteen minutes, I'm not sure.

When I look back, my eyes bug in surprise.

It's Tara. I consider her one of my best friends, ever since she moved to Goldheart and took over the local, iconic coffee shop. She's about my height with long dark hair and the prettiest hazel eyes. She says nothing as she touches my shoulder, and I fold into myself, the emotion so heavy from this week.

"Is Max gone?" Tara asks.

I nod.

"They were talking about some party?"

"His stepdad is retiring." Max will go back to San Diego and meet his destiny, the reason his stepdad offered me fifteen thousand dollars to disappear.

"Can I sit?" Tara motions to a small chair tucked in the corner, piled high with papers.

"Sure." I move the tower of paperwork for her. When Tara's seated, she rests her hands on her thighs and takes a deep breath.

"He'll come around. I just know it. It's a shock, is all," Tara says.

"I hope so." My voice quivers. "He called her. To say goodbye."

Tara shifts in her seat and her posture contorts. "That's a great sign, then."

"I hope so." I lean over and shove my fingers through my hair.

"Don't freak." Tara stretches her hands out like I'm a feral raccoon.

"What?"

"I saw Miriam Oliver talk to Max."

"What? What did she say to him?"

"I don't know. I tried my best to hear, Em, but I couldn't." I smooth down my ponytail. "Oh my God."

"No, I think it was good," Tara says.

"Still."

"Well, we'll see. Did Max say he would call you, or…?"

"I don't know. I'm such an idiot."

I tell her everything. I tell her about the phone call to Max's busted phone, the missed emails, the visit from his stepdad. How I threw my phone into the lake out of frustration and got a new number. I told her about the money and how I didn't tell Max about his stepdad because I couldn't figure out how.

"I would've thrown that stepdad so fast under the bus," Tara says, crossing her arms and leaning back. "Did you at least get some orgasms?"

The tears dry up as I think about our last night. I hold up three fingers, one for each flesh-shredding orgasm I received.

"Oooh." Tara rubs her hands together like she's making a campfire. "Tell me more."

"I came over and literally undressed myself and undressed him, and it happened. A lot."

Tara pats my leg. "Good for you, friend. I can't remember the last time I got laid. I'm worried a bat will fly out from down there if I ever tried."

"It had been ten years for me."

"Damn, you didn't have like a random hookup here and there?" The realization seeps into her expression. "Hold up, Max is the only guy you've ever slept with?"

"Yep," I say.

"You never slept with Burke? What a shame. I would've taken him for a test drive."

"What about Owen?"

Tara's smile disappears. "Who knows with Owen. I don't know how else to throw myself at that man. Do you think I have to show up in a dog suit or something? Ask for a canine exam?" When Tara moved to town, she accidentally ran into Owen, Goldheart's resident veterinarian at the Goldheart Neighborhood Market one Christmas Eve. They both realized they were going to have a quiet Christmas alone, so they decided to join forces and had a great time. They had been best friends ever since, and kept up the Christmas tradition this past holiday as well. Owen kept to himself prior to meeting Tara, and we've noticed him being more open and social, all because of her.

There was a point Tara thought it would turn romantic, and then it never did.

Tara always grimaces anytime someone teases her about Owen, but I always know there's a tiny flame of hope within her that one day Owen will come to his senses.

"Owen is a lost cause. He just loves the dogs, and not much else."

"I'm sorry. You and I could be platonic life partners."

"I like that idea," Tara says. "Although I have a good feeling about Max."

"I hope so," I say. Turning my phone over, I see nothing on the screen but a text from Shiloh, asking if I'm okay.

"I can bring over a bottle of wine tonight. Call in the calvary."

The calvary being Izzie, the town newspaper's editor, and Whitney. Annie and Shiloh, maybe, even though neither of them will drink.

"Sure," I say. "That would be nice."

"I can bring some sparkling cider for Olive."

"She would love that," I say. My heart feels lighter, more hopeful. Why not wish that he will come back? Our time together was so special. Maybe Miriam isn't a heinous bitch monster? All I can do is hope and trust that everything will work out for the better.

Olive and I were just fine until he came back. We'll just be as fine after.

"You will be okay. Whatever happens." It's like Tara read my mind.

"Thank you for being a good friend," I say.

"Anytime."

Saturday

I wanted to leave the second I stepped in the Muirlands Country Club's ballroom.

Instead, I sip my watered-down cocktail as I receive congratulations from my stepdad's friends, patronizing pats on the back, and stares from my mother's friends. The room is littered with "Congratulations, Fred!" banners, complete with his face partially covered with a surgical mask. There's also a Bon Voyage station, since my mom is finally getting her Around the World cruise my stepdad promised her two years ago, when the plans for me to take over and for Fred to retire first began.

They hired a cover band, and the lead singer is belting "It's My Life" by Bon Jovi into the microphone. His voice grates on my nerves. Everything about this party feels fake and forced.

How can everyone be so happy for a man who ruined my

life? He told me he cared about me, just to rob me of a chance to have my own family.

I've been coming to this country club for years, and the white walls never felt as stark and sterile as they do now. This sports coat feels like a straitjacket, the air too balmy and stale in this room. This cocktail tastes like garbage.

Murmurs float over me. I'm not sure if my mother told her friends about my love child, that she's finally a grandmother. It doesn't bother me. I've looked at the photo I took with Olive five times today. Whenever my mind drifts to anything other than Olive, my mind is snapped right back. To her voice, her unintentional jokes. How she cuddled into me when we read *Goosebumps*.

I think about her mother most of all.

All of the feelings I had that first week in Goldheart came back with a vengeance. She was exactly who I thought she was and more. I told her I loved her back then, and I left her —them—again. Finding out the trajectory of my life was changed because of a lie... It was a lot for me to handle.

Everything makes me want to curl into a ball in the men's locker room and stay here until the party is over. I left her. I left Olive. All to go to this stupid party all for something I'm not sure I want.

He's the villain in all of this. The kind older woman's words course through me as I stand here, watching that very man be congratulated. He was someone I looked up to my entire life and wanted to make proud. His approval was all that mattered at times.

Now, I couldn't care less.

"Honey, aren't you enjoying the party?" Mom asks. She's wearing a sparkly jacket and a long cream skirt, her wrist and neck dripping in my stepdad's diamond presents to her. She is thriving under the attention. It was always intoxicating to be in Fred Sawyer's inner circle.

"It's fine." I take another drink but it tastes like bourbon-flavored water.

"Emily and Olive can come live here," Mom says. "I'm sure Olive would love being so close to the beach."

Their entire life is in Goldheart—their family, the business, their friends. Olive has only known small town life amongst redwoods. Asking them to come to a town Olive has never lived feels cruel. "I'm not sure, Mom."

"Well, I'm sure you can convince them. An influential person of the community like you. What woman wouldn't want that?" Mom's smile drops when she sees my stoic expression. "What's wrong, Button?"

"It's just—" Everything.

Fred steps onto the stage next to the band playing, clapping, but his stance signals the lead singer to retreat and let him have the mike.

He is, after all, the man of the hour.

"Let's hear it for these guys." He can't even remember the name of the band, but he claps with floppy hands, and his friends mirror his enthusiasm with whoops and hollers, drunk off of champagne and power.

I've never felt more sober in my life.

"Thank you so much for this. It's shocking it's finally happening, isn't it, Molls?"

"Yes, dear," my mother says, raising her glass.

Fred sways, his short glass of amber liquid sloshing. "My beautiful bride has been on me for years to retire, and it's finally happening. I've served this community for decades, and it's been an honor to be *in your mouth*."

The crowd laughs, but I cringe and flinch. Fred constantly makes tiny jokes that sound like sexual innuendos. I used to laugh it off; now it just makes me sick.

"Never fear though, because my brilliant son, Maxwell Sawyer, will be stepping in so Sawyer Dentistry can keep you flush in veneers and crowns for years to come. Max, come on up here."

Oh God. I grumble as I walk toward the stage. It feels like an out-of-body experience to take the steps, to pass the drummer, who looks at me with pity.

I feel my stepdad's thin finger grip my shoulder, his sharp nails digging into my muscle.

"This man, right here." He jostles me, and I want to rip myself from his hold. A sea of his friends stand before us, looking up with glazed-over eyes. I take a deep breath and swallow.

"Max has been the best son a father can ask for. When I met him at two years old, I knew he was special. He would *make* something of himself."

What the fuck? I was two.

Anger I've pushed down for years bubbles within me, making it difficult to stand still.

"He has grown into a man I'm proud to hand this business over to. My life's work in capable and talented hands. And if he couldn't make me happier, he's made me a grandfather as well."

Fire courses through my veins. He *tried* to persuade Emily to get rid of the baby. He paid her off and intimidated her. My choice to be involved was ripped away from me. Now, he's only claiming my daughter as his grandchild because it makes him look great in his friends' eyes.

My fist clenches at my side as the crowd murmurs, sounds of glee rising up above the crowd. I wonder how many think it's Noelle.

My jaw tightens. Fred doesn't catch the glare I'm throwing at him.

"So, son, do you want to say a few words?" Fred asks, offering me the mic. I look down at it and back up at him. Most of the things I should say I should say in private, but the words crawl up my throat, ready to spew the truth over this crowd. He's pretending like he didn't ask the love of my life to abort our daughter.

Fuck him. Years of shutting up ends now.

I set down my drink on the stage's edge and take the microphone from him. It feels heavy in my hand.

"Thanks, *Dad*," I say, a little too close to the microphone. Only Fred catches my tone, but he laughs, a fist over his mouth.

"I love being a dentist," I start, placing a hand on my chest. "My father has been magnanimous enough to let me go on some dental missions to places in need, and that's when I'm happiest. Now, I've met many of you before, and you've watched me grow up. As you know, I never had a father before Fred walked into our life."

I look out in the crowd, and my mother's cheeks are wet with tears. A tiny voice tells me not to continue, to let it be, but I can't hold this in any longer.

"Fred…" I shake my head, looking to him. His shoulders hunch at my use of his first name. He's always been Dad. However, he lost that privilege about twenty-four hours ago.

Honestly, he should've lost it ten years ago.

"I'm glad I love being a dentist. Because it would really suck if you forced me into this and *also* forced me away from my child and the woman I was in love with."

The crowd makes a collective gasp, and the chatter begins. Gossip flows through the crowd as I continue.

"I have a child I didn't know about until this week. Her name is Olive. She's nine."

I let the crowd absorb that news. I can't look at Fred, or I'll lose my nerve. Staring at the ground, I wiggle the mic in my hand.

"She lives with her mother in northern California. I fell in love with her mother in a week about ten years ago, and we made the most perfect human. If I would've known she was pregnant, I would've picked up and moved in an instant. May not have finished dental school. But that wouldn't have worked for dear old Fred now, would it?"

I look at my mother, who's standing there, aghast.

"Of course my mother didn't know. It was all Fred's plan." I lean back like I'm the Joker, continuing with the lambasting. Fred reaches for the microphone, but I circle him like a wolf rounds a sheep. Holding out my hand, I continue.

"My life would've been very different if Fred had given me a chance to make my own decisions. Maybe I would've gotten married and had more children, doing dentistry in a tiny town with a lake, enjoying my life and being content. Instead, my life is hollow. I'm a shell of a person. Now, I'm not perfect. I could've been braver. But I wasn't."

My mother nods, just once, encouraging me to say my peace.

I lean in to get my mouth as close to the microphone as possible. "Oh, and if you couldn't tell, I quit. Fred, find someone else to take over. I'm done."

Fred rips the microphone from my hand and gives a politician smile to the crowd as he squeezes me to him, wringing all the breath out of me. "My son, Dr. Maxwell Sawyer, everyone."

I leave my drink as I walk down the stairs, pulling off my sport coat and undoing my top button. When I feel a hand on my arm, I whip around to see my stepfather.

"Where do you think you're going, Max?"

"Home."

"Aren't we going to talk about this?"

"Talk about what, *Dad*? There's nothing more to say. You lied to me. You lied to the woman I love. You told her I wanted her to get an abortion. What the fuck is wrong with you? That should've been a discussion between her and me."

Spit sprays from my mouth as my voice raises. My face is rigid and tense, my mouth hooked.

Fred grabs my arm and pulls me in an empty room, a space the country club uses for small dinner parties and gatherings. "Maxwell, keep your voice down."

"You fucked up my life," I say, my pointer finger punching his chest. "You *knew* what my dad did, and you turned me into him. I will *never* forgive you for what you did. Ever. We're done."

"Maxwell, be reasonable. I've given you everything. I married your mother. I put you in private school. I gave you a beautiful life."

"Was it, though?" I ask, feeling suddenly exhausted. "I didn't ask for any of this. This wasn't my choice. You even set me up with Noelle, since you golf with her dad and thought it would be funny if you were in-laws."

I expect Fred to blow up, but he's matching my shouting with a low, baritone voice that always sent shivers through my blood. "Hey, you loved Noelle. You dated her for three years! You like being a dentist. You run off every chance you get to help those poor people in that…what country was it?"

"Costa Rica," I say. Has he been paying attention to what I really want at all? It's what he wants is what I get.

"Don't throw away what we've worked so hard for. What we've planned for. I will pay for Emily and Olive to move here. I will give you the house."

The house in La Jolla is worth three million dollars. I shake my head. My mind flips to the dark wood and coziness of Emily's house, nestled amongst trees, a dark blue tiny home sitting close as a friend. I think about my daughter's giggles and the way Emily's face lights up when I tell a joke. I remember walking along the beach with her, dancing to "Wonderwall", and feeling the heat bear down on me. I remember it all, and I want it. With her.

"My family lives in Goldheart, so I will live in Goldheart."
I grab for the door and turn around. "Did you love me?"

"Of course," he says. "Of course I love you."

Nodding, I turn back to the hallway. "If you really loved me, you would've let me be with who I loved."

31

MAX

I'm shoving clothes into a duffel bag, my other pieces of luggage already full. I've ransacked my condo so violently, it looks like an intruder broke in looking for hidden cash. My AirPods are shoved into my ears as I listen to Metallica, fueling my rage as I pack, so loud I don't hear the banging at my door.

An alert comes through my headphones, and Siri reads out to me. "Mom said, 'Please open the door. I want to talk to you.'"

I pause "Battery" and pull my AirPods out, slip them into their case, and walk to my door. When I open it, my mother's worried eyes meet mine.

She closes the door and wrings her hands, approaching me like a feral animal.

"Max, I didn't get a chance to tell you this earlier, but... I'm so sorry. I didn't know what Fred told her. Fred didn't tell me she was pregnant. If I'd known..."

"Mom, that was years ago. It's his fault. He wanted to groom me to take over, but what he did was selfish and unforgiveable."

"He wants to talk to you." Mom inches closer to me, stepping inside of my bedroom. "He hopes you'll let him say his peace."

"Let him give me shit about the party? I don't think so."

"He understands you're angry—"

"He ruined my life," I yell. "He ruined Emily's life. My daughter's life. I was gone for *nine* years. She thought I didn't want them this whole time, and I....I became Dad. I'm just as bad as him. That asshole left us, and she felt the way I felt. That I wasn't good enough for him to stick around. I..."

I drop like a sack of bricks on my bed, my face in my hands. The bed shifts next to me, as my mom's soft tears join my own. Her hand rubs my back in soothing circles, like I'm five years old and I had a bad dream.

"I didn't know that your dad not being around still affected you so much."

"It's always hurt," I say. "When a parent doesn't want you, it really, really fucking hurts."

"I know, sweetie. I know." She wraps her arm around my head, pulling me into her chest. She pats my ear. "It's not too late for you to be the father you want to be, Max."

"I can't lose out on another second."

"I get that." Mom rocks me, and my heartrate slows. "What about her mother?"

"I want her. I want her so badly."

"Then you should go to her. It looks like you already have your mind made up." She sweeps her arm across my room, with open luggage and drawers.

"I do." I sit up, sniffling and wiping my nose. "I can't take over Fred's practice, Mom. I need to be with my family."

Mom rests her hand on my cheek. "I've never been prouder."

After I pull myself together, I leave my apartment and climb in the backseat of my parents' Suburban. It feels like I'm meeting the mafia, not my stepfather. He's in the driver's seat, sitting in complete silence when I climb in. Instead of getting in the front seat, my mom climbs in the backseat and grabs my hand.

In that moment, I feel her allegiance. Fred doesn't turn, doesn't move. All he does is flick his gaze to the rearview mirror.

"Son."

"Fred."

"I've had a lot of people ask me what happened at the party."

"It was pretty obvious, Fred. I quit. I'm not taking over your practice."

"I understood that. I just want...I just want to explain myself."

I really don't want to hear what he has to say, but still mutter, "Go ahead."

"Ten years ago, I saw how you were with that girl..."

"Emily." Her name causes a smile to emerge from my lips.

"Emily. It was different. You were different. I could tell you were willing to do whatever it took to be with her. We discussed your future, and I really did think you wanted to be a dentist. I didn't want you to waste all your potential working a manual labor job in a small town so you could be with her. You were too smart to settle for a mundane life just because of a girl, Max. You don't even know for sure if that child is yours..."

Heat flares in my temples. "She *is* mine. I would've still gone to dental school, Fred. I *wanted* to be a dentist. We would've made it work. I just wouldn't have worked for *you*. I know that kills you, that you wouldn't have someone to take over the practice. Guess you're just going to have to sell it."

His head nods, and I see his downcast eyes in the

rearview mirror. "Everything I did, I did because I had your best interest at heart."

"Did you change Emily's email on that scrap of paper?"

Fred stays silent.

"Did you mess with my phone? So I couldn't get service?"

Not a peep.

I grimace as I play words and scenarios over in my head. When I say what I need to say, I want it to have meaning. Fred needs to understand exactly what he did.

"Maxwell, all I did was because—"

"You made a little girl—my *daughter*—think I didn't want her. You made the love of my life think that I was some cad. A lovely woman named Miriam told me what you said ten years ago to Emily, and I can never forgive you for that. You *lied* to her, Fred. I wanted to be with Emily. I would have wanted that child with her. You ruined that for us. You stole ten years of my life."

"I didn't *steal* it," he says. "You were happy. I paid for your school. We helped you out with that down payment for this condo. We've given everything to you."

"That's not the point. I could've seen Olive grown up, taught her things, saw her walk and talk for the first time. Now, I'm doing damage control. Because of *you*." I swallow, pushing down my anger and resentment so it lives in my belly.

He nods, and take a deep breath through his nose, the air rattling. He turns and offers his hand to me. I take it, giving it a firm shake. It's not offering forgiveness. It's a business transaction. I'm turning down his practice, his course for my life. As far as I'm concerned, we're over.

I climb out of the car and head toward my apartment, climbing the stairs to my destroyed apartment.

While my heart feels heavy, the look on my mother's face burnt into my brain, a lightness courses through me. I feel free, like I'm finally doing what I want, not what others expect of me.

I plug my AirPods back into my ears, and the hard metal blasts into me.

I'm running toward the life I want. A life I choose. Towards the most beautiful girl in the world, who loves raccoons and Mike Wazowski. Towards the most beautiful woman in the world, who has had my heart from that first day at the snack bar.

The most beautiful home, away from beaches and palm trees.

I can't pack fast enough.

32

EMILY

Sunday

It's nice not crying for an hour.

I slump with exhaustion across from my parents, Olive by my side. They suggested Betty's Café for lunch, just the four of us to decompress after the week I had.

When Olive found me last night, curled in a ball, she said nothing as she tucked herself into me, lifted my arm, and rested it over her. Her soft snores started shortly after, while I stared into a corner, wide awake, thinking over everything with Max.

He hadn't called since he left, except to speak with Olive. The little stinker has been tight-lipped about what he said.

In my heart, I believe he will be back. That the first time was all Fred's fault, and there wasn't some subconscious desire on Max's part to run away. However, my brain is preparing me for an epic disappointment that will take me years to come back from.

"Honey, do you know what you want?" my mom asks, covering my hand with hers.

I've seen the menu a thousand times, but the words swim when I look at them.

"I'll just get the chicken club, I guess." I drop the laminated menu as it floats away, off the table.

It lands at feet covered by fuchsia Crocs.

When I look up, I see my nemesis. Miriam.

"Miriam, how are you?" my mom asks. My dad doesn't notice; he continues to pour sugar packets into his iced tea, but my mother's voice is laced with contempt.

"I saw your beautiful family and thought I would come say hi." Miriam stares at me, and I don't look up. It's best never to look dragons in the eye. Still, she says, "Emily, can I talk to you?"

I look at my mother and then at Olive, who is busy coloring a mermaid's hair blue on a worksheet Betty's Café gives to each kid customer.

"Why?" I ask, leaning back defiantly.

"Please, humor an old lady," she says, waving me over.

Looking across the table, I'm being encouraged by my mother. "See what she has to say. Tug your ear if you need help."

"Kit, is that necessary?" Miriam asks.

My mom throws up her hands.

I stand up, dropping the napkin in my lap on the table. Miriam motions for me to follow her outside, and the heat hits me like a sledgehammer. I cross my arms immediately as a shield against Miriam.

"What do you want, Miriam?"

"I wanted to talk to you," she says, exasperated. "First, I wanted to apologize for telling everyone you were pregnant all those years ago. That was not my place, and I'm sorry. I've been meaning to tell you I'm sorry for years, but it…it didn't happen."

"Why, Miriam?" I tuck my hands in further.

"Darling girl. I've always thought you were the most level-headed out of your siblings. 'That girl is going to make it,' I used to tell Leland. You were valedictorian and got that scholarship to USC. We never told you, but my friends and I used to sit around, talking about how proud we were of you."

I feel the "but" coming. For the most part, I stopped thinking of my alternate life a long time ago. There was another plane in the multiverse where I never met Max, never got pregnant. Maybe I would be in that big city, working and going to happy hours. Maybe I would learn to love martinis. But one day, I looked at Olive playing with dolls and trucks, and looked around at the home I bought with my own money and the stacks of orders I needed to run to the post office. That was the moment I accepted my life, as it was, and from that moment I stopped missing a life I never got.

"What's the point of this, Miriam?"

"The point is...I was shocked, is all. You see girls in this town get pregnant young all the time, and it's not shocking. But you, Emily, were too special—"

"I'm done with this conversation," I say, turning to the door.

"I talked to that boy for you."

My hand freezes on the handle. When I turn, my hair swings into my face. "What?"

"I talked to him. After you stood up to his poor excuse for a stepfather."

Did she tell Max to run? That I'm a case of wasted potential?

"What did you say to him, Miriam?"

The older woman is flustered, vibrating as she sticks her hands out to set the scene. "I heard you talk to that man, right after you found out you were pregnant. What I should've done all those years ago was find that boy and tell him about it, because I knew what that man was feeding you was malarky. You were so trusting, and I was so proud of you for negotiating. I told my friends about it, and your predicament got out, unfortunately. That's why we don't talk to Rue anymore. She has a *huge* mouth."

Rue does have a huge mouth, bigger than Miriam's. She once spread around town that she saw my brother and Shiloh looking cozy at the lake on New Year's, and we didn't believe it until it came out later that they were involved.

Miriam is burying the lede, but I let her talk.

"I told your man everything. That his stepfather strongarmed you into giving up. That you took the money and didn't waste it. You built a beautiful life for you and your daughter, Emily. I always hoped—" Miriam grabs her chest and looks up at me. There's tears filling her eyes. "As I saw each of your brothers fall in love, I hoped your time was coming. I watched you with Burke, and while he's *very* good-looking, I knew he wasn't right for you. Couldn't quite put my finger on it until I saw you with that handsome man who Olive looks so much like."

I raise my chin so I don't cry. "What did he say back?"

"Not much. Just nodded." Miriam reaches out and grabs my hands so quickly it startles me. She grips them, looking up at me. "He will come back to you. I just know it."

"How do you know?" I ask. "How?"

"I kinda picked him up from the airport. Well, I picked him up, and then he asked to switch in Natomas so he technically drove us home. That car came out of nowhere."

My eyes widen at this news. "What?"

"He's here." She points down the road to a bench, where a blond-haired man sits. I would know him anywhere. He looks and stands immediately, shifting from one foot to another.

"My sweet girl," Miriam says, pulling me down so she can

kiss my cheek. "I've never wanted anything more than the Finches to be happy. Most of all you, my dear. I'm so sorry for everything that happened. I hope this makes up for it."

Then, she disappears, and I have to face Max.

He came back.

"Hey," he says, walking towards me.

"Hey." Crossing my arms feels the most comfortable, creating a barrier.

"You look pretty," he says.

All I'm wearing is a white flowy T-shirt and blue shorts, but I nod. "Thanks."

Max walks closer. He could reach out and touch me, but his arms lay flat at his sides.

"How did the party go?" I ask.

"Well, I turned down the practice. Publicly. In front of his friends."

My heart flutters. "Did that feel good?"

Max's posture relaxes. "Amazing. I didn't realize how much angst I had about it. When I told him I quit, I felt free."

"How did he take it?"

"As well as you can expect." Silence grows between us. I'm not sure if he's still mad at me or if he's here to see Olive.

"Is this a quick visit, or—" I ask. I hold my breath as I wait for his answer.

"For now. I brought some stuff." He points to a pile of luggage, more than needed for a simple stay. I didn't see it when I approached him at first. "I still have to sell my condo and wrap up some things in San Diego. But you're here, and Olive is here. I want to be wherever you are."

"You do? I'm so sorry I didn't tell you sooner about Fred—"

His hand comes to my arm and his touch sends warmth toward my fingertips. "It's fine, Em. You were only twenty—"

"Still, I should've told you earlier this week instead of

letting you think that I didn't want you. Because I did. Are you mad I took the money?"

"No," he says with a shake of a head. "If anything, I'm mad you didn't ask for more."

Gripping his biceps, I say, "I wanted you so badly it hurt. When she was born, she looked so much like you, and I felt...haunted."

"I'm here now. No more ghosts." He pulls me into his arms and I hug him—I really hug him, smelling his cologne on his skin, feeling his hard chest through his shirt. Max clings to me like I will float away.

When we pull away, he leans in and kisses me, deep and hungry. The world goes away, just for a little bit, and it's just me and him. Max and Emily.

When we pull away from each other, breathless and panting, I hear an audible "Gross" from behind me.

"Mom, why do you have to kiss Dad like that? I mean, in *public.*"

Max's chin drops, and he presses our foreheads together. He sniffles.

"Was that the first time she's called you Dad?"

Max nods, a big grin across his face. "I got my wish."

I kiss him again, and Olive groans.

"You're going to have to get used to it, kid," I say. My daughter rolls her eyes. My parents stand behind my daughter, holding it together, but I know they're going to cry about it later.

"Hi, I'm Kit Finch, Emily's mom." Mom reaches around Olive to shakes Max's hand.

"It's a pleasure to meet you," Max says. "Truly."

"Randy Finch, Emily's dad," my dad says, shaking his hand as well. "Do you want to join us for lunch?"

"I would love to. Is there somewhere we can put my stuff, by chance?"

"Come on," Dad says, waving him over to his Suburban, parked in an angled spot in front of Betty's. "We'll put it in the trunk."

"Hey, Olive," Max says, walking toward our daughter.

"Dad," she says, looking up at him.

Max crouches down, his knee hitting the sidewalk. He looks up at her. "I just want you to know I'll never leave you again."

Olive studies him and then whispers, "Promise?"

Max offers his pinkie. Olive smiles and outstretches her own, hooking pinkies with her father. Mom is full-on crying watching this, and her crying makes me cry. Olive hugs him around the neck.

When she pulls away, she slips her hand in Max's.

"Mom, he came back. He told me he would."

I nod, the tears now covering my face. "He did, sweetie." Max reaches out and touches my cheek. I lean into it, and his thumb swipes away the tear. He offers, his hand to mine and I take it.

"My beautiful girls," he says. I kiss him one more time, much to the chagrin of our daughter before he helps my dad put his luggage in the car. We walk back into the restaurant, and Miriam turns in her chair, watching us. She notices my splotchy face. I mouth *Thank you*, and Miriam nods once, turning back to the Bad Biddies Club.

When Max and Dad rejoin us, they find an extra chair for Max and set it next to me. Max grabs my hand and holds it on his thigh. I catch him staring at me, several times, and he grins when I look at him.

This feels surreal, like I'm dreaming. However, his warm hand doesn't let go of mine the entire meal.

He's here. He's never leaving.

My whole body relaxes, maybe for the first time in ten years.

. . .

Max

"Sweetheart, can I talk to your mom privately for a second?"

"You just want to kiss again, don't you?" Olive asks, sticking out his tongue in disgust again.

She's on to me. "Maybe."

"Okay, fine," she says. "Can I have screentime?"

Looking to Emily for permission, I get a small nod. "Sure," I say.

Olive grabs the iPad on the side table next to the couch and runs upstairs, her feet slamming into the steps.

"Be careful," Emily yells after her. Her shoulders hunch as she turns back to me.

"I'm sorry I didn't explain before I left." Although we touched at the restaurant, I'm searching her eyes for explicit permission.

"You'll just have to make it up to me." She rests her hands on my shoulders, and I pull her by the waist to my chest. My breath shudders, and she chuckles. She knows what she does to me.

"So, what are we going to do?" I ask.

"You'll move into the tiny house," she says. I drop my lips to her neck, and she giggles. "You're trying to worm your way into the main house, huh?"

"Maybe." I take her lips with mine. She melts into the kiss, letting my tongue pass her lips, and I really kiss her, long and deep.

She pulls away. "We have to be smart about this."

"We do?" I ask. Resting my hands on my hips, I can't help but laugh at how flustered I make her.

"We've only really known each other for two weeks total. I mean, I need to make sure."

"Em, there's a human being up there that has half of each of our DNA."

"I know that," she says. She's pacing now. "I want to take it slow."

"But I lo—"

"Don't say that." She holds out a hand to stop me. "It's crazy. No one falls in love after two weeks."

A full-on laugh leaves my lips. "Really? I'm pretty sure I told you I loved you for the first time after five days. And you said it back, if I recall."

"We're adults now. You're unemployed."

"Well, when you put it like that."

"I just want to really get to know you. Without the drama or craziness. We have a great start, but I have to make sure, for Olive."

"I get it," I say, although all I want is to be reckless with her. If she wanted to run to the courthouse today and make it official, I would call and make the appointment. If she wanted to make another baby tonight, I would make her come while doing it.

However, whatever my love wants, she will get.

"I should get settled." Walking to the door, I turn around. "You're welcome, anytime."

She clasps her hands behind her back. "Thank you. I do own it."

"It's perfect. Because you can be very, *very* loud when I make you come."

A flush blooms on her cheeks. "Shush, Max."

"I mean, I won't sneak over here," I say. "Boundaries."

"You're welcome to have food here and eat with us," Emily says.

"Sounds like a plan."

"Perfect," she says. It's awkward for a second before she

runs towards me and kisses me, holding the back of my head as she leans into me.

My lips move to her ear, and I whisper, "I do love you, though."

She pushes me away, but I see a little smile.

"We usually go over to my parents' house on Sundays for dinner. Come."

"I would love to," I say. I move toward the door and turn around.

"Hey, Em?"

"Yeah?" She turns, and I swear a beam of sunlight casts a glow on her from the window. The freckles across her nose, her pink lips, her large green eyes. She's the most beautiful woman I've ever seen.

"I do have a question for you." I walk toward her, trying not to smirk. Taking her hand, I gaze into her eyes. I let her think what I want her to think, and she starts shaking her head.

"No, please don't. My brother Cam did that before his wife was ready, and it was just bad—"

"I'm not proposing. Yet." I cover her hand with mine. "Will you be my girlfriend?"

Her lips quiver with a smile as she looks down.

"Is that a yes?"

She nods and I take her in my arms, spinning her. As we kiss, we hear giggling and turn to see our daughter sitting on the steps, covering her mouth.

"Were you spying on Mom and Dad?" Emily asks.

"Maaaaybeeee," Olive says, scampering off.

"She's everywhere," I say, still holding her mother.

"She is. Good thing we have the love shack."

I wink at her before I leave to unpack.

. . .

When we arrive for dinner at the Finches, all of her brothers eye me, especially Cameron. He's taller than me by at least three inches, and broad where I'm lean. He stares at me off and on, in between tending to his very pregnant wife.

"So," he says, cornering me by the liquor cart. "You and my sister?"

"Yep," I say, pouring myself some bourbon, matching their other brother, Reid.

"Is this a long-term thing, or you gonna leave again?" he asks.

"I have to go back to San Diego to finish packing and sell my condo, but other than that, I'm here for good."

"Good," he says. He points to his eyes with his pointer and middle finger and then points them to me. Cam pats me on the chest. "Don't disappoint me."

"I'll try not to." I'm not sure if I should be worried or amused.

A cute blond woman bounds toward me like a puppy. "Hi! You must be Max. I'm Shiloh." I outstretch my hand, but she jumps in my arms for a hug. "It's so nice to meet you!" she screeches. When she dislodges herself from me, she also pats me on the chest. "You have a good one. I may not look like much, but I will hurt you if you hurt my girls."

I chuckle. "Understood."

"Good." Her smile spreads across her face. I smell Emily's perfume and turn to see my love.

"I've had two of your family members threaten bodily harm to me already." I circle her shoulders and kiss her hair part.

"Sounds about right. I would be scared of Shiloh. I've never seen her angry, but I assume it would be brutal."

"I bet," I say.

"Dad," Olive says, running to me. "The raccoons are out."

Hearing her call me Dad twists my heart in the best possible way.

Emily and I look at each other. "Mom and Dad don't usually have them. They must sense Shiloh is here," Emily says.

"You have to see them." Olive grabs my hand and pulls me to the front door.

"Okay," I laugh.

We walk out onto the gravel driveway, and she points to the clearing where the lawn meets the trees. Animal noises sound close as Olive points, her little hand in mine.

I kneel down so I'm her height, and I see their little black-and-white heads popping out. Emily kneels on the other side of Olive as she points them out, giggling as they tumble over each other.

At one point, Emily and I catch each other's gazes.

This was what was missing from my life.

I kiss her head, and then Olive's. Taking both of them into my arms, my heart swells.

I'll spend the rest of my life making up for the ten years I missed. But this moment, right now, is as precious as gold.

EPILOGUE

EMILY

Eight Months Later

"**M**om, come on. Let's not be late."

"There's no rush, Olive," I say, my daughter pulling me into the forest.

Today my daughter is ten.

She's grown two inches in the last year, and she's all arms and limbs. I see her dad in her more now that they're together every day. The way she walks, how she uses her hands to talk—it's all him.

However, the wishing well is just for us.

Since it's our birthday tradition, Max insisted we go alone before Olive's birthday party. I have my penny in my pocket, ready to make a wish for her. We try to still have mother-daughter moments, but having Max has been life-changing in the best possible way.

I have a partner, a lover, and the father to my child in my life. I fall more in love with him with each day that passes. Watching him with Olive makes me want another one. He joked last week that he wanted another baby as he peeled my clothes off of me, and I'm about to give in.

I made an appointment for next week to get my IUD removed.

Max lived in the tiny house for three months, but slowly, his stuff migrated to the main house. The first month he lived there, I would sneak over every night until one night Olive caught me coming back at eleven with her arms crossed.

"Mom, just let Dad sleep here," she says, like it was the easiest thing in the world.

We finally made Max's fatherhood official two months ago. We went through the song and dance of getting the paternity test—no surprise, Max is Olive's biological father—and then we officially updated Olive's birth certificate.

Father: Maxwell Nicholas Sawyer.

We sent copies to his stepfather.

Max knew Olive was his. It's hard to deny it when you look at her or see them shoulder to shoulder. However, we wanted to make absolutely sure that no one would question it ever again.

He slid into the dad role better than I could've imagined. This morning, he made Olive chocolate chip birthday pancakes, handing me a cup of coffee over her head with a kiss. At one point, he kissed Olive's head and looked up at me, and I had to text him to meet me upstairs for a quickie because I was overcome with how horny it made me seeing him cook and do dishes.

Olive and I reach the wishing well in the meadow, as majestic as I left it on my birthday eight months prior. It floods me with calmness and nostalgia for all the birthdays we've done this as a mother and daughter.

"Mom, I know you usually make a wish on my birthday, but do you mind if I make my own wish this time? Since I'm ten?" Olive asks, tucking her hand into the pocket of her shorts.

"Can I still do it?" I pull out a penny. "For tradition?"

"Okay, but I want to go first." Olive's eyes widen, noticing her rude tone. "Please."

"Okay, go for it," I say. My daughter approaches, and I can see her profile, her eyelashes fluttering closed.

"I wish—"

"You don't say it out loud, honey," I remind her.

"I wish," she says louder and then pauses. "I wish that my mom says yes."

"What?"

Olive tosses the penny and turns around, her mouth stretched in a smile. I look behind me to see Max with one knee on the ground, holding up a ring between his fingers.

My soul leaves my body as I drop to the ground as well, twigs scratching my knees.

"Emily Jean Finch, I'm sorry I'm ten years late, but I'm here now. I love you so much. It's time we make it official. Marry me."

Tears leak from my eyes. "Of course."

"Yes!" Max yells, holding his hand up so Olive can high-five him. Olive drapes herself over me, hugging my neck as Max slips a beautiful diamond ring on my hand.

"I helped, Mom," Olive says, pointing at the cushion cut, surrounded by tiny diamonds on a thin yellow-gold band.

"It's beautiful," I say through tears, kissing Max, then kissing our daughter.

Olive pats me on the arm. "Also, Mom, Dad's going to be a Finch."

"No, we'll be Sawyers," I tell Olive.

"Actually..." Max kisses my face, and I notice tears in his eyes. "I was wondering if I could become a Finch once we're married. Olive and I discussed it, and we both like the idea."

"You…want to change your name?" I ask. I've never heard of a man taking his wife's name. A sob leaves my throat.

"Yes, I would love to," he says. "It would be an honor to be a Finch. Especially with, you know, everything."

I kiss my new fiancé's cheek, knowing what he means. His relationship with his stepfather never recovered. It came out that Max's mom and stepdad hadn't been getting along for years and they hoped retirement would save their marriage. Turns out, lying about a grandchild and controlling Max was enough for Max's mom to finally ask for a divorce.

She's considering moving to Goldheart, and I offered her the tiny house. Other women wouldn't dare have their mother-in-law so close, but she swears she would find a place to stay where we could have our own space. "I'm not living in a tiny house longer than I have to," she said to us over the phone, and Max said he didn't blame her.

Max hasn't spoken to Fred in months. The thought of Max changing his last name to Finch did cross my mind, but it was special that he wanted to and decided on his own, after discussing it with Olive.

We get to keep our name and carry on the Finch legacy, with my siblings.

"Let's get to Ms. Martini's birthday," Max says, kissing my head. "And celebrate this." He thumbs my new piece of jewelry, and I can't help but grin like a fool.

We drive to the brewery, which I closed for Olive's family birthday. She had a friends birthday at the local skating rink, and I laughed as I watched my daughter skate backwards, showing off to her best friends, Kenzie and Brynn. The girls were so cute together.

Today is full of surprises, and it's not over yet. My siblings and I have one planned for our parents.

We park in our usual spot, and we wait for Max to open our doors.

Olive slips her hand in one of Max's, and Max takes my other one.

When we walk in, we're greeted by Shiloh.

"So…" She leans to the side, trying to get a glimpse of my left hand.

I hold it up, and she screams.

She immediately starts crying and wraps me in a hug. Jackson, my brother, proposed to Shiloh a few months ago, and they're planning an April wedding next year. She joked the other day that we should have a double wedding, and I pointed out Max hadn't proposed yet. Shiloh immediately looked guilty so I knew it was coming, in some capacity.

"He did it," Shiloh says excitedly to Jackson, who joins us. My brother looks happy, and it warms my heart how Shiloh helped him recover. If I think about their relationship too long, I will cry.

"Congratulations," Jackson says, shaking Max's hand. "You're finally making an honest woman out of her."

"Shut up," I say, hitting Jackson in the gut. He lets out an oomph, and I hear Shiloh say, "You kinda deserved it."

"I'm going to find Abigail," Olive says, searching for her cousin. She runs off and disappears, first stopping at my mom to say hi.

Max's boxes were barely unpacked when my daughter finally got a cousin, Abigail Katherine Finch. My brother Cam and Annie are the cutest parents and are already talking about getting pregnant again since Abigail is so easy.

"It's a trick," I told them, but they laughed it off.

Molly appears and takes me into a hug. "I'm so glad it's you," she says into my ear, and I want to cry all over again. Molly and I have had an opportunity to get to know each other, and we've become really close. She adores my mom, and I know they'll become best buds.

"Thank you," I say. "We're really excited."

"I decided I'm officially going to move," Molly says, and Max hugs her so hard, she makes a sound. "It just makes sense. It would be nice to have seasons again and be close to my granddaughter."

"You're more than welcome to the tiny house."

"Actually, I found another spot."

"Molly is going to move into Jackson's old apartment," my mom says, wrapping her arm around Max's mom's shoulders. "It makes sense."

"Mom, that job is still open for you if you want it," Max says.

"Only part-time," Molly says, sticking a finger up. "I want to enjoy being retired, *single*, and a grandma."

My love opened his own dental practice in Goldheart, focusing on serving underprivileged folks, taking all types of insurance and working it out with patients who can't afford it. Olive loves to hang out there and asked for a play dentist set for Christmas. It was a bitch to track down.

I ask him all the time if being a dentist is what he wants. My income can more than support us. He always reassures me that he loves being a dentist, but he wants to help folks too. It goes back to why he still wants to go to Costa Rica, and Olive has expressed interest in going when she's old enough.

"How does Dad feel about Molly moving in?" I ask my mom. "You two will be trouble."

Mom links arms with Molly. "Please, he has the dog. At least I'm not the third wheel anymore." Koda, the German shepherd, joined the family last year. That dog goes everywhere with my dad, and he started agility training for fun. My brothers and I joke we will always be second fiddle to a canine and my dad always laughs it off, but we all know.

"Where are Whitney and Reid?" Mom asks. We look around too, but we know why they're late.

"Where's the birthday girl?" our investor Dan Price asks from the entrance, holding a trolley of presents. Dan's wife Makenna follows, holding more presents.

"Dan, I told you to tone it down this year," I say. Dan and Makenna are practically members of the family. When our brewery was struggling four years ago, he stepped in, offering a hail Mary investment that turned this place around. In the last two years, we've been able to become not only profitable, but flourishing.

"I can't help it," Dan says.

"Uncle Dan!" Olive yells, running towards him, jumping into his arms. She looks down on the mound of presents. I'm not sure where I'll put all the stuff. "Is that for me?"

"Of course." He lets her down to her feet, and her mouth drops open in awe.

"Thank you so much." She hugs around his waist.

"I tried to talk him out of it, but he had one too many Coors Lights the other night, and before I stopped him—" Makenna says.

"It's fine," I say, waving my hand. "She's just getting money for college from me."

"I already got what I wanted most," Olive says, already snuggling up to Makenna.

"What's that?"

"My parents are getting married!" Olive says.

"Congratulations," Dan says, shaking Max's hand. Makenna takes a look at my ring.

Dan hugs me. I lean in and whisper, "We're doing it today."

"Okay, sounds good." His tone is serious as he pulls away, but smiles when he catches Mom's gaze.

"Sorry we're late," Reid says, running in with Whitney following, both out of breath.

"Jackson, Shiloh, come. It's time. Grab Dad."

Dad is standing by the food, arranging and rearranging it in front of the cake. Shiloh links arms with him and pulls him over.

"What's going on?" Dad asks, as he walks next to Mom.

"So," I start, "we have a surprise for you."

"What's that?" Dad asks, looking between all of us.

"You've given so much to us that we want to give back to you," Jackson says.

"So we pooled our money," Cam says.

"And with one generous donation from a romance author," Reid says, looking at his wife and winking.

"We're buying Dan out," I say. Whitney pulls out a cashier's check, for hundreds of thousands of dollars, and presents it to Dan.

We made him an offer last week to buy him out, and he barely negotiated with us. "This might make me a terrible businessman, but I love the shit out of you Finches," he said after we shook on the deal. The papers have been signed, and everything is final. The last piece is the check.

My dad is flabbergasted.

"The business is yours. A hundred percent yours," Dan says, folding the check and tries to stick it in his back pocket, but Makenna takes it and tucks it into her purse. "Congratulations."

"What?" my dad asks, his eyes filling with tears.

"No, you can't. It's too much," Mom says, tears already streaming down her face.

"Look at what you made," I say, sweeping my arms around the taproom that holds so many memories. All of my brothers look at their partners with love because they remember too.

"It's ours now. All ours."

My parents hug each of us, and all of our cheeks are wet.

Dan offers to take a picture of all of us in front of our logo on the wall.

"I had this made," Makenna says, pulling out a sign.

My mom crumples all over again.

The sign says, "We made this, and now we own this."

We surround my parents as Dan takes our picture to commemorate this day. Jackson and Shiloh stand on one side, excited to get married and grow their family beyond multiple fur babies. Cam, holding his daughter, who giggles as she touches his beard, stands next to Annie. Reid, happy and childfree with Whitney, the best uncle and aunt a mother could ask for.

It's not only the day where Max and I take one step closer to being the family we always wanted to be. It's the day that the Finches triumphed, that we rose from the ashes to make the phoenix of my dad's dream come true.

All of my brothers are in love and happy. My love came back to me.

We own Woody Finch Brewery completely.

My family is whole.

I can't help but smile through the happy tears.

THE END

WANT MORE?

To keep up to date with Jenny and be the first to hear about new releases and sales, please go to jennybuntingbooks.com to subscribe to her newsletter!

Loved *Heart of Gold*? Please consider reviewing on Amazon! It helps others find and enjoy this book.

Curious about the other Finch siblings? The Finch Family series is complete and available on Amazon in paperback and ebook!

For more details on upcoming projects, please find Jenny on socials! She has a readers' group on Facebook called Jenny Bunting's Adultish Readers, a Facebook page called Author Jenny Bunting, and she's on Instagram at @jenny-buntingbooks.

ACKNOWLEDGMENTS

Wow, we made it. The Finches are happy and thriving and they got their brewery back. All is right in the world.

There's many people who help me with every release. A special thank you for Sarah of Lopt & Cropt who has edited so many books for me, I've lost count. Thank you for your friendship in addition to the edits. I'm so glad we found each other.

To my cover designer, Kari March of Kari March Designs – what can I say that I haven't already said? You're the best.

I would like to thank my beta readers: Amanda, Beth, Erica, and Candice. Your suggestions made this book better and I'm so appreciative of your time and thoughts. You all are worth your weight in gold.

To my author friends, especially Ava Hunter and Kathryn Nolan, who helped me work out the tricky plot of this book and act as informal author therapists. I love both of you a whole lot.

To everyone who has read this series and other books I've written—you mean so much to me. Thank you for your support, your reviews, your shares. You all obviously have great taste.

Jeremy and Booker – Thank you for supporting this passion and encouraging me to chase creativity. Also, I'm so grateful you encourage balance, instead of letting myself burn out. My love for you both is infinite.

ABOUT THE AUTHOR

Jenny Bunting is the author of eight full-length romance novels and five romantic comedy novella titles, all self-published. Jenny dabbles in spreadsheets for her day job so she can do this on the side, as her passion. She would not give up Cheetos to a raccoon. Jenny lives with her husband and their German shepherd in the suburbs of Sacramento, California and she's sad that the Finch Family series is over.